D1376395

THE HANGMAN'S HYMN

The Carpenter's Tale of mystery and murder
as he goes on pilgrimage
from London to Canterbury

THE HANGMAN'S HYMN

The Carpenter's Tale of mystery and murder
as he goes on pilgrimage
from London to Canterbury

Paul Doherty

HEADLINE

First published in 2001 by
HEADLINE BOOK PUBLISHING

10 9 8 7 6 5 4 3 2 1

British Library Cataloguing in Publication Data

Doherty, P.C. (Paul C.)
The Hangman's Hymn
1. Christian pilgrims and pilgrimages – England – Gloucester
– Fiction 2. Executions and executioners – England –
Gloucester – Fiction 3. Great Britain – History – Medieval
period, 1066–1485 – Fiction 4. Detective and mystery stories
I. Title
823.9'14 [F]

ISBN 0 7472 2081 6

Typeset by Palimpsest Book Production Limited,
Polmont, Stirlingshire

Printed and bound in Great Britain by
Clays Ltd, St Ives plc

HEADLINE BOOK PUBLISHING
A division of Hodder Headline
338 Euston Road
London NW1 3BH

To Ned Richardson-Little
of Ferrier Avenue, Toronto

Chapter 1

Prologue

The pilgrims had found their road again. The rain had stopped, the mist had lifted. The morning sky was as blue as Our Lady's veil and the white wisps of cloud, mere fragments, grew smaller as the sun rose strong and hot, drying up the mud and baking the country trackways. On either side of the pilgrims stretched the sloping green fields of Kent: a veritable paradise, no wonder the pilgrims were in good fettle.

'By Satan's cock!' mine host growled. 'We'll have fair travelling today and a few good tales to boot!'

The prioress stroked the little lap dog nestling in her lap. She ignored mine host and, leaning down, whispered to her handsome, olive-skinned priest leading her gentle-eyed palfrey to walk a little faster. Mine host saw the movement and he hung back, his lip curling.

'Heaven's tits!' he breathed to the bright-eyed, cheery-faced Geoffrey Chaucer from the Customs House. 'But she's a fine one, isn't she sir, with her lovelocks peeping under her coif and that medal which proclaims love conquers all! Where's the poverty of Christ in her, eh? With her soft, woollen robes, cushioned saddle and embroidered harness . . . ?'

'In God's eyes we are all sinners,' Geoffrey quipped back.

'Aye, but He doesn't expect us to be arrogant or stupid with it,' mine host retorted. He spurred his horse on and stopped by the miller who, drunk already, was swaying in the saddle, farting and belching, his great tangle of bagpipes thrust under

1

his arm. 'Steady now,' mine host soothed, fearful of this giant of a man with fists like hams. 'It's just past noon and you're already sottish!'

'Pish off!' the miller retorted and, putting his lips to the mouthpiece, blew a long, wailing blast on his bagpipes; this startled the crows in a nearby copse and they rose, protesting raucously.

Mine host pulled a face and rode on, making his way past the different pilgrims. The little friar, hot and lecherous as a sparrow, winked lewdly at the wife of Bath, whose broad hips filled her embroidered saddle. The good wife's skirt rode high, allowing all to see the red-gartered hose beneath: her broad-brimmed hat was slightly askew, her face wet with perspiration. She gave a gap-toothed smile and winked as she caught mine host's eye. The tavern master travelled on, holding his reins loosely as he studied the different pilgrims. He was quietly amused at how they seemed to know each other yet, if the truth be known, he too knew a few, albeit secretly, a matter for pursed lips and whispers in the shadows!

There was the man of law, dark-eyed and close-faced. Didn't he know my lady prioress in a former life? Then the franklin, with his costly belt and purse, who always kept an eye on the summoner, that fat, lecherous, pus-filled scandal-monger: a gallows bird if ever there was one. And the pardoner, that strange-looking creature with his white, pasty face and dyed flaxen hair? Mine host was certain that his appearance was a disguise and the screeching voice a mere ploy to hide his true nature. And the quiet ones? Those who kept out of harm's way and always stayed in the background? The cook with that open ulcer on his shin which looked like one of his own blancmanges turned sour? Didn't he know the poor priest and parson who'd told them that ghostly tale the night before about the watchers and dark deeds in a lonely, haunted church in Kent? Indeed, there were even more sinister matters! Mine host tightened his lips as he approached the head of the column. The monk, a powerfully built man with a polished face and balding pate, fleshy lips and protruding eyes, always rode behind the knight, those dark empty eyes glaring hatefully ahead of him. Now and again the knight, Sir Godfrey, would turn and stare at the monk as if he knew his true nature. To the left and right of the knight rode his squire and his yeoman: they, too, resented the monk's presence and were ever-watchful.

Mine host took a piece of dried bacon from his pouch and bit at the salty meat. The knight had told them a fearful tale, about the strigoi, blood-drinkers in the King's own city of Oxford. How Sir Godfrey had taken a solemn oath to hunt them all down and kill them. Was the monk, with his full red lips, one of these blood-drinkers? A demon from hell? The monk abruptly turned in his saddle; he caught mine host's stare and sketched a blessing in his direction. The taverner glanced away. He shouldn't think thoughts like that. After all, the monk was a man of the Church but, there again, so many priests, friars and monks had fallen away from their true vocations.

Mine host urged his horse on. He always liked to ride in front, except when they confronted danger. He secretly saw himself as leader of the pilgrims though, if matters came to push, he would always concede to the wisdom and fighting abilities of Sir Godfrey.

'Ah, good taverner!'

Sir Godfrey grasped his reins in one hand and, with the other, wiped the perspiration from his sunburned face. He moved in the saddle in a creak of leather and clink of chain, the sounds of a fighting man.

'It's good, is it not, mine host, to be travelling the Pilgrims' Way to Canterbury, to pray before the blessed bones of St Thomas a Becket?'

'God be thanked, Sir Godfrey,' the taverner replied. 'But shall we have another story?'

'Aye, and a song,' the golden-haired squire piped up, his blue eyes and smooth face bright with excitement at the journey.

3

Sir Godfrey turned in his saddle. 'My lord monk has a good voice, deep and merry.'

The monk grimaced, his eyes fixed on Sir Godfrey.

'Come on, Sir Monk, be a merry fellow!'

The monk shrugged. 'My name is Hubert, Sir Godfrey, and my throat is dry.'

Mine host passed across his wineskin. The monk took this in one easy movement and squirted a stream of red juice into his cavernous mouth. He handed the wineskin back, gently burped and launched into a sweet, triumphant song of praise about some young woman who had caught the eye of a painter in a mansion near the Ile du Pont in Paris. He sang in Norman French; many knew that language but the monk's voice was so lusty and carrying they let him sing alone, enjoying the sound on this pleasant spring day. After he had finished they all cheered and clapped. They then stopped for a while at a well to quench their thirst and eat the dried meats and fruits they had packed away.

They continued their journey late into the afternoon listening to a story told by the squire. The sun lost its warmth as it began to set, turning the blue sky a fiery red. Some of the pilgrims became impatient. They were saddle-sore, weary, and hoped that, for tonight at least, they would shelter at some cheery tavern or well-stocked priory. The countryside was now cut by hedgerows which rose like prickly walls on either side. These cast long shadows and some of the pilgrims recalled the stories they had been told about assassins, blood-drinkers and ghosts.

They rounded a bend. Sir Godfrey had already stopped. The others clustered behind him or fanned out across the lane, trying hard to keep their horses away from the shallow ditches on either side. They had arrived at a crossroads where the trackway climbed before splitting and going a variety of ways. However, it wasn't that they were lost or confused. The pilgrims just stared in horror at the scene before them.

A huge, three-branched gallows stretched up against the

4

night sky. Beneath this stood a cart, its great dray horses hobbled, a youth grasping their bridles. On the cart stood three felons, hands bound; a group of bailiffs were busy fastening the nooses round their necks. On a horse near the cart, wearing the royal arms and carrying a white wand of office, sat a tipstaff of the court of assizes. He was dressed in dark murrey with a feathered cap on his head. A young, pointed-faced man, he was issuing orders. The felons, dressed in a motley collection of rags, their faces almost hidden by straggly hair, moustaches and beards, were protesting and shouting but the bailiffs held them fast. Around the cart stood royal archers, long bows slung across their backs; each carried a drawn sword. The pilgrims had been so engrossed in their own affairs, while the crossroads had been so well hidden by the hedgerows and trees, that it took some time for them to recover from their shock at this unexpected sight. The execution party, however, continued as if unaware of the pilgrims thronging only a few yards away. Indeed, mine host thought they might be seeing the ghosts from some dreadful execution which had been carried out many years ago. However, the tipstaff turned, holding up the white wand.

'Proceed no further!' he cried. 'In the name of the King!'

Sir Godfrey, his hand held up in the sign of peace, pushed his horse forward.

'My name is Sir Godfrey Evesden, knight banneret. I, and these gentle pilgrims, are on our way to Canterbury to pray before Becket's blessed bones.'

On the cart all movement stilled; the bailiffs and their victims now stared at the pilgrims. The tipstaff had doffed his hat as a courtesy to the knight.

'Sir Godfrey, I know your name. Mine is Luke Tiverton: chief tipstaff to the lords of assize now moving across Kent, dispensing the King's justice.'

Sir Godfrey nodded. 'Then, sir, why hang these men in such a desolate spot?'

'They are brought here because they carried out their horrible robberies, rapes, murders and other violations of the King's peace along these lonely lanes. They were caught red-handed by the sheriff. The assize lords have ruled that they are to hang on the nearest gallows to the place of their crimes!'

'Have they been shriven?' The poor priest nudged his sorry-looking nag to the front of the pilgrims.

'Aye, Father, we have but, if you want to do it again!' one of the felons shouted.

'Both God's justice and the King's have been done,' the tipstaff replied. He gestured towards the setting sun. 'My lords of assize have ruled that they must hang before dark and so hang they will. Sir Godfrey, you know the law. If no witnesses are present that is good. But . . .'

'Now,' Sir Godfrey added wearily, 'because we have arrived, we are those witnesses.'

'Sir Godfrey, you know the law.' The tipstaff stood up in his stirrups and stared over the pilgrims' heads. His eyes caught the prioress and the bold, beaming face of the wife of Bath. 'However, I see you have ladies of quality among you. They and any others, including members of the body spiritual, may turn away.'

Some of the pilgrims did so. Mine host suddenly remembered there was something at the back of his cavalcade he wished to see. The prioress had already dismounted. She stood with her back to the gallows scene. Her priest had his hand across her shoulder though mine host caught the man of law hurrying to assist her.

'I couldn't give a bugger!' the wife of Bath shouted. 'I've seen men hang and I'll see them hang again.'

She pushed her grey palfrey to the front where the squire, at his father's insistence, had turned away. However, the summoner, the monk and others craned their necks to get a good view. The evening breeze carried the tipstaff's voice as he read out the verdict of the court and many of the pilgrims chilled as the list of 'horrible' crimes was proclaimed: murder, sodomy, rape, breaking into churches, blasphemy, sacrilege, desertion from the royal levies, poaching. The long litany seemed endless. The felons on the cart, however, just stood staring impassively. The tipstaff's voice became a gabble. He finished, thrust the parchment back into his pouch and made a slicing movement with his hand.

'Let the King's justice be done!'

The bailiffs jumped out of the cart. The horses were unhobbled. One of the archers struck their hindquarters with a leather strap. The horses moved, pulling the cart away, leaving the felons to dance, jerking on the ends of the ropes like landed fish. They turned and twirled, kicking and spluttering as the nooses tightened.

The knight heard a commotion behind him but ignored it. He spurred his horse forward.

'For the love of God, man!' he snarled.

The tipstaff pulled a face, snapped his fingers and gestured at the bailiffs. Three hurried forward to grab the felons' legs and pull them down. Sir Godfrey heard a snap as one of their necks was broken; this act of mercy soon put all three felons out of their misery and finished the executions. The tipstaff ordered the bailiffs to check each body.

'Dead as nails!' one of them cried. 'They'll be cold and stinking within the hour!'

'Then do it now!' the tipstaff ordered.

A huge pot of tar was dragged from the cart. The bailiffs, armed with brushes, began to coat each cadaver in pitch so they would remain much longer as a grim warning to any other wolfs-heads or outlaws who came this way.

'We can pass now?' Sir Godfrey wrinkled his nose in disgust at the pungent smell from the cadavers.

'Sir Godfrey, may God be with you!'

The knight reined his horse in alongside the tipstaff.

'Which is the route to Canterbury?'

'Dead ahead, Sir Godfrey.' The tipstaff kept his face impassive. 'Two or three miles will bring you to St Bardolph's

Priory. However, I think one of your pilgrims is sore afflicted.'

While the execution party made to leave, the grisly corpses now hanging silently on the end of the tarred ropes, Sir Godfrey dismounted and made his way towards where the pilgrims thronged. His heart sank; on the trackway sprawled the carpenter, a dark-haired, cheery-faced man who kept to himself though he had a quick sense of humour and was always ready to help the other pilgrims.

'What is the matter?'

The physician kneeling beside the fallen man looked up, his sharp eyes crinkled in amusement.

'Don't worry, Sir Godfrey, it's not the falling sickness or the pestilence.' He glanced round at the rest of the pilgrims, now shrinking back. 'The poor fellow's fainted, that's all.'

He turned the carpenter over. The man's face was slightly bruised on one side, his skin as white as a sheet, his closed eyes fluttering, a streak of spittle at the corner of his mouth.

'Come on now.'

The physician grasped the man's shoulders and pulled him up. On a command his manservant came running up with a leather bag. The physician delved into this and took out a small pomade. Even from where he stood, Sir Godfrey could smell its acrid stench. As the physician waved the pomade, the carpenter's eyes opened.

'They have come!' he cried, gazing fearfully around.

'Who has come?' the physician asked.

'The nags of the darkness. The birds of the night. They'll never leave me alone! Agnes Ratolier's . . . !'

'Tush man.' Sir Godfrey knelt down, proffering his wine cup. The carpenter seized this and drank greedily. 'An execution has been carried out. Perhaps it was that, or hunger. Anyway, you fainted.'

The carpenter took a further gulp of wine and blinked.

'I am sorry.' He leaned forward, the colour returning to his face. 'They are dead, aren't they?'

8

'As Herod and Pilate,' the physician assured him. 'Come on man, it's getting dark and we must seek shelter.'

They helped the carpenter back up on to his horse, the physician offering to ride alongside him. Sir Godfrey urged the pilgrims on. They clattered by, eager to escape this place of death. Sir Godfrey noticed, as the carpenter went by the scaffold, how he averted his head. The knight sighed and remounted. So many secrets, so many mysteries here. When they had left the Tabard in Southwark only a few days ago, Sir Godfrey considered his companions a motley collection, eager to take advantage of the bright spring weather to go and pray before the shrine at Canterbury. Now he was not so sure. They were like himself, men and women who harboured great secrets, who were making this pilgrimage, not just because of the pleasant April weather or to see the sights, but to ask for divine protection: the personal favour of the great saint himself!

'Father?'

Sir Godfrey glanced up. His son came riding back through the gloom.

'Father, why do you tarry?'

Sir Godfrey touched his sword which hung from the saddle horn. He knew why his son was anxious. The monk had also held back. Seated on his horse in his gown and cowl, he looked like a great crow studying the three corpses hanging from the end of their tarred ropes.

'One of these days,' Sir Godfrey muttered, 'either before we arrive or when we leave the shrine, I am going to have words with Master Hubert!'

He dug his spurs in and, followed by the squire, clattered over the crossroads eager to join the rest of the pilgrims. The monk, however, sat as if fascinated by the corpses swaying gently in the evening breeze. A raven, probably hunting before nightfall, glided over like a lost, dark soul and perched on one of the arms of the gibbet. The monk caught the glow of its gleaming yellow eye. He stared at the twisted necks of the felons and ran his tongue around his upper lip in a display of fine white teeth, jagged and sharp.

'Bird of the darkness,' he whispered. 'So you'll feast on the flesh?'

The juices now ran strong and hot in his own mouth. He gathered the reins of his horse. It was so long, he thought, since he too had feasted yet he could not here. He had hoped to prey among the others but then he'd noticed Sir Godfrey Evesden. The monk, like other strigoi, recognised Sir Godfrey's fearsome reputation: a demon-hunter, a man ready to take his head as this raven here would the eyes of these dead men. The monk shifted, peering through the darkness. He could just make out the retreating backs of Sir Godfrey and his son. He would like to turn his horse, take the other trackway, but that might create suspicion. Yet he must eat and drink, the blood warm and cloying. What could he do? His horse stirred restlessly. If he fled through the night Sir Godfrey would certainly pursue him! He, that damnable son and the yeoman whose hands were never far from his sword and dagger.

The monk sighed. There was nothing to do except wait. He turned his horse's head, dug his spurs in and followed the rest, leaving the gibbet eerie and lonely under the watchful eyes of the raven.

The priory yard of St Botolph's was a hive of activity. The prior and guestmaster had come out, eager to welcome the pilgrims who would pay well for the use of their refectory and hall. Lay brothers held the horses, others took off saddles as well as bundles and panniers from the pack horses. The pilgrims had now forgotten the gallows, rejoicing in the warmth, light and fragrant smells from the priory kitchens. They were ushered over to the guest house. Some of the pilgrims could afford one of the small, white-washed chambers above; others would settle for a bed of straw in the hall or the refectory.

The pilgrims first visited the church to give thanks. The

dark nave was lit by candles fixed in small iron holders in the pillars. The air was warm and fragrant with the smell of incense. As they knelt in a group before the rood screen the poor priest led them in a hymn of praise and thanksgiving.

Afterwards they went to the refectory. Each pilgrim took their place along the broad trestle tables with Sir Godfrey at the top, the lady prioress on his right and the physician to his left. The carpenter had now recovered his good humour. When the brothers brought in traunchers of roast goose covered in sauce, as well as small bowls of vegetables and baskets of freshly baked bread, the carpenter ate as merrily and eagerly as the others. Jugs of wine, red and white, were passed round and, for those like the miller, large stoups of ale or beer. For a while the pilgrims chattered, discussing their journey and what they would do tomorrow. They all toasted Sir Godfrey, certain that it was the knight's strong leadership which had brought them so safely to this comfortable place.

Once the meal was finished they all sat patting their stomachs. The miller, who had been drinking since he had risen that morning, got up and tried to do a dance but then, clutching one of the pillars of the refectory as fondly and as warmly as he would a woman, slid gracefully down, stretched out and fell fast asleep. His snores reverberated like claps of thunder until the physician went across, closed his mouth and pinched his nostrils. The pilgrims raised a small cheer. The miller, when drunk, was a troublesome fellow. Mine host tapped his tankard.

'We have supped and drunk well,' he announced. 'Outside,' he pointed towards the latticed windows, 'darkness has fallen, given over to the creatures of the night.' He spoke dramatically and created the desired effect. After all, he was a taverner and, when people sat by a roaring fire, their bellies full of food and good ale, there was no better time to listen to some tale of ghostly terror. And hadn't the pilgrims agreed to this? To tell one story during the day and another of terror and mystery at night?

11

'Haven't we had enough horror for one day?' The franklin spoke up.

'Aye,' the summoner agreed.

He was still trying to get near the franklin's purse as he would love to pick it. The franklin knew this and the summoner now saw it as a game which he was determined to win before they reached Canterbury.

'Why did you faint?' Dame Eglantine the prioress took a sop of bread, dipped it into a small bowl of milk, and gave it to her little lapdog. 'I am speaking to you, sir.' She raised one elegant, be-ringed hand and pointed at the carpenter.

'Haven't you seen a hanging before?' the pardoner screeched, flicking back his flaxen hair. 'Lord save us, when the great rising was put down, they were hanging rebels along every road. The ravens and crows were so bloated they couldn't stretch their wings and fly.'

Dame Eglantine pursed her lips in distaste.

'Hangings be hangings.' The sharp, waspish-faced reeve spoke up. He'd drunk deeply and his glittering eyes were now looking for an argument. He'd love nothing better than to debate and demonstrate that sharp wit which he used on the poor peasants who didn't pay their proper dues and tolls.

The carpenter, however, stared down at his empty trencher.

'It's not the hangman I'm afeared of,' he declared. 'Dead is dead and that is it!'

'So what?' the physician asked.

'Do you believe in ghosts?'

'I certainly do.' The ploughman spoke up. 'You know that.' His hand went to cover that of his brother the poor priest. 'I truly think,' the ploughman continued, surprising the company with his sharpness of speech and knowledge, for, in truth, they considered him base born and ill educated, 'the veil between life and death is very thin and sometimes it can be crossed.'

'Especially when you are drunk.' The summoner spoke but his joke did not even produce a smile or a chuckle. All eyes were now on the carpenter.

12

'So, you believe in ghosts,' the carpenter said as if speaking to himself. 'But what about other horrors? Those who die but come back across the drawbridge out of the darkness, across that eternal moat between life and death. Who can sit here among us, flesh and blood! We think they are our own. Yet they are creatures of the night, spawned by hell's pit.'

'Have you seen such beings?' mine host asked excitedly, winking down the table at the knight.

'In my previous life,' the carpenter replied. 'Now I work in wood and, every time I touch it, like this table or the bench on which we sit, I say a quiet prayer to Jesus, born in a wooden manger and who died on the cruel cross. I can do no other.' He drank from his wine cup. 'I have seen such creatures,' he said again. 'Hags of hell and it started, well, it really started as a jest.'

'Tell us more.' Sir Godfrey leaned forward. 'Master Carpenter, the meal is finished, the doors are closed, the brothers will not interrupt us. We need a tale and, I think, your tongue is eager to tell one.'

The carpenter looked down at his hands.

'Can you do it?' mine host asked. 'Can you tell us your tale, carpenter?'

'Have you ever been to Gloucester?' the carpenter abruptly replied.

'On many occasions,' the wife of Bath said.

The carpenter smiled, his now solemn face transformed.

'Well, good wife, that's where I hail from. Not Gloucester itself but a small village outside, between the city and Tewkesbury, a fair place near the Severn.'

The wife of Bath smiled at this worker in wood and sucked on her teeth. If the truth be known she thought he was quite a handsome man and carpenters earned many a silver piece. She was lonely. How many husbands had she buried? She sighed. She had drunk so much she had forgotten, but the carpenter was a likeable fellow. She abruptly realised everyone was staring at her so she broke from her reverie.

13

'I have often visited Gloucester,' she repeated.

The wife of Bath felt her thigh touched under the table and lashed out. She glared across at the summoner who was trying to lift her skirt with the toe of his boot.

'Aye, it's a fair city,' Sir Godfrey intervened quickly and glared at the pock-faced summoner, his face now red as a piece of glowing charcoal.

'A veritable jewel,' the carpenter agreed. 'Bound by the Severn. To the north the Priory of St Oswald, just next to the Abbey of St Peter which houses the corpse of our present King's great-grandfather so foully murdered by his wife Isabella. To the south the castle. It's a godly city with the White Friars near Northgate, the Black and Grey Friars around Southgate. It's also a place of trade and commerce. Along Westgate and Eastgate you can buy anything your heart desires.' The carpenter paused. 'I had such fancies. But if you travel west,' he continued, 'beyond the city lies a forest dark and menacing. A place of shadows! Even the woodcutters and charcoal-burners are afeared of going there at night and they have good reason. Stay well clear of those moonlit glades where the lords of hell meet their worshippers! Oh yes!' The carpenter nodded. 'I will tell you a tale which will chill your blood. Never again will you look upon a scaffold without thinking of what I have told you!' He drew in a deep breath. 'Listen now . . .'

14

Chapter 2

Flame-haired Meg left Gloucester by Eastgate as she always did, across Goose Ditch, taking the Barton Road. Darkness was falling and the September weather was beginning to show the first hint of autumn. No sooner was she away from the lights and the safety of the town gates than a fine rain began to fall, made all the more vexatious by a strong, biting breeze. Meg pulled up her hood and grasped the ash cane more firmly. She walked, as she always did, slowly, lost in thought about the day's happenings.

Meg was from one of the outlying villages. Her father, a peasant farmer, had too many mouths to feed while her mother, grey-faced with exhaustion, dragged herself around their wattle-daubed cottage, too free with both her stick and sharp tongue. There was no work for Meg so she had come into the city and joined the rest of the jobless where they gathered in the porches of churches waiting to be hired. She had been fortunate. The taverner of the Golden Cockerel had espied her flaming red hair and pale face and offered her a job as a pot girl in the tavern. His customers always liked to see a pretty girl and Meg had become accustomed to the whispered comments, salacious remarks, the nipping and the pinching which she simply saw as part of a day's work. In her purse she now had two pennies, which would please her father.

Meg paused to stare up the trackway. The hedgerows on either side looked dark and sinister. The old oak trees which stood behind spread their great branches down, turning the lane into a darkening tunnel. Meg always felt wary of such a place. Usually there were other travellers, a chapman, a pedlar, some pilgrims from the abbey, but tonight, perhaps because the weather had changed, the trackway was empty. Meg walked on. Perhaps Mother might have made a stew. In the napkin she grasped, Meg carried some loaves the kindly taverner had provided. They were three days old but, if broken up and mixed with the stew, they would soften and fill her belly and those of her large family.

Now and again in the thicket alongside came a rustling; somewhere a night bird called. Meg kept her head down. It was best if she didn't let her mind play tricks. She had been in the abbey earlier in the day. She'd gone to sit there, a rest from the turbulence of the tavern. She had sat just within the doorway and studied the great Doom painted on the wall depicting Christ in Judgement. Meg had also seen a painting of Christopher carrying the Infant Jesus Christ. Meg now recalled the legend that, if you looked on St Christopher, you would never die that day.

'Do you have some food?'

Meg started. A figure stood near the ditch, just under the shade of the great oak tree. The figure moved forward, shuffling, her stick tapping on the trackway. Meg relaxed. It was only an old beggarwoman. In the fading light she could make out the grey wispy hair under the tattered hood, the slightly hooked nose. A bony hand came out.

'Do you have some food for an old one?'

Meg paused. She opened the napkin and thrust one of the hardened loaves into the old lady's hand.

'There, Mother. It's hard but soften it with water and it will fill your belly.'

The old woman's face cracked in a smile. Meg still felt uneasy; the face was old but the eyes seemed young and shrewd.

'Travelling far are we, my beauty?'

'Just to the next village, about half a mile. Why, do you

16

want some company?' Meg clutched the napkin tighter. She just wished the old woman would make her mind up and either go back into the shadows or accompany her.

'A day's business in Gloucester, eh?'

'I work in the Golden Cockerel.' Meg forced a smile. 'But, Mother, the day draws on.'

Meg brushed by her, walking a little faster, half listening to the thanks and fulsome blessing from the old beggarwoman.

'I don't like her,' Meg whispered.

She walked firmly, swinging the cane, then stopped and looked around. The old woman had disappeared. Meg tried to reason with herself. Why was she frightened of an old crone? Yes, that was it, Meg knew every inch of this trackway. Beggars usually stood by the city gates or some appointed spot. They would never try their luck on a deserted country lane as darkness fell.

'Ah well.' Meg turned a corner. Through the trees she glimpsed a spark of light, soon she would be home! She slowed her walk and, as she did so, heard the crash of wheels. As she paused and looked back, around the corner came a cart with a canopy, its two horses moving briskly, the driver flicking his whip. Meg drew to the side of the road. Perhaps he would stop and offer her a ride. She held her hand up and the cart stopped. Meg was surprised that the driver was not a man but a young woman, her plump face half-hidden in the hood.

'Do you want a ride?' she offered.

'Just to the next village,' Meg replied.

'Then climb in the back. Go on!'

Meg hurried round. The flap was already open. Another woman was there, a little older than herself, raven-black hair framing a long, white face. Meg climbed on the tail board and the woman grasped her arms.

'In you get,' she said.

The inside of the wagon was dark. Meg sat on a bundle of straw. She turned to thank the woman, and saw that sitting opposite her was the old beggarwoman. Meg's stomach clenched in fear, heart in her throat, she half rose. She didn't like the way the old woman was looking at her while the other was now blocking any way out.

'I'd prefer to walk.'

'Please yourself!' The woman pulled back the leather covering.

Meg stooped to get out. She saw a quick movement out of the corner of her eye but it was too late. The thick club smashed into the side of her head and sent her crashing back into the cart.

Near Blindgate, in Gloucester, Simon Cotterill, a carpenter from the village of Berkeley, was also fearful of his life. He'd supped and eaten in the Leather Bottle tavern then stepped out into Oxhead Lane, intent on returning to the garret he had hired above a shop in King Street. The dark shadows just seemed to rise from the ground around him. Six men, their faces hidden by cowls and vizards; all were armed with clubs. Simon had drawn his dagger but watched fearfully as the men pushed him back against the tavern wall.

'I've got very little money,' he gasped. 'I'm only a poor carpenter looking for trade.'

'In which case, Master Cotterill, you should look for work elsewhere and not go sticking your snout into other men's troughs!'

Simon's heart sank, his throat went dry. These were not footpads or night-walkers looking for easy prey. They knew who he was and had been waiting for him.

'We bring a message from Goodman Draycott.' The leader's voice was muffled. 'You are a landless man, you are no member of a guild. You haven't a penny to your name so why go courting his daughter, eh?'

'Alice is my business!' Simon retorted. He felt light-headed with fear, his stomach churning and pitching.

'No, no, Master Cotterill, Alice Draycott is not your business: we are here to teach you that.'

The men drove in with a whirl of clubs, punches and kicks. Simon's dagger was knocked from his hand. He tried to fight back but it was useless. The blows rained down on him hard and cruel, so that all he could do was cover his head and sink further down the wall. A kick to his ribs sent him sprawling and the bully boys were on him, banging his head against the cobbles, punching his face, rapping his legs with their clubs. Simon's whole body turned into a sheet of flame, he tasted blood in his mouth. He tried to shout but a smelly hand grasped his face.

'Remember your lesson, Cotterill!' the voice grated. 'No more dancing and singing round Master Draycott's house!'

Simon groaned and fell back. He felt his belt with its sheath and purse being pulled off, followed by his leather jacket and linen shirt.

'You won't look the noble suitor now, will you?'

The men walked off, laughing and talking among themselves. Simon pulled himself up and leaned against the wall. He felt the bruises on his face. His right cheek was swollen, his left ear was angry and sore while one of his bottom teeth was loose and his lips were split. He tried to get up but this only provoked the pain in his stomach and legs.

'Oh, God have mercy!' he groaned as the biting night wind caught his sore, chapped flesh. He tried to crawl back to the tavern door. A dog came rushing out barking, tail high, the ruff of his hair round his neck standing up. Simon sighed and turned away. He dragged himself to the end of the alleyway where, sore and exhausted, he lay down. He closed his eyes, trying to decide which part of his body hurt the most. What could he do? If he went back to his chamber his landlord would throw him out. Already he was two weeks behind in rent. He felt something furry and cold slide across his hand. Simon thrashed about, screaming even as the rat scuttled away.

'My son, can I help you?'

The friar was crouched beside him. A small, rotund figure with merry eyes, his face half-hidden by a luxuriant moustache and beard.

'I've been attacked,' Simon blurted through blood-caked lips. 'They've taken all I have.'

'Then, brother, you are about as rich as I am.' The friar helped Simon to his feet. 'Come on!'

'Where to?' he asked, now suspicious of anyone.

'Oh, I'm going to take you before the King.' The friar put Simon's arm round his shoulder and grasped the young man's waist. 'The hospital of St Bartholomew is not far. Come on!'

Simon thought the journey would last for ever. They passed between the Priory of St Oswald and the dark, gloomy mass of the Abbey of St Peter, into Westgate and along Bridge Street. Now and again they were stopped by members of the watch who, in the light of their lanterns, gazed suspiciously at the injured man. However, the friar assured them all was well and they were allowed to pass.

The hospital of St Bartholomew stood in its own grounds, a small park with orchards, lawns and sweet-smelling herb plots. They entered through a lych-gate and up the pebbled path to the main entrance dominated by a huge, wooden porch. The friar told Simon to sit on the steps and he pulled at the bell. There was a sound of footsteps and the door swung open. After a hushed conversation Simon was helped into the clean, paved hallway.

'Bring him along here!' a voice ordered.

Simon blinked at the dancing torchlight. The place was warm. Fragrant smells from the kitchen mingled with those of soap, oil and pitch. As he was led along a corridor he glimpsed statues in niches, crucifixes on the walls. The friar helped him into a small chamber and laid him gently on a narrow pallet bed.

'Just lie there.' The friar stepped back.

Another man loomed above Simon. He had a square, honest face with gentle eyes. He was dressed in a dark brown robe, and a great metal badge displaying St Bartholomew hung from his neck. The man examined him carefully. He then brought a bowl of sweet scented water and a soft cloth to wipe his wounds and sores. Simon turned his head. The friar was sitting on a stool just inside the doorway.

'Thank you,' he muttered.

It was the last thing he remembered. The other man had poured a drink into his mouth and, in seconds, he'd drifted into a deep sleep.

Simon woke the next morning, bruised and aching in every joint. Of the friar there was no sign but the burly individual who had tended him the night before introduced himself as Thomas Cowley, keeper of the hospital.

'You are in a sad state, my son.'

Cotterill told him about what had happened the night before. The keeper scratched his head.

'I know Draycott,' he said. 'A roaring bully of a man. You could complain to the mayor or the council but you'd get short shrift.' He helped Simon up against the bolsters. 'You'll be all right,' he added soothingly, noticing the carpenter's wince of pain. He gestured round the bare cell. 'It doesn't look much but it's the best we can do. We have few candles, just rushlights. No decoration on the walls or floors but the food we'll give you is nutritious: eggs, herrings and cheese.' He pointed to a bundle of clothes on the table. 'Those are for you. A pair of boots, a rather tattered shirt, a gown, tabard and hood. I might even be able to give you a sheepskin wrap. But, before you ask, you can't stay here. We are a hospital. Three days at the very most and then it's out of the door!'

Simon shook his head. 'I'm grateful. I arrived in Gloucester full of high hopes. I am a carpenter from Berkeley. I was working on the castle when Master Draycott and his daughter visited the lord.' He shrugged. 'You know how it goes: a glance at lunchtime, a sweet smile at supper.'

'And so you came here?'

21

'I came, Master Cowley, because I truly loved Alice Draycott.'

'And does she love you?'

'I haven't had a chance to find out. I've been seven days here. My money's all gone. Yesterday I knocked on Draycott's door. I was told to go away. I thought there was no malice in the man.'

'But now?'

Simon heaved a sigh. 'There's no work for me back in Berkeley and I have no family there.'

'And, in Gloucester, you are not a member of the guild?' Simon nodded mournfully.

'Ah well.' Cowley got to his feet. 'Friar Martin is coming back later this afternoon. Perhaps he can help.'

Friar Martin did. The little fat friar's liquid brown eyes filled with sadness as he, too, listened to Simon's tale of woe.

'So, you've got no family, no money, no job, and not even a corner to call your own?' The friar shook his head despondently. He sat, sandalled feet apart, hands on his knees, staring down at the floor. 'There is a job.' He lifted his head. 'It's, er, a post recently vacated.'

'Why?'

'The person . . .' The friar smacked his lips and combed his tangled beard with stubby fingers. 'Ah well, I won't tell you a lie, he was hanged.'

'Hanged?'

'Yes, I am afraid hoist by his own petard would be a very suitable phrase.'

'Brother, what are you saying? Who was this man?'

'He was called "No Teeth".' Friar Martin smiled wryly. 'Well, that's the only name he ever gave; his mouth was like that of a newborn babe. Not one tooth to boast about! He always had to eat everything softened, mixed with milk like a child.'

Simon ran his tongue round his mouth, feeling the sores on his gums.

'Brother, if there is a post and it pays money?'

'Oh, it pays very well,' the friar continued in a rush. 'I'll tell you honestly. No Teeth was an assistant hangman to the city council.'

Simon groaned.

'No, listen. No one knew where he came from, he was like you. He wasn't bad at his job but he was very sensitive about having no teeth. One night in the Green Hoop tavern someone started making fun of him, one of these apprentices full of arrogance and spite. No Teeth talked in rather a peculiar way and the apprentice mocked him. No Teeth, my companion, my friend-at-arms, my brother in Christ, drew his dagger and killed him. Five days later, having appeared before His Majesty's justices at the Guildhall, No Teeth was taken out and hanged on the common gallows near High Cross on the corner of Northgate. You know where that stands?'

Simon nodded. 'But you called him your companion?'

'That's right,' the friar replied. 'One of my tasks is to visit the condemned and offer them the spiritual comfort of the Church.'

'How many hangmen are there?' Simon asked.

'Four in all. We make up a happy band of brothers. There's Shadbolt, he's the chief hangman. He had three assistants until No Teeth's execution: Merry Face, you'll know why we call him that when you meet him, and Flyhead are the two whom you will join.'

'And I'll know why you call him that when I meet him?' Simon echoed.

The friar sighed, shuffling his feet.

'Just wait there.'

He went out and returned a short while later.

'According to the hour candle, the market horn is about to be sounded. I think you'd best come with me. Don't worry about saying goodbye. I'll explain to Master Cowley later.'

Simon, already dressed, put on his new-found boots and followed the friar out of the hospital of St Bartholomew.

It was a fine day and the crowds were out along the streets and lanes among the stalls and booths. People were shouting and greeting one another. Apprentices were still trying to catch the eyes of prospective customers. Constables and beadles patrolled the streets. Refuse carts were busy; beggars thronged the bakeries and cook shops, looking for stale bread. A young man, dressed in white, was walking up and down, a variety of hides and skins of fox, cat, squirrel and rabbit draped across his arms and shoulders, or strapped round his body with pieces of rope, a desperate attempt to entice customers to shop at his master's stall. A number of dogs, attracted by the smell of the hides, were also following him and this novel idea of selling merchandise had provoked more humour than custom. Elsewhere children were playing football with a pig's bladder filled with oats or chasing a hoop, making it stand and roll with the little hollow sticks they carried.

Simon looked around anxiously. Perhaps Master Draycott was out or, even better still, Alice? She might catch his eye, be sympathetic, but all he could see were the faces of strangers.

They went down Westgate past the churches of St Michael and Holy Trinity to where the great market cross stood. Here the market officers patrolled, slapping their white wands of office against their legs. Pompous and full of their own importance, they insisted that all selling and buying cease forthwith on payment of a fine or even a short stay in the stocks which stood at the end of the street. Nevertheless, these and the people they were trying to control soon scattered when a group of young men dressed in finery thundered through on mud-spattered destriers, dogs yapping behind them. The horsemen pounded by, more concerned with the hawks and peregrines on their wrists than the good citizens of Gloucester, who quietly cursed the young bloods who'd spent the day playing while others worked.

At the end of Westgate, the crowd was more dense, more difficult to push through. Carts and wagons were preparing to leave the city; disconsolate farmers shepherded the cattle,

24

geese, ducks, pigs and other livestock they had failed to sell to the slaughterers, fleshers and poulterers. Friar Martin led Simon away from these, down an alleyway, thin as a needle and smelling foul as a midden-heap, on to the execution ground. Here the crowd was held back by city bailiffs. In the short space before them a huge branched gallows soared up into the sky. The crowd jostled each other while water-tipplers, apple-sellers and purveyors of sweetmeats swarmed around looking for trade. Friar Martin climbed on to a low-bricked wall and stared over the heads of the crowds.

'They are coming!' he announced.

The crowd grew silent. Simon glimpsed a great banner bearing the civic arms of the city, a group of archers and then a death cart trundled into the space before the gallows. The executioners were dressed in black leather with red masks over their faces. One drove the cart, the other two sat with the three prisoners.

'Follow me!' Friar Martin whispered.

The little friar pushed his way through the crowd, every so often shouting who he was and why he had to be there. The people respectfully drew aside. Simon felt strange as he followed the friar across the empty space to where the executioners were now dragging the condemned men out of the death cart.

'Good day, Brother!'

A huge, burly fellow, the driver of the cart, swung himself down and stood, feet apart.

'God bless you, Master Shadbolt,' Friar Martin replied.

The chief hangman turned. The prisoners were lined up, a sorry sight in their rags, hands and feet tightly bound.

'Do any of you wish a final word with the good brother here?' Shadbolt asked.

One of the prisoners, his face bruised, his right eye almost closed, hawked and spat.

'Piss off, Shadbolt! Do what you have to! Let's be in hell before sunset!'

'I always try to oblige my customers.'

The other executioners were now taking ladders, placing them against the scaffold posts. They ran up these as nimble as squirrels and attached hempen ropes through the iron hooks on the end of each branch. The crowd was now restless. Pieces of offal, mud, dirt, even the corpse of a dead rat were thrown in the direction of the scaffold.

'What did the men do?' Simon whispered.

'They are outlaws, poachers from the Forest of Dean. They stole the King's venison.'

Simon closed his eyes and muttered a prayer. He felt the friar nudge him.

'Are you squeamish, Simon?'

'I just think it's a pity, Brother, that good men are hanged because they are hungry.'

'Do you now?' The friar raised his eyebrows. 'Do you really, Simon?'

'Yes I do.'

The prisoners were being jostled towards the ladders when a strange thing happened. Simon had seen other men executed at Berkeley, both in the castle and outside in the village. They were usually strung up like rats, left to dance, their death throes sometimes seeming to last for ever. Their bodies were then daubed with pitch and tar and displayed in an iron gibbet as a warning to others.

This, however, was different. White sacks were pulled over the condemned men's heads, completely concealing their faces. Simon had heard of such a practice: an act of mercy so others couldn't see the terrible contortions of death. Shadbolt treated the prisoners gently. Their bonds were cut and they were taken up the ladders. When they reached the top, one of the assistants, who had gone up before, placed a noose round each condemned man's neck, pushing down the great knot just behind their left ear. Soon all three prisoners were ready. A city official walked forward. Pompous and fat-bellied, a ridiculous beaver hat on his head, he read the list of indictments then, with a flourish of his hand, shouted: 'Let the King's justice be done!'

The chief executioner swiftly moved each ladder. The condemned men were launched into the air to dance and jerk. The assistant hangmen scrambled down the scaffold, grasped each of the felons' ankles and pulled them down. Within a very short while all three hung silent, legs and arms loose, bodies swaying slightly at the end of the rope.

Immediately the crowd broke up. The city officials wandered away, as did the archers. The hangmen, however, sat at the foot of the scaffold; pulling their masks up over their eyes, they shared a wineskin. Simon thought Friar Martin would go across and join them but he stayed where he was, his only gesture being to sketch a cross in the direction of the three dead felons.

Once the crowd had dispersed, the ladders were put back, the hangmen climbed up and released the ropes. The corpses were placed in the carts and immediately covered with a tarpaulin sheet.

'What now?' Simon asked.

'Well, they'll be taken to Austin Friars cemetery near Southgate. There's a piece of common land which stretches down to Goose Ditch, they'll be interred there.' Friar Martin dug into his purse and pressed a coin into Simon's hand. 'Just across there you'll see Catskin Alley. Halfway down is a small tavern.' He grinned. 'The Hangman's Rest. Once the corpses are buried we'll meet you there. Go on,' he urged.

Simon walked away, still feeling sore and bruised after the attack the previous evening, his mind all in a whirl. He stopped and looked back at the gallows. He was in his twenty-fourth summer, the year of Our Lord 1388, and what did life hold for him? There was nothing for him at Berkeley. He had been raised by an aged aunt and knew full well the bitter dregs of poverty. He had been taught his trade by a local joiner, a master craftsman who had worked here on the Abbey of St Peter. But what else? He, Simon Cotterill,

27

was not a member of a guild and had scarce received a warm welcome in Gloucester except at the hospital of St Bartholomew and from that little friar now climbing on to the death cart.

Simon scratched where the tabard given to him at the hospital rubbed his neck; the harsh serge cloth had raised a small weal. He stared up at the sky. Autumn would soon give way to winter. He remembered what the master craftsman had told him, that life was like a greasy pole, you climbed or you slid back into the mud. Would that happen to him? Would he be forced to join the hordes of landless men who roamed the roads looking for work? He walked on, reached Catskin Alley and found the Hangman's Rest.

Despite its name the tavern was cheery, the taproom large and spacious. Hams, flitches of bacon and vegetables hanging from the rafters to be cured gave a sweet aromatic smell which made Simon's mouth water. The tables were of good walnut, the stools three-legged and firm while the window seat was even cushioned with quilted cloth. A fire crackled in the hearth and from the kitchen came the clash and clatter of pots and pans. The rushes on the floor were green and supple. On the walls were drawings of gibbets, scaffolds and death carts. In one niche the skull of a man had been placed: underneath this, in a clerkly hand, a piece of parchment described the skull's former owner as one 'AEFULWULF, a monk who had fled his monastery and turned to robbery near the river crossings, before being captured and hanged in the year of Our Lord 1312'.

The taverner came out of the kitchen, a tall, wiry individual dragging his left leg behind him as he walked. He looked Simon up and down.

'You are not a beggar, are you, yet I can see your clothes weren't made for you.'

'I'm a friend of Friar Martin,' Simon replied.

The flinty-eyed taverner's face remained impassive.

'He wants me to work with him.' Simon resented having to

explain but he did not wish to be thrown out and have to kick his heels in the alleyway.

'A new recruit.' The taverner's face creased into a smile. 'I was once a hangman myself till I fell from the scaffold tree.' He tapped his damaged leg. 'A grisly profession. So, friend, welcome to the shadows between life and death!'

Chapter 3

In the mayor's secret chamber above the Guildhall near King's Cross, the two leading aldermen sat at the long, polished walnut table. They were waiting for their leading citizen, the mayor, to continue his deliberations. The mayor, however, seemed lost in his own thoughts. He stared at the great civic sword placed in the centre of the table, its blade unsheathed. The precious stones in the hilt caught the candle glow and shimmered in small flashes of light. Outside the lead-paned windows, darkness was falling. The casements were all shut, just in case voices were raised and those outside, eager to eavesdrop, heard about the horrors which had been discovered near the King's city of Gloucester. On the shadowy stairwell outside, archers wearing the city livery, steel conical helmets on their heads, stood guard with drawn swords. Near the doorways below men-at-arms thronged, ready to support the bailiffs and tipstaffs against any disturbance of this important meeting.

'My lord mayor.' Draycott, merchant and alderman, scratched his grey, close-cropped hair and played with the guild chain round his thick neck. 'My lord mayor,' he repeated. 'Why are we here at such a late hour? And where are the clerks?'

He looked over his shoulder at the green-baized table where the scribes would usually sit, taking careful note of the important matters being discussed. The mayor, Sir Humphrey Baddleton, didn't even bother to raise his eyes but kept running his fingers round grim set lips though, now and again, he would absentmindedly scratch his greying beard. He was fascinated by the sword, a symbol of his power. He would like to seize it, use the point to dig out the evil canker threatening the King's peace and the harmony of the city.

Sir Humphrey surveyed the opulently furnished chamber: the embroidered tapestries on the walls, the shields with their gaudy escutcheons; trunks, chests, metal-reinforced caskets; the shelves laden with silver, gold and pewter cups, the civic plate of the city. He stretched out and sipped from his wine cup then he leaned back in the quilted chair, resting his elbows on the arms, his fingers playing with the lion's head carved at each end. The chamber was warmed by the capped braziers standing in each corner. A movement out of the corner of his eye made Sir Humphrey stare down at the two pet white rabbits which he took everywhere. A small eccentricity which the mayor was proud of. He was wealthy, powerful and had the time and riches to breed a special type of rabbit as well as plump doves and pigeons for his dovecote. Yet, in his heart, Sir Humphrey knew this was all nonsense. Such playthings were not for these dark times.

Draycott raised his head to intervene again but his companion, John Shipler the furrier, nudged him sharply. The mayor's temper was short and quick; even on the merriest of occasions he did not take kindly to interruptions, and they would just have to wait. They knew something terrible had happened.

At the far end of the table sat the mayor's sergeant-at-arms, his principal officer. The man sat rigidly, now and again moving in a creak of leather and chain mail. He had arrived late in the afternoon, followed by a cart closely protected by archers, its contents a casket, hidden under bales of straw. The casket now stood in the small anteroom. They had glimpsed it when the mayor's officers had ushered them up here, closing and locking the door behind them.

'I am sorry.' The mayor scraped back his chair. 'I'm trying to find words to describe how all this happened.'

'What has happened?' Draycott demanded.

'You have heard about the disappearances?'

His two companions looked puzzled.

'For the love of God!' the mayor barked. 'Young women, in and around the city, have disappeared.' He clapped his hands. 'Like puffs of smoke!'

'Tavern wenches,' Draycott intervened. 'Alehouse girls, daughters of peasants.'

'Aye, Master Draycott.' The mayor's bulbous eyes glared back. 'They were someone's daughters.'

'But . . . but . . .' Draycott stammered. 'My lord mayor, it's well known, these girls are, well, they are loose in their ways, they go hither and thither . . .'

'Who said they were loose in their ways?' Sir Humphrey retorted. 'And what has happened, Master Draycott, that suddenly, within a few months, aye, no later than the feast of Pentecost, these young wenches take it into their minds to disappear? Well, you are wrong!' He snapped his fingers. 'You'd best come with me! I hope your stomachs are not tender.'

He walked into the anteroom. This was usually a place where manuscripts and ledgers were stored. Now it had been cleared. A coffin lay across two trestles covered by a black pall. Once his colleagues were assembled, the mayor dragged this off and, without a word of warning, moved the lid to reveal the corpse of a young woman. Her throat had been cut, and the body almost drained of blood, lay white and lifeless. The red hair made the liverish mottled face only more gruesome.

'Oh my God!' Shipler, hands to his mouth, ran out of the chamber.

Draycott stared in horror. 'By the rood!' he exclaimed. 'And by all the saints! What has happened to her eyes and mouth?'

The smell from the corpse was now beginning to fill the chamber. The alderman hurriedly took a pomander from his wallet and pinched his nostrils. The mayor nodded at his sergeant-at-arms who, using his dagger, turned the face so they could see the full horror of what had happened. Flame-haired Meg's eyes and mouth had been stitched with thick, black cord.

'You've seen enough.'

The coffin lid was hastily replaced, the black pall thrown over it. The mayor crossed himself, his companion followed suit and they both walked back into the council chamber. Shipler was crouching over a pot he had taken from a shelf. He rose, his face white, dabbing at the corner of his mouth with the edge of his cloak.

'Master Draycott.' The mayor smiled thinly. 'We have no servants here, so perhaps you could serve us all wine?'

Draycott nodded hastily. Once the goblets were full the mayor tapped the table.

'Since the feast of Pentecost,' he began, 'we have had a number of young women disappear in or around Gloucester. Young wenches. Some served in taverns, a few followed more nefarious occupations. They had one thing in common. They travelled in and out of the city. Accordingly, both I and my sergeant-at-arms believe that they were abducted from country lanes.'

'Abducted?' John Shipler the furrier spoke up.

'Abducted,' the mayor repeated. 'Well, that's the best I can think of. Now there's been no trace of them but the wench whose poor corpse you have just viewed worked in some alehouse and was last seen leaving the city a few nights ago. Her family live in a hamlet a few miles down the Barton Road. She never reached home. Her father, a tenant farmer, came in to make enquiries both at the sheriff's office and with the coroner. Neither they nor the girl's former employers could provide any information as to her whereabouts.' Sir Humphrey took a sip of wine. 'In the normal course of events her disappearance would have been unmarked and unnoticed. However, yesterday afternoon, two foresters out with my Lord Berkeley's hunting dogs crossed Rushdene Brook in the Forest of Dean. One of the dogs, inexperienced, ran off and the foresters, with the help

34

of verderers, went looking for the animal. It was young and in its prime, much prized by its owner. The dog was being trained as a limner, to smell out game for the hunt. They tracked it deep into the forest and found it in an open glade, digging at the soil beneath a rock. The foresters were curious. The dog was muzzled and leashed, then they dug a little more themselves, and that's what they found.'

'But why?' Draycott asked. 'Who would kill a poor girl in such a way?'

The mayor looked at his sergeant-at-arms. The soldier coughed and cleared his throat.

'The highways and byways,' he said, 'are often plagued by wolfs-heads and outlaws.'

'Aye, we know that,' Shipler broke in. 'And I've sought better protection from the sheriffs.'

'Hush! Hush!' the mayor intervened. 'Now is not the time for criticism and back-biting. Continue now . . .'

'The girl was apparently taken from the Barton Road,' the sergeant-at-arms continued sonorously. He did not like these fat merchants and resented their criticism and muted accusations. 'She received a blow on the side of her head and must have been taken four or five miles deep into the forest. Her throat was cut, her eyes and mouth sealed in that barbarous way.' He paused, tapping the table, letting the truth sink slowly into these merchants' thick heads. 'Can't you see?' he continued mockingly. 'If she were to be ravished it would have happened near the trackway but her gown was never removed. There is no mark or bruise upon her except for her throat being slit and her eyes and mouth horribly disfigured.'

'What the officer is saying,' Sir Humphrey added, 'is that this young woman was abducted, knocked senseless, taken into the forest and used for some nefarious rite.'

'Witchcraft!' Draycott exclaimed.

'Yes, Master Draycott, witchcraft! And this is no petty trick or spiteful accusation. We know the Forest of Dean is often used by those who practise the gibbet rites. We have often heard of fires glimpsed there at the dead of night. Of bizarre scenes. Yet these are usually dismissed as fanciful notions.'

'But why were her eyes and mouth sewn together?' Draycott asked.

'I'm the Mayor of Gloucester, not a warlock!'

The answer provoked smiles and muted laughter.

'From the little I know,' Sir Humphrey continued, 'the practitioners of the black arts need a blood sacrifice. The eyes and mouth are closed in such a barbarous way to prevent the soul leaving, so the sacrifice is complete, body and soul, for the demons they worship.'

'But what can we do?' Draycott moaned. 'It would take a king's army to scour the Forest of Dean. And even then . . .'

'Even then they wouldn't find anything,' the mayor concluded. 'Now, this is not just a matter of the church spiritual. Gentlemen.' Sir Humphrey paused. 'Fellow merchants . . .' The last two words were deliberately emphasised. 'Can you imagine what will happen if the news becomes common knowledge? God knows the truth is bad enough, but when the rumour-mongers, the gossip collectors, the whisperers on the wind, publish the story, well, if it's news in Gloucester tomorrow, by the time the bell tolls for the Angelus, they'll know it all in Bath and Bristol. Who would want to come to a city where warlocks and wizards can sacrifice young women and practise their rites? People will become frightened to go here or there. To put it bluntly, trade will suffer.'

Sir Humphrey picked up his wine goblet and rolled it between his hands. Now he had their attention. Murder, disfigured corpses, was one thing, a fall in profits was much more serious.

'And then, of course,' he continued, 'we'll have the perjurers and liars pointing to this person or that. Old grudges and grievances will surface. Fingers will be pointed. All of us here serve as justices. Can you imagine how busy we will become?'

'So, what do you propose?' the sergeant-at-arms asked.

'The same as I do, sir, when there are mice in my house! I don't go looking for them! I bait a trap and wait for them to come to me. Now listen . . .'

In the Hangman's Rest, Simon Cotterill was making the acquaintance of his new colleagues, Shadbolt, Merry Face and Flyhead. Shadbolt was straightforward enough. A veteran of the King's wars: grizzled-headed, scar-faced, a man of few words but of undoubted authority. Merry Face, so-called because of a disfigurement to a muscle in his right cheek, which made him look as if he was always smiling, cheerfully confessed to being a former cleric, forced to leave his benefice in Leicester because, as he put it, of certain misunderstandings regarding a miller's wife and the contents of the offertory box. A youngish man, Merry Face, despite his disfigurement, was bright-eyed and quick-witted. Flyhead was older, a lean, vicious man, his teeth no more than black stumps. He was given his name because his bald pate was covered in black blotches which looked as if he were hosting, as Merry Face put it, a council of flies. Friar Martin, who was with them, quietly informed Simon that Flyhead might have been a priest.

Tankards of ale were ordered; bowls of diced chicken and pewter plates containing soft, white bread, a mixture of vegetables and the tavern's delicacy, grilled veal in a herb sauce, were placed beside each of them.

Simon could scarcely remember when he had eaten or drunk so fast. The hangmen seemed well replenished with silver. Simon noticed how their black jackets, leggings and boots were of the finest quality. Shadbolt's shirt was white and crisp while the leather war belt, slung on the floor beside him, was broad and shiny, the scabbard of his long Welsh stabbing dagger ornate and cleverly wrought.

They were all treated with great respect by the landlord who filled tankards and dishes whenever Shadbolt raised a hand. Simon was quickly accepted as one of their company. He was wondering how the evening would end when Shadbolt

slammed down his tankard and seized his hands, grasping them
so hard Simon winced.

'Well, boyo. You want to hang your fellow kind?'

'Er, no,' Simon stammered. 'To be precise, sir, I don't want
to hang anyone but I am poor and starving.'

'Sixpence a week,' Shadbolt replied. 'A shilling on execution day. You also get, though not as fine as this, jerkins,
leggings, boots and a war belt as well as a stipend at Christmas,
Easter and midsummer. The council expect you to be law-
abiding, not to get drunk in office and carry out your duties
faithfully. What do you say, Simon Cotterill, carpenter?'

Merry Face, Flyhead and Friar Martin were all looking at
him curiously, as if assessing his true worth. Shadbolt drew a
knife and, before Simon could flinch, cut him lightly on the
little finger of his left hand. The blood trickled out on the table.

'Do you swear to be one of our company? Day and night,
in fair weather and foul?'

'I swear!' Simon replied.

'Good, Master Cotterill, you have just taken your oath with
us.' Shadbolt re-sheathed his dagger. 'Break it and I'll cut your
throat!'

Fresh tankards of ale were ordered and, when the tapster
had served them, Shadbolt raised his.

'To the dead! To the hanged! To those who swing between
heaven and earth!'

They all accepted the toast and Simon Cotterill, carpenter,
became assistant hangman in the King's city of Gloucester.

Over the next few weeks Simon learned his trade. It included
a bewildering array of tasks because the executioners were not
only busy on hanging days but on other, diverse duties: the
maintenance of the scaffolds; the purchase of hempen ropes;
the upkeep of the cart; the exercise of the dray horses. Simon
soon became used to the black leather garments which made
him feel stronger, more powerful and, when he drew the red
mask over his face, like a knight in armour preparing to do
battle. The hangmen were not only responsible for executions

but also a whole range of punishments imposed by the courts in Gloucester: the branding of forgers and blasphemers; trimming the ears and slitting the noses of felons convicted for a third time; the fitting of branks around the mouths of women found guilty of contumacy, blasphemy and malicious gossip.

Simon found these punishments grisly, gruesome and, at first, quite harrowing. Most of the victims were hardened felons but those who were being punished for the first time screamed and resisted. Shadbolt soon realised that Simon had what he called 'a tender heart', unlike Flyhead who took a malicious glee in carrying out his duties. Accordingly, Simon was often just a witness rather than a participant. The birching of whores was also left to Flyhead and he always laid on with relish, smacking his cane across the plump, white buttocks of some street-walker caught soliciting, either out of hours or in the wrong place.

Execution days were different. Simon was expected to play his part. He quickly learned how to climb the dizzyingly high scaffold, fasten the noose round the felon's neck and turn away the ladder. He accepted Shadbolt's express orders that the condemned felon's face should also be masked and the executioner swing on the legs of the hanged so as to ease them, as quickly as possible, from this life to a more blissful state.

Simon soon hardened his heart. Most of the felons condemned, either at the assizes or the city courts, deserved their punishments. At the same time, however, Shadbolt and the others kept him well away from the prisoners. The condemned cells were cavernous chambers beneath the Guildhall. One of the principal tasks of the hangmen was to accompany Friar Martin down to visit the condemned. Shadbolt would measure the doomed felon with his eyes while Friar Martin offered him the comforts of Holy Church. Merry Face and Flyhead often accompanied them but never Simon. The first time he ever met the prisoners was when they were taken out, either in the morning or late in the afternoon, and hoisted up on to the condemned cart. He would sit with them but, as Shadbolt wryly remarked, they were not the best of company. Most just sat dour-faced. Others were drunk, a few cried and begged for mercy.

Simon became curious as to why he was excluded from any visit to the condemned cells as well as when the corpses were removed to the derelict wasteland in the cemetery of the Austin Friars. He would always be told to stay by the gallows and take the ropes down, remove the ladders and wait for them to return. Once, he asked the reason for this exclusion. Shadbolt just grinned and shook his head.

'In time, my son,' he declared sonorously, 'in time, you will enjoy the full rights of our profession.'

Friar Martin and the other two quietly agreed so Simon left the matter alone, though he grew uneasy and curious; Shadbolt called his little group the 'Hanging Crew' and composed hymns and songs for them to sing. They would meet in the Hangman's Rest and drink till they heard the chimes at midnight; one of the concessions the hangmen in Gloucester enjoyed was that they were not bound by the curfews and licensing laws. These were convivial meetings and the wine and ale flowed like water while the landlord served the most savoury dishes. On other occasions, particularly around a great feast like Michaelmas, they would stroll through the markets, attend the fairs and be greeted obsequiously by leading citizens and members of the Guild. Shadbolt's 'Hanging Crew' lived under the shadow of death and this gave them an aura much envied by others. The young whores and street-walkers also sought them out and Simon had his fill of tender wenches, ever ready to offer him their favours free.

At times Simon felt as if he had died and descended into hell and was feasting in some dark, sepulchral chamber surrounded by demons. Shadbolt would hire the taproom of the Hangman's Rest; the whores and street-walkers would be invited, Friar Martin would say grace and the revelry would last into the early hours.

At first the young carpenter was taken by this but, as the

weeks dragged on and autumn turned into winter, Simon hid his growing unease. He was barely aware of the days passing. His mind and soul seemed to be centred on that great soaring gibbet in the marketplace, the rumbling of the death cart, the roar of the crowd and those bodies jerking at the end of their ropes. Simon also became increasingly suspicious about the secrecy of Shadbolt, his companions and Friar Martin and quietly wondered at their constant supply of silver. They were paid well but Shadbolt lived like a lord while Merry Face, one night in a drunken stupor, claimed he had enough wealth to buy a house in Westgate. Simon considered going back to Berkeley, but one look at the beggars clustered in the alleyways around the cathedral, and he changed his mind. Winter was coming on and, as Shadbolt reminded him, beggars rarely lived to see springtime.

He did try to meet the love of his life, flaxen-haired Alice Draycott. One day he accosted her in the marketplace, where she was buying needles and a roll of lawn for the feast of All Saints. She was civil enough but distant; she scrutinised him from head to toe and smiled quietly as he jingled the silver in his purse.

'You look well, Simon. A man of war in your black leather.' She picked up her purchases and handed them to the maid standing behind her. 'But I always thought you were a carpenter, a good one, not a common executioner.'

And, before Simon could reply or object, she was past him, marching stiffly away, head held high.

Simon saw her on a few more occasions in the marketplace but she was colder and would stare in his direction as if he didn't exist. Shadbolt found out about this and teased Simon mercilessly. The carpenter didn't object; Shadbolt was shrewd enough to detect his unease and now he could offer the lovely Alice Draycott as the cause of his sadness.

Simon eventually hired his own chamber above a clothier in Capstall Lane, well furnished with bed, mattress, bolsters of goose feathers, quilts and testers, cushions, stools, chests and even a large aumbrie for the clothes he bought. He would often excuse himself from the revelry at the Hangman's Rest and go back to his chamber. Yet he'd only sit and stare at the coloured canvas painting he'd bought from an artist who worked near the cathedral. Simon came to dread sleep, when nightmares plagued his mind and roused him sweating in the early hours.

One day Simon felt these gruesome nightmares were invading his waking hours. He had gone for a walk and decided to visit the marble sarcophagus of Edward II in the Abbey of St Peter. He was going down Archdeacon Street when a man brushed by him. Simon apologised. The fellow turned slightly and hurried on.

'By all heaven's angels!' Simon gasped.

He was so surprised he stood stock still and, by the time he had recovered his wits, the man had disappeared.

Simon went into an alehouse, a shabby, ill-lit place. He sat absentmindedly in the corner, ordered a cup of mead and looked across at a tallow candle, placed in a barrel in the centre of the alehouse, watching the flame rise and fall in the draught. Simon was certain that the man he had bumped into was a poacher whose execution he had witnessed.

'It can't be!' he whispered.

A chill of fear gripped him. Was his mind beginning to wander? Were these nightmares coming to haunt him? He stared out of the doorway at the fading daylight. Were all the victims he had hanged out there waiting in the gloom? He finished the mead more quickly than he had intended and rose uncertainly to his feet to make his way back through the lonely streets to the Hangman's Rest.

Shadbolt, as usual, was holding court. Simon smiled and sat on a stool at the corner of the table. The conversation and laughter echoed like a distant sound.

'Is anything wrong, Simon?' Shadbolt pushed his face close to his. 'Are you wetting your breeches, boy?'

'Leave him alone!' Friar Martin intervened. 'Simon, what's wrong?'

'Nothing, nothing.' Simon tried to assert himself. 'What are you talking about?'

Shadbolt winked and tapped his fleshy nose.

'Just rumours, Simon.'

'About what?'

'Do you remember Pie-hot Prunella?'

Simon grinned. How could he forget the plump little strumpet he had danced with so assiduously?

'She's married a baron?' Simon asked, trying to show his good humour.

Shadbolt shook his head. 'Oh no!' He loosened the kerchief round his neck and dabbed at the sweat. 'Pie-hot's disappeared. And do you know we've just been discussing that. Rumours are growing as thick as weeds in a garden that something nasty has come to Gloucester. She's not the first to disappear and they say those at the Guildhall know all about it.'

'What do you mean?' Simon asked.

'Rumour.' Shadbolt glanced sideways at Friar Martin. 'And our good friar here, well, you tell him the story, Martin.'

The friar folded back the voluminous sleeves of his gown. With his merry eyes and bristling beard, the friar looked like some good-natured gnome. Simon often wondered what his order, the Austin Friars, thought of his consorting with hangmen and whores. Martin simply declared that the Church's place was to be in the company of sinners.

'Well, I've heard rumours.' He glanced over Simon's shoulder to ensure no one was listening. 'There's talk of witchcraft!'

'They are always chattering about that,' Simon protested. 'Especially in the forest lands. Every alehouse in Berkeley had a ghost story about Satan and his coven meetings in the darkness.'

'Aye, and some of it's true,' Merry Face broke in. He spoke

43

thickly as he always did, the right corner of his mouth fixed and unmoving. 'We've all heard of the fires at Samain and on St Walpurgis' night.'

'Never mind that!' Friar Martin said. 'What's more important is that two good brothers of the Dominican Order have come from Blackfriars in London. They're claiming that they are simply travelling on to Bristol but that's not true. They are staying longer than I thought. Brother Shadbolt here has seen those same Dominicans at the Guildhall.'

Simon was now paying attention. He'd heard of the Dominicans, eloquent preachers and members of the Inquisition.

'If the devil's work is being done it will end on the gallows,' Shadbolt declared, leaning back against the wall. He tapped his nose. 'Mark my words, this will keep us very, very busy. So, cheer up, Simon, and tell us all your troubles! Not poor Alice?'

'It's not that.' Simon decided to tell the truth. 'I had an eerie experience. I was in an alleyway the other side of Gloucester. Now, I admit daylight was fading . . .'

'And?'

'I knocked into a man. He turned and I glimpsed his face.' Simon paused while the tapster served more tankards of ale. 'Before God, I don't tell a lie!'

'Come on lad!'

'About two weeks ago we hanged a poacher,' Simon continued in a rush. He looked at Friar Martin. He repressed a chill of fear, for the friar was staring at him hard-eyed. 'I'd swear on oath, on the sacrament, that it was the man we hanged. But that's not possible, is it? I mean, a man who's been hanged can't come back?'

He expected guffaws of laughter to greet his revelation but his companions stared coldly at him. Simon gulped nervously.

'I mean, it's ridiculous. Once a man's hanged, he's hanged, is he not?'

Shadbolt abruptly laughed but Simon wondered why the smile never reached his eyes.

'It's that Alice.' The chief hangman clapped his hands. 'She's turned your wits at last!'

Chapter 4

Simon found the atmosphere of their meetings grew more strained over the next week. So much so, that it was almost a relief when Shadbolt told him to take the execution cart and one of the dray horses across the Severn. He was to go into the Forest of Dean to buy supplies, planks of timber and other requirements, for the gaol and scaffold at Gloucester.

'Take your time.' Shadbolt clapped him on the shoulder. 'Enjoy the country air. Try and clear your wits.'

Simon did enjoy it. Autumn had turned the leaves a golden brown. The air was fresh but not icy-cold and the forest on either side of the pathway was alive with game. Birdsong rang clear and far-carrying. The rain had stopped and most of the days were crisp and dry.

Simon did take his time. He even made a visit to Berkeley and spent the night in the Cross Keys tavern where those who had known him in former days gaped, open-mouthed, at his new-found wealth. He visited the castle, seeking out friends, but found there was nothing like good fortune to turn men's faces sour. He returned to the forest, buying up supplies, stopping at the different alehouses for refreshment or to hire a straw bed on the taproom floor.

About six days after leaving Gloucester, Simon realised it was time to return. He took the trackway down to the Severn. The gentle, swaying movement of the cart and the clip-clop of the horse's hooves lulled him into a half-sleep. The day was a fine one and, to stop himself dozing, as well as slake his thirst,

47

Simon left the main trackway, going up to an evil-looking hovel which served as an alehouse. The place was really no more than a cottage, wattle-daubed walls and a thatched roof with an ale bush pushed under the eaves. He hobbled his horse and went inside. Two narrow windows provided light. Smoke from the hearth in the centre mingled with the rancid smell of a thick, tallow candle. Simon would have left but he had made the journey. He ignored the hens standing on the side of the vats soiling the wood with their droppings and asked for a stoup of ale. The harridan of an alewife served it, her manner surly. She banged the tankard down and flounced away. To Simon's surprise the ale proved tangy and fresh. He looked around; the other customers were charcoal burners and a wandering chapman. The latter sat in the corner, his broad-brimmed hat pulled over his eyes. He clicked his dirty fingers and ate some bread from a pewter dish. Simon watched him out of the corner of his eye, noticing that every so often the man would pour a little ale on the meat and bread to soften it up, kneading it with his knife. The fellow kept his head down. Eventually he finished and put the plate on the floor. The alewife came by and almost slipped on the greasy platter.

'No Teeth!' she shrieked.

'Shut your gob!' the man snarled back and gazed fearfully around.

Simon looked into his tankard, pretending to be half-asleep though the hair curled on the nape of his neck. This was the second time he'd met a man supposed to be hanged. Was it a coincidence, mere trickery?

'I'm sorry, Cuthbert,' The alewife almost shouted the chapman's name. She brought across a stoup of ale. 'Here, drink this free!'

Simon was convinced that the man opposite was the former hangman of Gloucester, supposedly executed for killing a man in a tavern brawl. He ordered another stoup of ale. The time dragged on. When eventually the chapman got up to leave, Simon followed. He unhobbled the horse. The chapman passed him.

'Sir!' Simon called. 'Whither are you going?'

'South to Bristol.' No Teeth kept his head turned away.

'You are welcome to a free ride,' Simon said. 'But what are you selling?'

'Gewgaws, ribbons for your beloved, or needles for your wife.'

'Sit up beside me,' Simon invited. 'Come on! I may even buy!'

The chapman needed no second invitation. He climbed on the cart. Simon grasped the reins, gently easing the horse and cart along the muddy trackway on to the road down to the Severn. All the time he chattered about how he was a peasant farmer out at Berkeley, now intent on selling the supply of wood he had bought in one of the markets at Bristol. The chapman heard him out but, when Simon asked him where he had been and what his business was, the fellow only grunted. Simon continued chattering. The chapman asked if they could stop. He turned his face, wizened and dirty, and displayed red, sore gums.

'I've drunk so much bloody ale,' he rasped. 'I need to piss!'

Simon watched him go into the trees. He got down from his seat and took out a small arbalest, slipping a bolt into the groove. He then stood beside the cart. The chapman came back, tying his points, and climbed up. Simon went round the back of the cart and came up beside the chapman. He winched the cord back and held the crossbow up. No Teeth's jaw sagged.

'For the love of God!' he protested. 'I am only a poor chapman! I have neither gold nor silver, only a few pennies!'

'I'm not interested in your coins or what you carry,' Simon replied. 'But let me introduce myself. Simon Cotterill, once a carpenter, now assistant hangman in the King's city of Gloucester, one of Master Shadbolt's hanging crew.'

'I don't know what you are talking about.' No Teeth's agitation, however, was more than apparent. His hands trembled and he swallowed so hard that the Adam's apple in his scrawny throat bounced and jerked. Simon came closer and nipped the back of No Teeth's vein-streaked hand.

'I don't believe in miracles, No Teeth, but here we have a man who should be dead, mouldering in his grave, feeding a legion of worms. Yet you are sitting here as bright as a spark. Now you can protest your innocence, in which case I'll take you down to the nearest village and ask the constable to hold you.'

'I'll kill that prattling alewife!' No Teeth groaned, hands covering his face.

'Or,' Simon replied, digging one hand into his purse, 'I can give you a silver piece and let you go, on one condition! You tell me the truth.'

No Teeth looked up at the trees.

'I made a mistake. I should have gone into Wales and stayed there.' He glanced at Cotterill, his eyes full of tears. 'But I was born here,' he whined. 'I became homesick.'

'That can be cured,' Simon replied.

No Teeth shrugged. 'Then get back on the seat, put down the crossbow. You are stronger and brawnier than I am. I'll tell you my tale, then I'll be gone.'

Simon arrived back in Gloucester late the following evening. He took the cart and horse to the stable behind the Guildhall and made his way to the Hangman's Rest. Shadbolt took one look at Cotterill's face and told Flyhead to clear the whores and the other hangers-on out of the taproom.

'What is it, Simon? Come!' Shadbolt leaned over and filled a tankard. 'You look like a cat who's taken the cream.'

'I've found out,' Simon said. 'I know now why I'm never allowed to visit the prisoners or attend their funerals in the cemetery of the Austin Friars.'

Shadbolt closed his eyes. Flyhead scraped back his stool.

'I wouldn't do that.' Simon half turned his head. 'Flyhead, sit where I can see you and you, Merry Face. Friar Martin, I expect no interference! My wits are not wandering,' he continued. 'I did see that poacher, the one who's supposed to be hanged. He didn't die, did he?'

'Oh come!'

'Oh come, come you, Master Shadbolt. I've also met No Teeth. He was drunk and garrulous as ever. He was hiding in an alehouse in the Forest of Dean.'

'The little dog turd!' Merry Face retorted. 'He was supposed to be across the Severn in Wales, either there or Cornwall.'

Shadbolt chewed the corner of his lip.

'What are you going to do, Simon?' he asked. 'Turn us over to the sheriff's men?'

'Don't be ridiculous!'

The hangmen looked uncomfortable, except for Flyhead who was just gaping open-mouthed.

'It's really an act of mercy,' Friar Martin explained, his fat face a sheen of sweat. He had lost his usual, jovial ways.

'An act of mercy?' Simon asked. 'And one, I wager, which also brings you great wealth.'

Shadbolt put his tankard down.

'Enough.' He looked round the table. 'Sooner or later Simon was to join us. I suppose No Teeth has told you the truth, so let me tell you it once again.' He wetted dry lips. 'We are hangmen, Simon, the city's executioners. We carry out lawful punishment against reprobates, outlaws and wolfs-heads but you've seen some of them. Why should a man hang because he takes a plump deer and lets the juices squirt into his chidren's mouths? There are two groups: those who deserve God's mercy and pay a little and those who deserve God's justice but can pay more.'

'And who decides?' Simon asked.

'I do,' Friar Martin said. 'I always visit the condemned in their cell. It began about three years ago. There was a young boy of fifteen, he'd taken one of the King's swans from the

Severn. His father was a trader. The poor man was beside himself with grief, the boy was frightened out of his wits because he would hang. I came and talked to Master Shadbolt, the father offered one mark.'

'I agreed,' Shadbolt interrupted.

'I heard the boy's confession.' Friar Martin took up the story. 'On the morning of his execution I gave him a cup of wine with an opiate in it, which made him drowsy, his body slack. Beneath his jerkin I fashioned a stout leather collar. Show him, Master Shadbolt.'

The chief executioner fumbled beneath the table and brought out his sack. He took out four collars of varying lengths. They had been cunningly devised, the leather thick and stitched. Simon felt them; they were reinforced, padded with a strong heavy clasp on the back. Along the edge they had curving hooks, and looked like the collars fastened on a mastiff or guard dog.

'Had those made specially,' Shadbolt said. 'Look, I'll show you.'

And, before Simon could object, Shadbolt was up behind him. The collar went round his neck, the clasp was secured.

'Now!'

A piece of rope was looped over Simon's head; his hand went to his dagger hilt.

'Don't worry,' Shadbolt scoffed. 'I'm not going to kill you! See, Simon, how the rope fits on the collar beneath the hooks. The noose knot, which will go round behind your left ear, will be blocked by the clasp; the collar itself will be hidden under the jerkin.'

'And by the mask over the felon's head?' Simon asked.

'Precisely.'

Shadbolt was tightening the rope; Simon felt pressure on his throat but the collar held firm.

'It takes the weight.' Friar Martin smiled.

'But, surely someone would detect this?' Simon put his hands behind his neck and undid the clasp.

'Well,' Shadbolt explained, 'as you have suspected, the collar itself is hidden by the sack and the condemned man or woman's jerkin or gown. Moreover, people are not looking at a felon's neck but his legs, his body. Now, when we have decided that a victim will be saved, the noose is secured round the collar. The felon is pushed off the ladder. Believe me, Simon, the shock of that alone is enough to make a man dance, jerk and swing.'

'It is still very painful,' Flyhead added. He was acting uneasy, his face pallid and sweating. 'The muscles in the neck and shoulder, I understand, ache for days afterwards. It's an experience no one ever forgets.'

'Now,' Friar Martin leaned forward, rubbing his hands. 'Only a few have the sense to hang still. I'll be honest, most faint in a dead swoon. Overcome by shock.'

'And so the bodies are cut down,' Simon continued. 'And thrown in a cart and covered with a sheet. Wouldn't anyone notice? There are archers, tipstaffs?'

'It's strange.' Shadbolt smiled. 'People will turn up to see a man hang. Yet, have you noticed, Simon, how frightened they are of a corpse? They can't leave fast enough. The poor prisoners lie unconscious in the cart and we take them off to the death house at the Austin Friars. On a few occasions we've made a mistake. God knows why but the heart fails and the person is truly dead.'

'But on most occasions?' Simon asked.

'On most occasions the collar is taken off. They are revived and payment is made. Friar Martin here gives them fresh clothing and, as you know, the Forest of Dean is only across the river.'

'And who will object?' Merry Face laughed, a strange neighing sound. 'The felon? He does not want to be taken again. His family?'

'And if suspicion is ever raised,' Shadbolt added, 'we can always say something went wrong. The condemned man has had the fright of his life, he is only too eager to leave the area. The family, if he has any, are happy while we are considerably richer.'

'So, many of the graves at Austin Friars are empty?' Simon asked.

'No.' Friar Martin smiled from behind his tankard. 'Don't forget we have a hospital there for the poor and infirm. After a corpse has lain in the earth for a few weeks it looks like any other.'

'And what happens?' Simon asked, 'if the Justices order the body to be gibbeted outside the city, placed in a steel cage for all to see?'

'Yes, that can pose problems,' Shadbolt admitted. 'But, as Friar Martin said, one corpse looks like another, especially if it's coated in thick tar.'

'And you make a profit?' Simon asked.

'Oh yes. Silver and gold. What you've been eating and drinking over the last few weeks.' Shadbolt leaned forward and placed his great paw on Simon's shoulder. 'And now you are part of this, Simon, you're one of us, aren't you?'

'For goodness' sake,' Friar Martin added. 'Drink the cup with us, Simon. What does it matter? Do you really want to see men hang? Have the life choked out of them? Don't worry, sooner or later you would have been brought in.' He shrugged. 'It was just a matter of time, of making sure.'

'And no one suspects?' Simon asked.

'Suspects!' Shadbolt laughed. 'No one suspects, Simon. It's been done before and it will be done again. Are you one of us, yea or nay?'

Simon glanced round. Flyhead was glaring at him. Merry Face had his hands on the hilt of his dagger. Friar Martin was drumming his fingers on the table.

What does it matter, Simon thought. He felt a great sense of relief, a weight being lifted off his shoulders. Over the last few weeks, he thought he had participated in the deaths of others but now . . .

'How many escape?' he asked. 'Is there a list?'

Shadbolt tapped the side of his head.

'In here, young Cotterill! For every five condemned, let us say two walk free.'

'But you are leaving yourself at risk,' Simon persisted. 'I saw a man in the alleyway and I met No Teeth!'

'That's because you've sharp wits, Simon,' Friar Martin replied. 'Others wouldn't look and, if they saw anyone, they'd dismiss it as a fanciful notion.' The friar's face grew stern. 'But I tell you this, when we reach an understanding with the prisoners, we enter into a contract. They put as much distance between themselves and Gloucester as possible: the two you met broke that contract.'

'What Friar Martin is saying,' Flyhead said as he glowered evilly, 'is that if we meet them again, we kill them. The poacher should have more sense and, as for No Teeth, did he tell you what he was doing?'

'Yes he did.' Simon, more relaxed, sipped from the tankard. He lifted a hand. 'And, before you ask again, Master Shadbolt, I am in your company. What you decide I agree upon, that is my blood oath! Life or death you have my word!'

Simon could feel the tension ease. Friar Martin called for the tankards to be filled and more candles to be brought. Once this had been done he leaned forward.

'You were saying, Simon, about No Teeth?'

'He claimed to have a little silver left,' Simon told them. 'And he had come back to the Forest of Dean to hide.'

Simon was about to continue when there was a pounding on the door. Shadbolt put a finger to his lips. The taverner went across and drew back the bolts. A tipstaff entered, sweaty-faced and breathless.

'Master Shadbolt, you and your companions, your presence is demanded at the Guildhall!'

'At this hour?' Shadbolt asked.

'My lord mayor is insistent. You are to go there now. I am to accompany you.'

The company rose, groaning and protesting. Shadbolt looked

worried and stared narrow-eyed at Simon who shook his head.

'I have said nothing,' told them quietly. 'You have nothing to fear.'

They put on their war belts, grabbed their cloaks and followed the tipstaff out into the alleyway. He hurried ahead, along the lanes and runnels, the hangmen of Gloucester trailing behind, hooded and cowled, mysterious in the glow from the lanterns outside the houses they passed. Now and again they would be disturbed by some beggar pleading for bread. On one occasion they all withdrew into a narrow recess to allow a group of lepers, dressed in soiled white sheets, to go by clanging their bells and whining through decayed lips for alms. Dogs barked at their passage. Cats scampered from the midden. Rats squealed and scuttled away. They crossed the deserted marketplace; only the occasional light from a window or the sound of music from some wealthy household broke the silence.

At the Guildhall, however, all was activity. Men-at-arms and archers guarded the entrances and courtyards. The wooden wainscoted passageways were filled with retainers. Shadbolt could get no sense from any of them. The tipstaff led them up the main staircase and into the council chamber. This long, spacious room was now lit by cresset torches and candelabra; beeswax candles stood along oval tables where the mayor and two of his councillors were gathered. Behind the mayor stood the sergeant-at-arms of the city dressed in half-armour. Simon caught the eye of Master Draycott. He held the alderman's gaze and was pleased to see the fear in that glance.

'What have we here?' Flyhead whispered. 'A council meeting at the dead of night? Has the King died? Has a rebellion broken out along the Marches?'

The mayor beat his knuckles on the table. He glanced over his shoulder at the sergeant-at-arms.

'Clear the chamber!'

The men-at-arms and archers were ushered out. Only the

sergeant and executioners remained. The mayor waited, staring down the table at Shadbolt.

'Master Shadbolt,' he began. 'How many men are here? Including yourselves?'

Shadbolt counted. 'Why, my lord mayor, eight.'

'And if I held a court,' the mayor asked. 'I would be judge, yes?'

Shadbolt nodded.

'And Master Draycott here would be prosecutor of the King's court?'

'If you say so, my lord mayor.'

'While John Shipler,' the mayor indicated the ferret-faced little merchant swathed in furs who sat on his left, 'he could offer whatever defence the prisoners wanted?'

'What prisoners, my lord mayor?'

'In a while you'll see. But tell me, Master Shadbolt, how many would be left?'

'Why, my lord mayor, five men.'

'Five men good and true.' The mayor smiled thinly. 'It's enough!' He snapped his fingers and looked over his shoulder. 'Sergeant-at-arms, bring up the prisoners! Master Shadbolt, find stools for you and your companions!'

The hangmen did. Simon felt strange. Here he was at the dead of night in the council chamber of Gloucester and, if the lord mayor was to be believed, a secret trial was to take place.

The door opened and two Dominicans, like ghosts in their black and white habits, came into the room. They sat on a bench just within the doorway, arms crossed. A short while later the door was flung open and the sergeant-at-arms pushed three hooded figures into the chamber.

At first Simon didn't know whether they were male or female, because their faces were hidden deep in their cowls. They stumbled rather than walked. All turned to look at them. The sergeant-at-arms pulled the hoods back and Simon felt a chill of fear. The one in the centre was stooped, with steel-grey hair framing a lean, cold face with hooded eyes, hooked nose and a twisted, sneering mouth. The other two were younger, plumper, but were similar in face and demeanour. Their black hair straggled down to their shoulders and they had high cheekbones and slanted eyes. They looked defiant and, in spite of their bruised faces and bound hands, unabashed by the council.

The more he looked at them, the more Simon felt a sense of dread, a cold, numbing fear. As a hangman he had been in the presence of murderers, men who took human life at the drop of a coin, who could slit a throat and then sleep as innocently as a babe. These three were different. They had apparently been rough-handled by the gaoler and soldiers but they stood arrogant, undismayed by the great gleaming sword which lay down the centre of the table, its sharp point directed towards them.

'Why are we here?' the older one sneered.

The mayor brought his fist crashing down upon the table.

'How dare you?' he snarled. 'How dare you treat this court with such contumacy!'

'So, we are being tried,' the old one riposted. 'In which case, where is our defence? Where is our accuser? Where is the jury? And, above all,' she added maliciously. 'Where is our judge?'

'I am your judge,' the mayor replied. 'And there are enough good men and true to hear the evidence!'

'Men! Yet, whether they be good or true is another matter.' She stared round, slyly sneering at Friar Martin. Then, for some strange reason, her gaze rested on Simon. The young man wished he could run, flee. The old crone's face seemed to change, grow younger, though the eyes remained ancient in their sin. She blinked and her gaze moved on. Simon felt as if he had been brushed by the angel of death. 'What crimes have we committed?' She jerked her head back, staring down at the mayor.

'Murder,' the mayor replied. 'The practice of the black rites: witchcraft; the worship of demons!'

The old woman laughed. 'You have no proof.'

'What is this?' Shadbolt whispered into Simon's ear.

One of the younger women turned. 'Silence in court!' she jibed.

Simon caught her gaze. He felt repelled by the sneering malevolence in the young woman's eyes. She wasn't beautiful, not even comely, but she exuded power. A woman used to riding men, satisfying their wants, be they physical or spiritual.

'Keep a civil tongue in your head!' Shadbolt shouted back.

The woman made a rude gesture with her thumb then turned and whispered in the old one's ear.

Simon's unease grew. He wished he wasn't here. The chamber was dark and it was growing colder. When he breathed in he caught the stench of the charnel house, of decay and putrefaction. Something very evil, a dark malevolent presence, was in this chamber and he wanted to have none of it. Yet what could he do? He realised what must be happening. The three women before him had been accused of some dreadful wrong which the mayor and his colleagues could not reveal. A court had been convened; the horrid crimes, whatever they were, would be tried in secret and punishment would be carried out. He looked across to where Friar Martin sat on a bench at the far end of the room. The friar had drunk deeply. Usually he became sleepy, but now he sat, feet apart, his gaze going to the Dominicans then back around the council chamber.

'You have asked for evidence.' The mayor broke the silence. 'Master Shadbolt, you have just joined us. Our good friends the Dominicans who, I believe, are staying at the Austin Friars, have already given their verdict.' He tapped the table with his fingers. 'Go into the antechamber.' He nodded his head behind him. 'The sergeant-at-arms will show you.'

Simon glanced quickly at the witches; their arrogance had disappeared, they looked expectantly at each other. The old crone shuffled her feet and muttered under her breath.

Simon followed Shadbolt and the others through the door held open by the sergeant-at-arms. His sense of dread increased. The antechamber was lit by two cresset torches. The window at the far end had been shuttered. The air was rank with the putrid smell from the caskets, three in number, which lay across the trestles. The sergeant-at-arms removed the lids. Simon felt his heart beat more quickly. He heard the groans and gasps of disgust from his companions. He saw then looked away. He could not believe his eyes. Three corpses, all presumably of young women, now much decayed but it wasn't that which turned his stomach and terrified his soul. More, the black thread which had been sewn to tightly seal their eyes and mouths.

Chapter 5

The trial was a simple recording of judgement. The witches, Agnes Ratolier and her two daughters, Eleanor and Isabella, were found guilty of the charges of sorcery. When the mayor asked if they had anything to say in their defence, old Agnes just hawked and spat vile phlegm.

'You have been found guilty,' the mayor told them, 'of murder, treason and terrible conspiracy. Your crimes are too fearful to describe. They are an abomination both to God and man. So, by the powers invested in this secret court, you are to be condemned. You will be hanged by the neck until you are dead!' He joined his hands together. 'My verdict is that of the King and Holy Mother Church.' He nodded at the two Dominicans. 'Sentence will be carried out immediately. Sergeant-at-arms, take them down!'

The witches were hustled out. The younger one was smiling, the other was crooning softly to herself, while their mother looked serene. Her gaze took in the court as if memorising every detail.

Once the council chamber was cleared, the mayor rapped the table.

'Sentence must be carried out immediately!'

'I would advise against that.' One of the Dominicans spoke up. 'My lord mayor, our task is finished. As you know, we have examined the witches. They are as guilty as Judas. Nevertheless, they should be offered the consolations of the Church and the opportunity to recant.'

'Shouldn't they be burned?' Draycott asked.

His question was greeted by a murmur of assent. 'Shouldn't their bodies be consumed by flames?' he insisted. 'As their souls will burn in those of hell?'

'I disagree.' Friar Martin spoke up. 'I am confessor to the condemned but I am also official chaplain of this council. These matters should be kept secret. No fire, no hangings at King's Cross. Let them perish at the scene of their wicked crimes, in the darkness of the Forest of Dean.' He shrugged. 'It is the only way both justice and secrecy can be served.'

Friar Martin spoke sharply and fervently; the Dominicans nodded.

'It is fitting,' one of them said.

'Can we do that?' Shipler whined.

'The law recommends it.' Shadbolt spoke up, eager to support Friar Martin.

'I have asked,' the mayor intervened quickly, 'in a petition to the council in London that this process be kept secret so the common weal is not disturbed and public order is maintained. To put it bluntly,' he added wearily, 'if the witches were burned, it might attract attention. Even in the depths of the Forest of Dean such a fire might draw the curious. I agree with Friar Martin. Tomorrow night after dark, let them be taken back to the place where they carried out their abominations and be hanged. Master Shadbolt, you and your companions will be responsible for carrying out lawful sentence and ensuring they die according to the full rigours of the law.' He drank from his goblet. 'You will remain in the Guildhall till you leave then stay at the scene of execution for three days.' He paused. 'Three days they'll hang, then spike their hearts and bury them deep.' He looked at Shadbolt. 'You, your companions and Friar Martin will receive special payment as well as permission to draw from the council's stores for whatever you need.' He raised his hand. 'Before we leave each man will take an oath, swearing himself to secrecy on pain of forfeiture of life and limb in this life and his soul in the next!'

Simon shivered. The Dominicans, the mayor, the two members of the council were pale and cowed. Matters were not
helped by the dancing light from the candles and torches. He
was afraid; a cloying evil had swept into this chamber and
still lurked in the shadowy corners or up along the darkened
rafters. His companions felt the same. Flyhead's face jerked
and moved. Merry Face had his hands clenched before him as
if deep in prayer. Even Shadbolt, who always boasted to be
frightened of no one, surreptitiously wiped the sweat from his
cheeks. Friar Martin was busy running his Ave beads through
his fingers, eyes half-closed, lips moving in silent prayer.

The proceedings ended. One of the aldermen acted as clerk
as each one stepped up to take the oath. Afterwards, the
sergeant-at-arms showed them up to chambers where straw
mattresses had been laid, together with blankets, baskets of
bread, dried meat and flagons of ale and wine.

'You will stay here,' he ordered them, his fingers drumming
on the pommel of his sword. 'By all that is holy, I've never
seen such filth!'

'Why the three days?' Simon asked. 'Why not hang them
and be done with it?'

'It's the custom,' Friar Martin replied, 'for witches to
know the full rigours of the law, a safeguard against any
devilish tricks.'

The sergeant-at-arms wagged a finger. 'I hope you lads make
those witches hang. Let them know what it is to die. They
showed no compassion. Let them receive none.' He grasped
the latch of the door. 'Four burly executioners and a stout
friar will be more than enough for three witches shackled in
chains.'

'How will we know where to take them?' Merry Face
asked.

'There's a verderer, calls himself Deershound. He was there
at the capture. I will lead you to him.'

The sergeant-at-arms left. Shadbolt immediately took a
tinder and lit every candle. He filled five goblets and shared

them out; his face was still pale and sweat-soaked. He lifted his own cup in a silent toast.

'You heard what the sergeant-at-arms said,' he said. 'There will be no mercy for these. Hang they must and hang they will!'

They soon drained their cups and refilled them. Merry Face lit a fire in the small hearth. Food was shared out and, as the first streaks of dawn appeared through the window, they relaxed. The horrors they had witnessed receded a little to be replaced by an anger, a determination that these dreadful women suffer the full punishment awaiting them.

They spent the rest of the morning sleeping and dozing. The gallery on which their chambers stood was closely guarded by men-at-arms and archers. They were only allowed to leave to use the privy in a small recess at the far end of the gallery. Water bowls and jugs were brought up for their ablutions. Late in the afternoon the sergeant-at-arms returned.

'They want to see you,' he reported.

Shadbolt, sitting on his mattress with his back to the wall, shook his head.

'I've got a good view of them. I don't need to see them again.'

'They want to see the friar,' the sergeant-at-arms persisted.

Friar Martin reluctantly got to his feet.

'I'm not going down by myself. Cotterill.' He winked. 'You want to be one of us. You haven't visited the cells. Now's your chance!'

Simon reluctantly agreed; he and the friar followed the sergeant-at-arms along the gallery and down to the cavernous cellar of the Guildhall. The passageway was narrow, dank and gloomy, lit by the occasional cresset torch. Dungeons and cells were ranged on either side. The turnkey took them to a door at the far end.

'The bitches are in there,' he whispered. 'I don't know what's going on.' He wiped his nose on the back of his hand.

64

'Mind your own business!' the sergeant-at-arms snapped. 'And, remember, you never go in there. They'll have one meal before they leave and I'll see to that.'

The turnkey shrugged, turned the key and swung the door open.

The cell was cavernous and surprisingly clean. No rushes lay on the floor; the furniture consisted of just one rickety table and a stool. A tallow candle glowed in a niche. The three witches lay sprawled against the wall beneath a small barred window. As the sergeant-at-arms slammed the door behind him, all three moved in a clink of chains. Simon wrinkled his nose at the sour smell.

'What's the matter, young one?' Agnes Ratolier mocked. 'It's not a lady's parlour.' She leaned forward. 'It's good to see you, Friar.'

'What is it you want?'

Ratolier's eyes shifted. 'Tell the sergeant-at-arms to stand away from the door.'

Simon looked over his shoulder. On the far side of the door the sergeant-at-arms closed the grille.

'It's only right!' Agnes shouted. 'No one should hear our confession!'

'Is it confession you want?' Friar Martin asked, crouching down before them. 'Do you wish to confess and be shriven?'

'In that case I should leave,' Simon offered.

Agnes beckoned him closer, indicating he kneel next to the friar. Simon obeyed. The old woman exuded an imperious authority, as her small, black eyes held his. Simon didn't know whether he was frightened of them or of being accused of cowardice by the rest.

Up close the three witches looked even more daunting and formidable. Isabella and Eleanor had cleaned their faces, although their hair was tangled and hung like rat-tails down to their shoulders. They were comely enough, with regular features and large eyes, slightly slanted. They reminded Simon of two cats. Agnes didn't look so ancient now: her face was not so lined and seamed but smoother, the nose not so hooked, the lips more full. Simon blinked. Were they practising their black arts? Friar Martin, too, seemed in a trance.

'What do you want?' Simon stammered. 'If it's confession . . .'

'Shut up!' Agnes Ratolier hissed. 'We can offer you gold, more than you've ever seen!'

'For what?' Friar Martin asked.

'You know well.' Agnes gazed slyly at the priest. 'No Teeth came and sought me out. I know everything that happens in Gloucester!'

'What do you mean?' Simon asked.

'What do I mean, young one?' She sniggered. 'I mean the hangmen of Gloucester run a pretty game: some they hang and some they don't! Why can't we come to an understanding now? Use those pretty collars as you have on others? Come on, boy.' Agnes Ratolier's voice became more cloying. She gestured to her two daughters who crouched on either side. 'And, when we are freed, you can come and visit us. What a night that would be, eh? All three in a bed.' She looked him up and down. 'And, if it's your fancy, why not four?'

Simon's mouth went dry. He wished he hadn't come to confront these three women crouching and staring at him.

'More gold.' One of the daughters spoke up.

'More silver,' the other echoed. 'And pleasures neither of you have ever experienced.'

Friar Martin abruptly got to his feet.

'What are you talking about?' He crossed himself and grabbed Simon by the shoulder. 'Bitches from hell!' he spat out. 'I've got nothing to offer you in life, and nothing in death. I've seen the devil's work, those poor wenches!' He took a step forward.

The three women glanced up at him.

'You are going to hang!' he hissed. 'And I am going to enjoy it! I am going to stand in the forest glade and watch you dance! Nothing in the world, not all the gold and silver in the King's treasury, can save you!'

He walked to the door and hammered on it.

'Master Cotterill!' Agnes Ratolier's voice was now a whine.

'Come on, Simon!' Friar Martin shouted, hammering on the door.

'Please!' the old woman begged him.

Simon looked down to notice that Agnes' face was now aged, her jaw slack. Tears brimmed in her eyes.

'What is it?' he asked sharply.

'We are all finished.' She shook her head, her whole body quivering in a rattle of chains. 'One favour please!'

'It depends!' Simon felt a pang of compassion for these three women doomed to a horrible death.

'Before you leave Gloucester, get a scribe to write a letter . . . !'

Simon made to object.

'No, no, nothing much!' She shook a vein-streaked hand. 'I have a kinsman here! Address it to the kinsman,' she pointed a finger, 'of Agnes Ratolier at the Silver Tabard tavern near Blindgate. Say, "Agnes has said farewell, all is lost. I beg pardon and will he pray for me?" Give it to the taverner before we leave. He will pay you well.'

'Is that all?' Simon asked.

'That's all.' She smiled in a row of cracked teeth.

'Simon!'

He looked over his shoulder to where the sergeant-at-arms and the friar stood in the doorway.

'There is nothing I can do for them,' Friar Martin declared loudly.

Simon followed him out.

'And there's nothing we can do for you, Friar!' The shout was mocking, echoing along the narrow, gloomy passageway.

'If I ever meet No Teeth again,' Friar Martin whispered, 'it will be a case of no ears and no nose as well!'

Once back in their chamber, Friar Martin told the rest what had happened. Shadbolt agreed.

'We can do nothing for them,' he said.

Simon told him what the Ratoliers had asked of him. Shadbolt sniffed, tapping his feet on the floor.

'I don't suppose it can do any mischief,' Friar Martin observed. 'You can form your letters, Simon?'

'Of course I can, I went to the parish school.'

The rest returned to their discussion about the wickedness of the three women in the dungeons below. Simon got the sergeant-at-arms to bring a piece of parchment, ink-pot, quill and some sealing wax. He wrote the message in large clumsy letters, rolled the parchment up, sealed it and tucked it into his jerkin.

Darkness fell. They had a last meal and collected their war belts. Each man was given a sword and dagger, and an arbalest or longbow which included a quiver of bolts or yard-long shafts. Boiled leather jerkins were also provided. The sergeant-at-arms came and took them down to the Guildhall yard where their large covered wagon had been prepared. Supplies of food and drink were loaded on. The witches were brought up from the cells. In the poor light they looked like three spiders shuffling across the cobbled yard and up into the cart. Shadbolt climbed into the driver's seat and took the reins, Merry Face beside him. Friar Martin and Flyhead climbed into the back to guard the prisoners. Simon was told to walk behind.

'We'll pass Blindgate,' Shadbolt said quietly to him as the sergeant-at-arms prepared to leave. 'We'll stop for a while there. You deliver the message and make sure you get well paid.'

A short while later the cavalcade left, the sergeant-at-arms issuing his last instructions just before the gates were opened.

'We'll go through St Mary's gate, down Blindgate, past the Priory of St Oswald's and take the route into the Forest of Dean. Just where Little Meadow begins, the verderer, Deershound, will join you. He will take you into the forest – do what you have to and then return.'

The gate swung open. The sergeant-at-arms, followed by the wagon, Simon walking behind, entered the dark, winding streets of the city. The curfew bell had long sounded. The mayor must have insisted that tonight's curfew be strictly adhered to. The lanes and runnels were deserted except for the occasional dog or wandering cat. Simon walked at the tail of the cart from where he could hear Merry Face crooning a tune and the ominous rattle of chains. The dark mass of St Peter's Abbey loomed up. On the corner of Oaklane Alley stood the Silver Tabard. Shadbolt reined in, explaining to the sergeant-at-arms that he had a message to deliver to the tavern-keeper.

'It's a personal matter,' he said.

'Very well,' the sergeant-at-arms shouted back through the darkness. 'But no more than a few minutes!'

Shadbolt looked round the cart and nodded. Simon went and hammered on the door. A greasy-haired slattern opened it.

'I have a message,' Simon whispered, 'for your master.'

He heard footsteps; a tall, thin-faced man, his cheeks holed and pitted, came up behind the girl. He sent her away but kept the door on the chain.

'What is it?' he asked.

'A message from your kinswoman, Agnes Ratolier! Are you the tavern master?'

'I am.' Bony fingers came out.

'I was told I'd be paid, well paid.'

The tavern master quietly cursed. 'Then paid you will be.'

A hand came out. Simon glimpsed the small stack of silver coins.

'Give me the message,' the voice said, 'and these are yours.'

Simon handed it over. The coins were dropped into his outstretched hand and the door slammed shut. Immediately, the sergeant-at-arms ordered the cavalcade to continue.

They left the city, entering the winding country lanes. Now the sergeant-at-arms rode back.

'Deershound will be waiting for you at the crossroads. He'll be hooded, carrying a bow and quiver.'

The cart was now rattling over the potholes and ruts in the lane. Simon heard the Ratoliers' curses and Shadbolt's cheery insults back.

It was a clear night. The rain clouds had broken and the full moon provided some light. Even so, at the crossroads Deershound appeared as if from nowhere, stepping out from the trees on to the trackway. The sergeant-at-arms reined in, and leaned down to whisper to the hooded man, who nodded.

'You know what to do,' the sergeant-at-arms shouted. 'This is as far as I take you.' He waved farewell and thundered back down the lane.

Shadbolt climbed down. The verderer Deershound introduced himself, a tall, slender man, with a shock of red hair framing his pale face.

'You can find your way in the dark?' Shadbolt asked.

'I can find my way blindfolded. Are the bitches in there?'

'Shackled and chained,' Shadbolt replied. 'They'll soon be gone and we'll be back in the city.'

'I was there, you know,' Deershound continued. 'I was there when they captured the three hags.'

'Aye, and we shall remember that.' Agnes Ratolier's voice rang through the darkness.

Deershound swallowed hard and turned his back on the cart.

'How was it done?' Flyhead asked, climbing down.

'The council laid a trap. They hired a whore from the city to leave every night through different gates. She was followed by archers who kept to the fields the other side, well away from view. The night before last she left by the east gate. The poor girl didn't know what she was doing except that she was well paid to walk for at least an hour and then come back to the city. Old Ratolier stopped her and begged for money. The whore became frightened, cursed her and walked on.

'A short while later, much to the surprise of the archers, a cart pulled out of a lane and went alongside the whore. She was offered a ride but refused. She had been paid to walk for an hour and walk she would. They tried to coax her in and, when this failed, one of the young women got down and struck her with a club.' He blew his cheeks out. 'The cart then took the forest paths. I was with them then. We seemed to journey for hours. We crossed Devil's Brook, a place deep in the forest, you'll see it, and went into a small clearing. They took the girl out and laid her on a slab of stone. By then she had recovered her wits and was screaming. It's a wonder she wasn't heard in Gloucester. They had candles lit; the old one had a knife in her hand when we burst out of the trees. The whore was released and well paid.' He grinned. 'She was told to go to Bristol and never return.

'The hags put up little resistance. Your sergeant-at-arms, there, the one who brought you here, noticed fresh graves had been dug in the clearing. The ground was still soft from the rain so, well, you know the rest.' Deershound shook his head. 'I've been twenty years a verderer, I've seen things in that forest which would chill your blood but, those corpses, their throats slit, their eyes and mouths sewn together . . .' He lowered his voice. 'God knows what powers these women have.'

'Perhaps they just like killing,' Merry Face declared, loud enough for the witches to hear. 'They like to wield their power and see the hot blood spilt. Not very powerful now, are you?' he called over his shoulder. 'Who'll come and rescue you now, eh?' He made a mournful sound. 'Where are the creatures of the night and the lords of the air?'

'All around you!' came the soft reply.

'Enough!' Shadbolt ordered and climbed back on the cart.

Merry Face also climbed up; Deershound went ahead and they entered the forest. Simon, plodding behind, tried to keep his wits, thinking how much silver he had earned and quietly vowing that when this business was done perhaps he, too, should slip away to Bristol and start again. He had had enough

71

of gibbets, dungeons, whispers in the dark, the likes of the Ratoliers. He could stomach it no longer. He would take his small treasure hoard and buy his own shop. Perhaps, one day when he had become accepted, join a local guild, meet a comely wench, marry and settle down. He'd forget his nightmare days as a hangman of Gloucester.

Simon kept quietly repeating this to himself as they went deeper into the forest. The route they followed was clear though it snaked and turned. From either side came the sudden dark sounds of the night: the hoot of an owl, the yip of a fox, the crashing and slithering in the undergrowth.

On one occasion Simon climbed on to the cart where Friar Martin and Flyhead guarded the witches. The two men sat huddled in the corners while the three women whispered among themselves, now and again chuckling as if they shared some secret joke. The atmosphere was oppressive, the stench of ill-washed bodies offensive. Simon was pleased to get out and go and walk along the moonlit trackway. He felt as if he were in a dream. Here he was, walking in the dead of the night, taking three witches to an execution. Now and again he would step sideways and glance further up where Deershound loped through the night, stopping now and again to urge Shadbolt on.

They must have journeyed for hours. Simon's legs grew heavy and his eyes began to droop. Sometimes he'd stumble or slip in and out of a dream. Then it was over. Deershound shouted, the cart abruptly stopped then turned, following the verderer into the tangle of trees. The ride was so jolting Friar Martin got down from the cart and helped walk the horses. Simon noticed how the friar had become very silent since they had left the Guildhall. Usually he was jovial, the life and soul of the company, but now he acted like a frightened, beaten man plodding unwillingly onwards.

They reached the glade. Deershound and Friar Martin took cresset torches out of the back of the cart. They lashed these to a pole, stuck it into the ground and lit them. Simon looked about.

A sombre, hidden place, where a stream gurgled and bubbled as it slipped through its narrow banks. The trees were squat and ancient, rounder and thicker than even the pillars in the Abbey of St Peter. He glimpsed the large white slab of rock which came thrusting up from the earth, shallow pits beside it.

'A place of sacrifice,' Deershound told him. 'In ancient times the tribes who lived here hung their victims from the oak trees.'

'In which case,' Shadbolt remarked merrily, coming in between the verderer and Simon, clapping both of them on the shoulder, 'the ancient rites are about to be repeated.'

'I've done my task.' Deershound broke free of Shadbolt's grasp.

'Come, come,' the chief hangman said angrily. 'We are in the Forest of Dean at the dead of night. We need to know the way back.'

'You are supposed to stay here three days,' the verderer replied. 'And I can't stay with you. Go back, turn left on to the trackway, keep to it and it will take you back out of the forest.'

And, with Shadbolt's curses ringing in his ears, Deershound loped back into the trees.

'He has got more sense than any of you!'

Simon turned. Agnes and her two daughters were now sitting in the mud at the back of the cart.

'Yes!' The torchlight made Agnes' face look even more evil and grotesque. 'He knows better than to stay here. Your God doesn't reign in these dark parts.' Agnes Ratolier turned and, stretching out her neck, clicked her tongue at Friar Martin.

'Christ rules over all!' the friar insisted, but he turned away.

Simon heard the low rumble of thunder in the far distance.

'Well,' Shadbolt said. 'I'm not going to sit and be baited in the darkness by these three hags!'

He strode away, shouting orders as if any sound or movement would break the dark oppressiveness.

73

Merry Face and Flyhead soon had three ropes attached to the overhanging branches of the oak trees. The canvas canopy of the cart was removed. The three witches were made to stand and, under Flyhead's directions, the cart was backed under the execution tree. It was a slow, cumbersome exercise. The dray horses, usually placid and calm, now became restless, rearing their heads, bucking within the shafts.

Eventually Shadbolt quietened them but the witches started to laugh, bodies shaking till their chains rattled. Simon hastened to help Flyhead and Merry Face, who were already up on the branch. The nooses were tied round the witches' necks. Simon climbed on the cart, making sure each noose was tight, the knot just behind their left ears. As he did so, Agnes tried to brush his groin with the back of her hand but he pushed her away. The other two hags stared, eyes bright with excitement, and Eleanor even pursed her lips into a kiss.

'Cotterill!' Ratolier turned, her head slightly askew with the tightness of the noose and the hempen knot pushed in behind her ear.

'What is it?' he snapped.

'Did you deliver my message?'

'Yes.' He jumped down from the cart.

Friar Martin approached.

'Is there anything you wish to say before sentence is passed? Is there any comfort Holy Mother Church can give?'

'Go back to your drinking!' Agnes shrieked. She forced her head back, looking up at the stars, and muttered something in a tongue they couldn't understand. 'I shall see you all again!' she yelled, even as Shadbolt struck the horses and the cart pulled away.

Chapter 6

At last the three corpses stopped jerking and hung silent, swaying in the breeze. Merry Face called them rotten fruit. For a while the hangmen studied their handiwork; the cadavers, the chains still round their wrists and ankles, moved eerily in a clink and clatter.

'You heard what the lord mayor said,' Shadbolt reminded the others. 'They are to hang for three days, then we are to spike their hearts and bury them.'

'Why three days?' Flyhead asked, staring round the firelit clearing. 'Why can't we just cut the bitches down and have it over and done with?'

'It's a powerful counter against witchcraft,' Friar Martin broke in. 'If the body hangs for three days, the soul truly leaves. Once body and soul are completely separated, the corpses are nothing!'

'It's also the law,' Shadbolt added. 'In London.' He put his head down.

Simon realised that this was the first time any of them had talked about their past.

'In London,' Shadbolt continued quickly, 'river pirates must stay on the gallows for three turns of the tide.'

'What did they really do?' Simon asked. He stared across at the shallow graves. The soil was now falling back as if the earth wanted to forget and cover up the horrors revealed there.

'Do you know.' Friar Martin leaned against the cart and stared, hands outstretched to the fire. 'I was going to ask our

75

Dominican friends that. Why did these three hags sacrifice young women?'

'And what did they get in return?' Simon persisted.

He looked across at the corpses, heads down, necks awry. In the dancing firelight their faces looked grotesque. Friar Martin followed his gaze.

'Well, I'm not looking at that for three days!' the friar muttered.

He opened a chest in the cart and took out three white hoods which, with Flyhead's help, he put on the cadavers. Simon tried to repress the qualm of fear as the friar stretched up. It seemed as if the three corpses came to life, pitching and moving. Shadbolt came and crouched by the fire.

'I had a word with the sergeant-at-arms,' he said. 'Apparently the witches were interrogated in his presence by the Dominicans. He wasn't too sure who the dark lords or demons were these night hags sacrificed to. Whether they be devils or the old gods who used to be worshipped here. Anyway, the witches mocked their interrogators. When asked what they received in return: was it life or wealth? old Agnes Ratolier replied, "Powers which people like you can only dream of!". When the Dominicans persisted, she just went back to her chuckling and mocking insults.'

'Where did they live?' Flyhead gestured round the clearing. 'I mean, this was their temple, their chapel, but they must have had a cave or a house?'

'It was never found. They had a lair but it would take an army to comb the forest and find it.' He lowered his voice. 'I suppose one day some lovers, looking for a place to hide, will stumble upon it. A place of horrors, of skulls and bones of young men whose flesh they have chewed.'

'Shut up!' Flyhead snapped.

The teasing would have continued when, abruptly, out of the darkness a large owl floated, wings softly beating the air, its shadow racing across the glade. Simon froze and looked up. The bird seemed to be hovering as if there were quarry below, then it went and sat on the branch of the gibbet tree, its head turning, looking towards them.

'A bird of the night,' Friar Martin whispered.

Simon swallowed hard. Flyhead sprang to his feet.

'I don't like this!' he gabbled.

A rumble of thunder echoed through the night.

'There's a storm coming,' Merry Face said but Flyhead was running towards the trees, a rock in his hands.

'Piss off!' he screeched and threw the rock with all his might. The owl simply lifted off, feathered wings beating the night air. It disappeared into the darkness, floating like a ghost among the trees. Simon was so tense he jumped to his feet and, collecting more bracken, placed it on the fire.

'Why don't we bury the bodies now?' He glanced at his companions. 'We've got three days of this.'

'Cotterill's right.' Flyhead came back, crouching before the flames, eyes rounded in his white, liverish face. 'I don't like this at all, Master Shadbolt.'

A long, ululating howl came out of the trees.

'In God's name!' Flyhead's hand went to his dagger.

Again the howl, long and sombre.

'It's like that of a wolf,' Shadbolt declared. 'When I was a hangman in London we had quarters in the Tower: that's where our guild used to meet. The old king had a wolf, a present from some prince. At night, when the moon was full, it used to howl like that, fair chilled our blood.'

Again the howl shattered the silence. Flyhead was now dancing from foot to foot.

'For the love of God!' Shadbolt snarled. 'Keep your nerve! It's only some wandering farm dog; it's well known they bay at night.'

Simon was not convinced. Friar Martin was also agitated, his usual jovial face now slack and pale, Ave beads wrapped tightly round his fingers. Simon thought he saw a movement among the trees, something silvery, shadowy, like a plume of smoke. He got up and walked across, passing the sacrificial stone. He turned and gasped. Was that blood? A dark, wet stain spreading across its white surface? He knew when this was over how they would all tease each other about how frightened they were. He drew his dagger and approached the great wedge of rock. However, when he crouched down, he could see nothing, no stain, no mark, so he rose and walked into the trees. Hiding his fear he undid the points of his hose and relieved himself. Afterwards he walked even deeper into the forest, drawing his dagger again. He wanted to show the rest that he was brave, that it took more than the sounds of the night to alarm him.

'Simon!'

Someone had called his name. A whisper as if someone was playing hide-and-seek. He turned; a movement caught his eyes but, when he looked, that grey shape, what seemed to be a plume of smoke, had disappeared. He stared up through the branches; the sky was overcast, the clouds massing. The rumble of thunder grew louder and, through the trees, Simon caught a flash of lightning. He walked back to his companions.

'There's nothing there. Master Shadbolt, let's bring out the wine.'

The chief hangman did, sharing out the pewter cups, filling them to the brim. They toasted each other but Flyhead threw his down and sprang to his feet.

'What on earth! It's blood!' Flyhead screamed. 'Shadbolt, is this a trick?'

Shadbolt's face was full of fear, tears glistened in his eyes. Simon smelt his own cup. It was fragrant, so he sipped and tasted good burgundy.

'You are letting your wits wander.'

Simon picked up Flyhead's cup and sniffed at it, but all he could smell was wine. Shadbolt grasped Flyhead's arm.

'Sit down!' he whispered hoarsely. 'Otherwise you'll have us all jumping at the elves and goblins out in the woods. You are letting this place affect your humours.' He refilled

Flyhead's cup. 'There!' He sipped from it. 'It's only wine. Come on, man, drink it!'

Flyhead drained it in one gulp. The jug was passed around as well as the linen cloth carrying salted bacon. The fire, the food and the wine soon had them merry. They were laughing and joking when Simon heard the singing, a low crooning through the darkness. He put his cup down. Now the others heard it.

'It's the old bitches' song,' Merry Face said. 'Some ditty they were singing.'

Simon turned. It was as if old Agnes Ratolier, swinging on the end of the hempen rope, had opened her eyes and was staring at him through the white hood, singing him to sleep, a macabre lullaby. Simon recalled her insolent eyes, the twist to her lips. He glanced across at Friar Martin.

'Brother, can't you do anything? A prayer? A blessing?'

'God knows, Simon, I've been praying since I came here.'

Simon rose and crossed the glade. The singing had died away. He ignored Friar Martin's protests and took the white hoods off the condemned.

'Flyhead!' he shouted. 'Bring across a firebrand!'

The hangman obeyed. Simon surveyed the grisly scene, all three witches hung, eyes closed.

'Put the hoods back on!' Friar Martin ordered. 'Come back and finish the wine. This is a gloomy place, it's playing tricks with our minds.'

Simon hastened to obey. He was just about to slip the final hood over Agnes' grey, wiry hair when he was sure the head moved, the eyelids blinked. After he pulled the hood down, he found he couldn't stop trembling. He walked back and joined his companions by the fire.

'I am sorry,' he said. 'But I do not like it here. I think we should be gone.'

'We can't,' Shadbolt reminded him. 'We are under strict instructions from the mayor and the council. For all I know, that sergeant-at-arms may well come back to ensure their orders are being carried out.' He tossed the dregs of his wine on to the fire. 'We are the hangmen of Gloucester. We fear nothing. We either sleep in the cart or on the ground. When the sun rises it will be better.'

They had hardly made themselves comfortable when the storm came, the rumble of thunder sounded above them and the first raindrops fell. In a short while the rain came down in sheets, pounding the earth, driving them into the wagon where they sat huddled, fitfully dozing. Nevertheless, it was not just the rain but the sounds from the forest: cries; snatches of song; voices raised, which frayed their nerves and broke their resolve.

Friar Martin was insistent that they move and, as the cacophony of noises grew, and the rain fell even heavier, Shadbolt reluctantly agreed. The horses, which had been hobbled some distance away, were brought back and placed between the shafts of the cart. They hurriedly fixed the traces, put aboard their possessions and left the macabre glade.

Marking trees and using stones as signs, the hangmen kept a clear idea of where they were going and the path they took. The rain never let up. They travelled for hours and, just as dawn broke, Simon, who had been going before them, found a large, disused house, the fence around it long collapsed, the outbuildings much decayed. However, the large hall was warm and dry despite the smells of the animals which had sheltered there. He gleefully returned to his companions and described what he had discovered.

'One of the royal hunting lodges,' Shadbolt said. 'In the reign of the old king's great-grandfather, the Forest of Dean provided much sport and hunting.'

Simon's find was greeted with crows of triumph. They cleaned the lower rooms. Fires were lit, stores brought in. One of the chambers was even used as a stable for the horses. Flyhead went out hunting and brought back two rabbits. Shadbolt was a good cook, and the hunting lodge was soon full of the sweet smells of woodsmoke and roasted rabbit meat. They ate and drank well. At the end Shadbolt leaned back against the wall, licking his fingers.

'I know what,' he said. 'We'll stay here. We'll soon find the glade where the three hags hang. In two days, lads, our task will be over and we'll trot back to Gloucester to collect our earnings. Just think,' he leaned forward, 'we now have the mayor and the council in the palm of our hands.' He grinned. 'There's nothing they can ever do against us: they are in our debt.'

Everyone agreed. Outside, the morning light grew stronger as they speculated on their future good fortune. Even Simon was beginning to wonder whether perhaps he should stay on when he heard a sound from above.

'Hush! What's that?'

'Oh, don't start again!' Flyhead moaned.

'No, no, listen!' Simon held his hand up.

They heard it, a footfall, as if someone were walking backwards and forwards.

'You heard it first!' Shadbolt said. He picked up Simon's war belt and threw it at him. 'Go and see!'

Simon reluctantly wrapped the belt around him, took a firebrand and went out into the cold, gloomy passage. Tendrils of the thick early-morning mist were seeping in. He climbed the stairs, rotten and mildewed, the timber cracking under his boots. Eventually he reached the gallery which stretched away like a black tunnel in front of him. Chambers ran off either side, nothing more than black holes, the windows open to the grey morning light. On one or two, doors still hung, creaking on their sagging leather hinges. Simon drew his dagger, listening to the sounds: the distant call of a bird, the cracking and shifting outside as animals scurried through the undergrowth. He kept his nerve steady.

'Simon! Simon!' The voice seemed to come from further down the gallery.

He swallowed hard and walked along, his dagger out before him. He heard footsteps as if someone were walking up and down in the chambers he had just passed.

'Are you all right, Simon?' Shadbolt's voice echoed up the stairs.

Simon didn't reply but edged into a room. Holding up the firebrand he looked around. It was empty, dirty, reeking of some forest stench. He was about to leave when the door suddenly slammed shut behind him and when he tried to find a handle or latch there was none. He heard a tapping on the door and looked through the metal grille. Agnes Ratolier's face, eyes bright with malice, lips twisted in a spiteful sneer, was glaring through at him. Simon stared back in horror.

'I told you,' she hissed, 'I'd see you again!'

Simon struck with his dagger at the grille. He heard a laugh, low and throaty, then the door swung open, knocking him aside. He dropped the torch. For a while he sat on one knee, holding his bruised head, then grabbed the firebrand and ran out. The gallery was alive with noise as rats scrabbled away to hide. Simon sheathed his dagger and ran to the top of the stairs. He jumped down, his high-heeled boots cracking the wood as he almost crashed into his companions. He thrust the torch into Friar Martin's hands.

'What is it?' Shadbolt asked.

'What do you think! I wish to God I was away from here and from you! I've just seen Agnes Ratolier's face, the bitch didn't die! She's up there!'

'That's impossible!' Merry Face whined. 'We saw them hang. There were no tricks.'

Simon grasped the torch from Friar Martin and thrust it into Merry Face's hand.

'In which case,' he yelled, 'go upstairs and prove me wrong!'

Merry Face handed the torch back.

'What shall we do?' Flyhead moaned.

Simon grasped Friar Martin's sleeve. 'You are a priest. Can't you say some prayers? Bless this place?'

Friar Martin was trembling, eyes blinking, mouth opening

and shutting, a man caught in a dreadful panic, the terrors seething through his body.

'Simon! Shadbolt! Merry Face! Friar Martin! Flyhead!'

The chorus of voices came from outside. Shadbolt seized the torch and went out on to the steps of the hunting lodge. The others clustered about him, peering through the swirling mist.

'Ah, Master Shadbolt!'

The chief hangman dropped the torch. Simon glimpsed them: three figures standing under the outstretched branches of a tree. He could make out the outline of their features, the long, straggly hair. Ratolier and her two daughters.

Shadbolt ran inside, the others followed. They shut the door and hastened back to the room where they'd stored their provisions and arms. Friar Martin had recovered his wits. He immediately blessed some water and salt, scattering it around the floor. He then blessed the chamber and crouched in a corner, eyes closed, hands grasping his Ave beads.

'Stay here!' he urged them. 'Do not go outside!'

The others stood, trying to calm their wits. Simon notched an arrow to a bow he had found. Then the terrors began: knocking and tapping on walls; their names being called. Branches and stones were hurled through the unshuttered windows.

'Why don't they come?' Shadbolt asked. 'If they're spectres or phantasms, why don't they attack?'

'I don't know,' Simon replied.

And then, in answer, Agnes Ratolier's voice cut the silence.

'This is only the beginning!' she chanted. 'The game's commenced!'

Simon's blood went cold for he knew this night was going to change his life. These three ghouls from the darkness were not common criminals but true witches, whose executions had not resolved anything. He dare not share his fears with his companions. Indeed, Flyhead was so terrified Simon had to force the crossbow out of his fingers, fearful that the hangman, overcome by fright, might release a bolt and kill one of his companions. They kept the fire built up. Simon watched the mist through the open window, waiting for it to break. When it did, the noises and the terrifying imprecations ceased. Friar Martin clambered to his feet, groaning and moaning at the aches in his body.

'What shall we do?' Shadbolt asked.

'Go back to that glade,' Simon said decisively.

He glanced around and felt a spurt of secret pride. Somehow or other his relationship with his companions had changed. He was no longer the follower but the leader. Merry Face and Flyhead looked shaken to the core. Friar Martin seemed lost in his own world. Shadbolt was grey-faced; a muscle high in his cheek kept twitching and he seemed uncertain about what to do.

Simon left the hunting lodge. Everywhere he could see the signs of disturbance: bits of wood and rock, some tiles which had slipped down from the roof as if the lodge had been shaken by a violent wind. His boots squelching in the wet grass, he crossed to the spot where the three witches had been standing and, crouching down, saw the imprint of boot marks in the soft mud. Then he walked to the back of the hunting lodge. The dray horses were standing quietly in their makeshift stable, still nuzzling at their pots of feed. The wagon, pushed under the gaping roof of an outhouse, looked as if it had suffered no damage. Simon clambered in and sat on the wooden bench. From the hunting lodge he heard Shadbolt calling his name but ignored it. What had happened to them? Had the three witches really died? Had the Ratoliers miraculously cheated death, releasing themselves from those tight nooses to pursue them here? Simon shook his head.

'That's impossible!' he whispered.

He drew his dagger and watched the growing daylight wink in the blade. Recalling the poor education he had received, he smiled to himself. He knew his letters and his numbers. He could write and read a little but he'd always been told that he would be an excellent carpenter and the working of wood had been the trade of the Lord Jesus and of his stepfather Joseph. The Guild of Carpenters proudly proclaimed this, pointing out that carpentry, the shaping and moulding of wood, required as much mental skill, the use of logic as well as common sense, as any study at the Halls of Oxford or Cambridge.

Simon was also surprised at himself. He thought he would be like the rest, quivering with fear. Yet, secretly, he almost relished the challenge: a break from the tedium of everyday existence, the cloying squalor of his life as a hangman. He recalled an old soldier, an archer who had served in the King's wars: the fellow had been given a small pension and lived by himself in a cottage on the outskirts of the village. As a boy, Simon used to visit him and listen to the old man's tales of the savagery of war and the glory and panoply of battle.

'It's not the battles,' the old man had hissed through toothless gums. 'Battles cause the blood to tingle, make the heart leap like a bird. It's what goes on before that deadens the soul: the boredom of the march, the tedium of the camp.'

Simon re-sheathed his dagger and climbed out of the cart. He gazed up at the sky where the clouds were breaking.

'I know what you mean, old man,' he said to himself. 'I'm sorry, I thought you were a fool, but now I know you spoke the truth.'

Simon crossed himself. Those witches had died yet they'd used some secret power to bring themselves back to life. Simon recalled visiting the Silver Tabard before they'd left Gloucester. Was the message he had delivered something to do with this? Had some sacrifice been carried out? But, if that was the case, why had Agnes Ratolier tried to bargain for her life? And why had she called out his name before the others? And why hadn't they killed him? Or done further damage? Was it because Friar Martin had prayed? Simon crouched down to scrape the mud off the toe of his boot. As a child he had heard all the stories about the witches of the Forest of Dean, the hags who could fly through the night, those who worshipped demons and constantly lived in the halls of darkness. He'd dismissed them as fables.

'Simon!'

Shadbolt was leaning through an upper storey window.

'I'm here,' Simon called.

He walked back into the hunting lodge, where his companions looked heavy-eyed and still frightened.

'There's no one there,' he told them. 'The horses and cart are untouched.'

'What shall we do?'

'What shall we do? What shall we do?' Simon mimicked. 'Flyhead, is that all you can say? I am going to tell you what I think.' He ticked the points off on his fingers. 'First, we are in mortal danger. What we experienced this night is of hell rather than earth. And no, I don't know how it happened. Secondly, I think Friar Martin, by his prayers and blessings, saved us from a hideous fate. I urge all of you to pray that if you are not in God's grace, He speedily restore you to it. And, if you are in God's grace, pray that He keep you there.'

'What else?' Shadbolt grated.

'These three fiends attacked us but have now disappeared.'

'So?' Friar Martin insisted.

'I don't know how these three ghouls have returned to life but they intend to do us a mischief.'

'I'm going to flee.' Flyhead strapped on his war belt.

Shadbolt seized him by the shoulder, his face turned ugly.

'You'll do nothing of the sort!' he threatened, swinging the hangman round. 'We are in this together. We have nothing to fear. We carried out lawful execution.'

'But we didn't.' Simon spoke up. 'In my view, Master Shadbolt, we should never have left that glade. Friar Martin, you are a priest. You know about things supernatural, of what exists between heaven and hell.'

'If you speak the truth, Simon,' he replied slowly, 'we are truly in Satan's nightmare! Lost in the valley of darkness!'

'I know that,' Simon retorted. 'I would like to know how we get out?'

'I have little knowledge of these matters,' Friar Martin protested. 'But, on our return to Gloucester, I will make careful study.'

Simon squatted down before him. 'Brother, for the love of God!' he pleaded.

'What I tell you is only guesswork.' Friar Martin lifted his head. 'But we have three witches involved in bloody sacrifice to the dark lords. Now, at the beginning, such creatures ask for the good things of life: wine, silks, feather-down mattresses, good food, all the luxuries. But, as you know,' he smiled bleakly, 'these things are only passing. Their demands probably became more insistent, their sacrifices more bloody and grotesque. They may have asked for powers over others as well as themselves.'

'The Ratoliers?' Shadbolt jibed. 'Who offered to bribe us?'

'True, they bargained for their lives,' Friar Martin continued as if speaking to himself. 'And we refused. So they called upon the keepers of the shadows to come to their assistance.' He sighed. 'The message left at the Silver Tabard; I suspect that, before we left Gloucester last night, another sacrifice took place.'

'In a tavern!' Merry Face exclaimed.

Friar Martin glanced up contemptuously. 'Hasn't it dawned on you yet, clodpate! The Ratoliers were members of a coven, and though they were taken others still remain. You don't think those Dominicans travelled all the way from London because of three smelly hags?'

'Continue,' Simon demanded.

Friar Martin swallowed hard. 'I belong to the Order of Austin Friars. Or at least I am supposed to. There have been rumours, quiet whispers in the religious houses around Gloucester, about a powerful coven being at work. From what I gather young women have been disappearing for months, perhaps even years, but what do the fat lords care about some poor wench? It was more the number of victims. Something had to be done.'

'And you think,' Simon asked, 'that the other members of this coven made a sacrifice?'

'I do.' Friar Martin wiped the sweat from his brow on the back of his hand. 'Last night I wondered about that storm. The way we were driven out of the glade; the frightening tricks played on our nerves, disturbing the humours of our minds. Perhaps if we had stayed, if we had spiked and buried those witches, this would never have happened.'

'Oh, what can we do?' Flyhead wailed.

Simon got to his feet. 'Return to the glade. Come on, let us see what has happened!'

They hitched up the cart and piled on their possessions and fled from the hunting lodge. They found the trackway soft and muddy. At times it dipped and the hollows were filled with water, the soft mud clogged the wheels but, at last, they reached the path leading back into the glade.

Simon ran ahead. The clearing was dark, still dripping with rain, but on the execution tree, the makeshift gibbet, all that remained were three empty nooses hanging down from the branch beneath which the chains had been neatly piled. Of Agnes and her daughters there was no sign. Simon felt uneasy. It was so cold here. He was about to go back and inform the rest when he saw the red marks daubed on the great white crag of rock. Simon hastened across. He spelt out the letters and the chilling warning they carried: 'I told you that we would meet again!'

Chapter 7

The carpenter's discovery agitated and perturbed the other executioners.

'We should return to Gloucester,' Flyhead announced. 'I know,' he added lamely, 'we should all stay together in this business.' He smiled weakly at Simon. 'God forgive us for bringing you to this.'

'If we go back,' Shadbolt remarked, 'we will all be in serious trouble. We should never have left the glade.' He flicked the reins. 'Three days we've got to stay here and three days we will.'

The others, encouraged by Simon, entered the glade. They unhitched the cart, hobbled the horse then inspected the makeshift altar and its grisly message.

'I would like to say it's paint.' Friar Martin spoke up. 'But it could be blood.'

'Some animal perhaps?' Simon offered. 'Or a bird? Whatever, we have two more nights here. I think we should prepare.'

A fierce discussion took place which threatened to turn into a violent quarrel. Merry Face and Flyhead were urging once again that they should leave. Shadbolt and Simon, with the tacit support of Friar Martin, argued that they should stay. In the end Merry Face and Flyhead conceded, especially when Friar Martin offered to say a Mass in the glade, using the end of the cart as an altar.

'Holy Mother Church,' he declared flatly, 'says a Mass can be celebrated in such circumstances.'

The cart was prepared and two candles lit. Friar Martin placed a wooden cross between these; he had also brought his black, velvet-lined box containing a chalice, a small phial of altar wine and some unconsecrated communion wafers. He began the Mass as darkness fell, using the service from a Book of Hours. He spoke in Latin but Simon recognised, from the tone of the friar's voice and the fervour in his face, that he was beseeching the powers of heaven. He then gave them communion and, before he pronounced the Mass was ended, once again blessed water and salt which he sprinkled round the edge of the glade.

'If this goes on,' Shadbolt whispered to Simon, 'we are going to spend the rest of our days as sanctuary men, never daring to leave a church.'

In the end the Mass must have proved effective: the night was untroubled, apart from the usual forest noises. They all slept well and woke much refreshed the next morning. They went hunting, ate, drank and generally relaxed. Flyhead even began to scoff at his own fears. Simon hoped against hope that, perhaps, the night at the hunting lodge would be the sole visitation of terror and the powers of hell would leave them alone.

Just before eventide, as dusk fell and the mists crept in from the trees, Friar Martin celebrated another Mass, giving them communion and blessing their encampment.

Afterwards they sat round the fire, eating and drinking. Simon felt a prickle of cold on the nape of his neck and, every so often, he would turn and stare into the blue-black darkness, wondering what hideous horrors lurked among the trees.

The attack came just as the moon slipped behind the clouds: a low moaning and a cry of desolation brought them quickly to their feet, hands going for knives, daggers, bows, whatever protection they could find. Shadbolt didn't even wait but, raising his longbow, sent two arrows swiftly into the trees. Simon took note. He knew so little about his companions. The chief executioner's skill demonstrated that once he must have been a master bowman.

'Why not loose again?' a voice mocked from the darkness.

Shadbolt was going to but Simon seized his arm.

'Don't!' he warned.

Friar Martin agreed. 'They are playing upon our fears. God help us all but none of us should move out of the firelight.'

It turned into a night of terrors. The three witches appeared, dressed in their shabby, tattered gowns, hoods pulled over their heads. They moved along the trees, prowling like wolves round the edge of the camp, mocking and cursing, taunting and inviting the hangmen to come out and meet them.

'You are in our hands!' Agnes Ratolier screamed. 'You can pray, you can whine and that priest may prattle to his heart's content. But your bodies are for the worms and your souls are for hell!'

The sounds of the screams, the mocking laughter, chilled their blood. Shadbolt loosed another arrow but his hands were shaking and the witches were out of bowshot.

As the night drew on, the Ratoliers' attack became more insidious as they began to call out the hangmen's secret sins. Simon sat dumbfounded at the litany of vices placed against the souls of his companions: lechery, violence, homicide, robbery, rape, desertion.

'They are lies!' Shadbolt put his face in his hands, his face soaked in sweat. He pressed his fingers to his ears. 'They are all lies!'

Merry Face sprang to his feet, hurling insults back, as if trying to drown the ominous chanting of Agnes Ratolier and her daughters.

At the first streaks of dawn the witches disappeared. They vanished as swiftly as they had come, leaving the forest quiet. The group round the fire sat drained and exhausted.

'Why?' Shadbolt asked, springing to his feet. 'Why us?'

'Friar Martin,' Flyhead cried. 'I wish to be shriven!'

'Bollocks to that!' Merry Face objected. 'Perhaps it's only

this forest which is cursed? We've been here three nights: I say we return to Gloucester and leave immediately.'

'Wait!'

Flyhead had pulled his cowl over his head and now sat cross-legged, arms hidden up the sleeves of his gown.

'I want to make a confession. I listened to those screams last night and I realise the evil of my life. I am to blame for this.'

Simon, resting against the wheel of the cart, caught the desperation in Flyhead's eyes. The man's face seemed to have aged, his eyes red and rheumy. Shadbolt crouched down beside him as the others drew close.

'What are you talking about, Flyhead?'

'Do you remember No Teeth?'

When Flyhead glanced quickly at Simon, shivers seized the young carpenter. He had a premonition of what Flyhead was about to confess.

'Do you remember No Teeth?' Flyhead repeated, looking up at the lightening sky.

'Of course we do. He killed a man in a tavern and was hanged,' Shadbolt snarled. 'You should know, Flyhead, you were deputed to carry out the execution.'

'I . . . I . . .' Flyhead stammered. 'It's what you said, Friar Martin, about there being a coven in Gloucester.'

'Go on,' Simon insisted. 'Flyhead, I have a suspicion about what you are going to say.'

'No Teeth was a strange one.'

'We all know that,' Merry Face said.

'Ah, it was more than that. He kept to himself, remember? Often disappeared?'

'So what?'

'He had a doxy,' Shadbolt revealed. 'A toothsome, little wench with hair as yellow as ripened corn and eyes as blue as the sky. She used to make me itch. I always wondered what she saw in No Teeth.'

'She came and lived with me,' Flyhead retorted.

'What!'

'Well, she used to. But then, about three or four weeks ago . . .'

'She disappeared, didn't she?' Simon asked.

Flyhead nodded. 'I don't know where she went. One day she was there, the next minute she was gone.'

'Perhaps she'd left to go and join No Teeth?'

'That's what I'm trying to say,' Flyhead replied. 'Do you remember No Teeth was condemned by the justices? Master Shadbolt, you were away and Merry Face, you were ill with the rheums?'

They both nodded.

'I told No Teeth that he was safe; that he'd have the collar round his neck.'

'You said you put it there,' Friar Martin said. The friar's hand went to his lips and his eyes rounded in horror. 'What did you do?' he gasped.

'It was the wench.' Flyhead scratched his brow. 'Since I met her I used to spend every minute of the day and night thinking about her, those lips, the neck, the breasts, the way her hips swayed when she walked. I lusted after her.'

Shadbolt seized Flyhead by the jerkin and dragged him to his feet, pushing him against the cart.

'You hanged him, didn't you, you bastard!'

Flyhead, now sobbing quietly, opened his mouth to reply. Shadbolt stood back and smacked him across the mouth. Flyhead sank to the ground holding the blood bubbling through his lips. Shadbolt was about to kick him. Simon drew his dagger and came in between them. The chief hangman stepped back breathing deeply through his nose.

'Well, well, Master Cotterill.' He narrowed his eyes. 'What do we have here? Are you now master of our happy band of brothers?'

'I want the truth,' Simon replied. 'Beating and kicking Flyhead will achieve nothing.'

Shadbolt was about to disagree but Friar Martin grasped him by the shoulder.

'Leave it!' the friar commanded.

Flyhead wiped the blood on the back of his hand. The look he threw Shadbolt was of pure murder. And Simon wondered if this, too, was the work of the witches, setting them all at each other's throats.

'Yes, I lusted after her. I moved the rope. No Teeth died.'

'But didn't you accompany him to the graveyard?' Shadbolt turned to Friar Martin.

'No.' Friar Martin shook his head: 'I couldn't watch No Teeth be strung up, even if it was a charade. I stayed in the Friary.' He pulled a face. 'I dug the grave.'

'I cut him down,' Flyhead added, 'took him to the pit, threw him in and thought that was the end of it.'

'And No Teeth was buried?' Shadbolt whistled between his teeth. 'You are sure he was dead?'

'As I was those three bitches were strangled. But I did it quickly.' He shrugged. 'I knew I'd done wrong.'

Simon opened the wineskin and poured a generous measure into a cup. He recalled his meeting with No Teeth, his quiet impudence, and realised that he had not been so clever. Indeed, had No Teeth really sought him out?

Friar Martin pushed his cup across.

'A drink for a friar, Simon?'

Simon filled his cup. Shadbolt was tapping the ground with his boot. Merry Face crouched, digging his dagger, time and again, into the dirt. Flyhead had got up and walked away into the trees.

'The first thing I am going to do,' Shadbolt said, 'is go to the common graveyard in Austin Friars and see if No Teeth's corpse is still where it should be.'

'A waste of time,' Simon assured him. 'I'll tell you what, Shadbolt, the answer is obvious and quite simple. A coven exists in Gloucester steeped in black magic. The Ratoliers were members, probably its leaders. No Teeth was also a

94

member of this coven. Such groups are usually thirteen in all. There must be at least nine other members.' He scratched his chin. 'What puzzles me is that No Teeth bore no rancour. He hides but the Ratoliers are different. I wonder why?'

'I don't think No Teeth hid in the shadows.' Friar Martin slurped from the cup. 'His doxy has disappeared, hasn't she? I'm sure she's been taught a sharp, brutal lesson. It also explains why No Teeth didn't leave the area. I'd be careful if I were you, Flyhead. I'm sure our former comrade is desirous of having words with you.'

'But we are safe from him?' Shadbolt wondered. 'We did him no wrong.'

'The Ratoliers see us as their enemies,' Simon declared.

'And I don't think we are the only ones,' Merry Face added. 'I wager the mayor and the alderman will not be allowed to sleep quietly in their beds.'

Simon took his cup and walked towards the edge of the clearing. He pinched his thigh because, sometimes, he felt as if he was in a nightmare and would surely wake up. Nevertheless, he could not doubt what he had seen and experienced over the last few days. When he heard Shadbolt shouting at the rest to get in the cart he sighed, drained his wine and walked back to join his companions.

They left the clearing within the hour, taking the trackway down to the crossroads following the verderer's directions. Late in the afternoon they began to pass the occasional hamlet and lonely farmstead. Shadbolt said he was thirsty so they turned off to rest and drink at the only wayside tavern in the locality, the Scarlet Dragon. This was a large, spacious hostelry which had seen better days: the plaster was peeling, the wood was chipped and weatherbeaten. Mullioned glass horn once filled its windows, but this had now been replaced by strips of horn or left vacant like sightless eyes. The taproom was gloomy and dank. At first Simon could only make out small, rounded tables, together with the beer casks and wine tuns which served as stools, then he glimpsed a long trestle table with a coffin on top.

'What's the matter?' he asked a chapman sitting just within the doorway.

'A corpse has been found,' the fellow replied. 'It's been sheeted and coffined now the coroner has given his verdict.'

Simon nodded. In these country parts, the victims of sudden death were often displayed in taverns or on the steps of churches for people to view in the faint hope that witnesses might come forward. Merry Face picked up the coffin lid.

'Oh sweet Lord!' he whispered.

Simon pushed him away and looked himself. At once he recognised the corpse as that of the verderer, Deershound, his face white as snow, dark rings under his eyes and a long, red gash like a gaping mouth that seared his throat from ear to ear. The half-open eyes, the bloody mouth, the tufts of hair sticking up strangely made his stomach heave and he turned away.

'Jesus miserere!' Simon whispered.

The others, too, now gathered round.

'Did you know him?' The taverner came out of the kitchen, a small, thickset man with balding pate, greasy face and pebble-black eyes. He was wiping his hands on a blood-covered apron.

'We know of him,' Shadbolt replied tentatively.

He beckoned the others to join him at a table over near the window, nothing more than a square opening which looked out on to a bramble-choked garden.

'Aye,' the taverner replied, following them across. 'It's Deershound. He often came here to slake his thirst.'

'What happened?' Simon asked.

The taverner shrugged. 'Well, you know the Forest of Dean, full of poachers and wolfs-heads. Deershound was not popular with them. Thanks to him many a poacher ended up on the gallows for taking the King's venison.'

'What happened?' Simon insisted.

The taverner drew his brows together.

'What did you order?'

'Five pots of ale.'

The taverner turned to the pot boy.

'And your best,' Simon added. 'None of your slops.'

The taverner looked back. He was about to object but then glimpsed the silver coin Simon held between his fingers.

'Of course, sir. You heard the gentleman, Tomler: our best ale and a piece of pie. I am sure the gentlemen are hungry.'

'Venison,' the taverner added slyly. 'Bought, of course, in the market.'

'Of course,' Shadbolt said. 'But what happened to Deershound?'

'From what I gather, the royal foresters found him hanging like a rat from a branch, throat slit from ear to ear. A rope had been put round him and he had been hoisted up on a tree. Were you friends? The coroner wants to meet anyone who knew him.'

'We didn't know him,' Shadbolt replied.

The taverner caught their hostility. He sniffed and walked away.

'So, Deershound's dead,' Shadbolt said mournfully. 'And that's only the beginning.'

'You think it's the work of the Ratoliers?' Merry Face piped up.

'Keep your voice down!' Flyhead grumbled. 'Master Shadbolt, I think we should finish our ale, eat our pie and get out of here. The day is drawing on. I don't want to be caught in the forest at night.'

They all agreed. They drank the ale, wolfed down the pie and went back to the cart.

They reached Gloucester just as dusk fell. The city gates were already closed but Shadbolt produced his warrant and the watch let them through. The streets were deserted and empty, still soaked from the recent rain. Simon felt as if the city had changed since they had left, as if the grisly news from the forest had already swept through the narrow lanes and runnels.

'Do you think something's happened?' he asked as Shadbolt cracked the reins, urging the horses on.

'I don't know.' Shadbolt kept his face impassive. 'I tell you this,' he whispered so the others behind couldn't hear, 'I think it's time we disappeared.'

'I wouldn't advise that,' Simon replied tersely.

'We'll see.' Shadbolt clicked his tongue.

They entered the Hangman's Rest, leaving the horses and cart in the small cobbled yard. The sly-eyed innkeeper bustled across the deserted taproom.

'You've been gone for some time, Master Shadbolt. Secret business for the council, eh?'

'What do you mean?' Shadbolt asked.

'Oh, nothing.' The taverner stepped back hurriedly. 'But last night someone was asking after you.'

'Who?' Shadbolt rasped.

'Well, I couldn't say. She was cowled and hooded, a young woman I think. Came here asking after you. "Where're the hangmen?" she asked. "Master Shadbolt and his companions?" "Gone to a hanging," I joked.'

'And?' Simon asked.

'Well, the woman chuckled. She said you'd be back soon but to give you a message that she hoped to see you again.'

Simon glanced quickly at his companions. Shadbolt's hand went to his mouth. Merry Face and Flyhead looked as if they were going to cry while Friar Martin grasped his Ave beads.

'Bring some ale!' Simon said hastily.

The taverner did and the stoups were drunk quickly.

'None of us should leave,' Simon told the group. 'I know what you are all thinking, that the further you get from Gloucester the better. However, I'd strongly advise against it.'

'Oh my God!'

Flyhead was staring at the small casement window at the far side of the taproom. He half lifted his hand. Simon looked across. For no more than a simple glimpse, he was sure that

Agnes Ratolier's face was pressed up against the window, eyes crinkled in amusement, mouth gaping in a sardonic smile. Merry Face went to rise but Simon pushed him back on the stool.

'Master taverner!' he called out.

The taverner hobbled across.

'What news from the city?' Simon asked.

The fellow pulled a face. 'Nothing of note.'

'Any trials?' Shadbolt asked. 'Have the justices sat?'

'Now, that's strange,' the taverner replied. 'We have a clothier who comes here to break his fast each morning. He had been up to the Guildhall last night, said it was closely guarded, the mayor was meeting in secret. There are whispers and murmurs in the city that something's gone wrong but no one knows what.'

'I'm going home.' Merry Face sprang to his feet.

'And we'll come with you,' the others added.

They drained their tankards, eager to be gone. Flyhead, however, kept to his stool, looking at Simon.

'It's business as usual,' Shadbolt declared, as if he wanted to convince everyone that all was well.

They made their farewells, Shadbolt saying he would take care of the cart and horses. Once they had left Simon glanced across at Flyhead.

'Are you going with them?'

Flyhead put his tankard down. 'I'm a dead man, Simon.' He blinked and gnawed nervously at his lips.

'What do you mean?'

'I am supposed to be a priest, a man committed to do good works.'

Simon leaned across and gently grasped the man's scrawny hand. 'You are not a bad man.'

Flyhead glanced away.

'Simon, I am supposed to be a good one. I am what I want to be. I refuse to be what God wants me to be, that's the difference between a sinner and a saint.'

Simon studied this scrawny, hard-bitten hangman.

'Yes.' Flyhead smiled, catching his glance. 'That business in the Forest of Dean has made me think. You defended me, Simon. You challenged that bastard Shadbolt! So, I've a duty to discharge before I die!'

'Don't talk so despondently,' Simon replied. 'There must be a way out of this. I say we go down to the Silver Tabard tavern, take mine host by the throat and choke him until he tells the truth.'

Flyhead sighed noisily, blowing his cheeks out. He snapped his fingers and ordered the pot boy to refill their tankards.

'I am a dead man,' he repeated. 'And it's only right.' He gestured towards the door. 'As for those three, Simon, they are steeped in sin. Shadbolt's a soldier, a mercenary. He was an *écorcheur* in France.'

Simon lowered his tankard. Even in Berkeley he had heard of such savage outlaws. Men who had burned, sacked, pillaged and raped; who took French prisoners and stripped them of their skins, torturing them cruelly until they gave up their hidden wealth.

'And the other two?' He asked.

'Merry Face is no better. A man steeped in sin. Friar Martin's a drunken buffoon. They make a good hanging crew. Talk of the blind leading the blind. In their case, it's more that those who should be hanged, are hanging others.' He sighed. 'How long do you think we can go on, Simon? If the Ratoliers don't kill us, one day the city council will find out about our deceitful stratagems and bring us to book. We are not so clever.' Flyhead sipped from his tankard. 'You ask the taverner here. It almost seems God's law that hangmen die violent deaths.'

'But you are changing?' Simon tried to hide the panic rising within him.

'Oh, for the love of God, Simon! I'm a former priest! Look at me, I drink, I wench. However, let me come to the point.' Flyhead put his tankard down and leaned across the table. 'You are different, Simon. You are a carpenter, a good man. You don't have the mark of Cain upon you. I feel responsible for you. I mean, if I am going to die, it's time I put my affairs in order, prepared my soul.' He forced a smile and raised a hand against Simon's objections. 'Don't lie,' he pleaded. 'I know what I am but you are different. So . . .' Flyhead sipped from his tankard and surveyed the taproom; the taverner was over by the beer barrels flirting with one of the scullion maids. 'Listen carefully,' he continued. 'You are an innocent, Simon, and, if I can do some good before my life is finished, no, don't interrupt, then I will. We are faced by a great evil: like mischievous children playing a game, we don't realise what dark corner of the garden we have entered. There is no doubt that the Ratoliers are members of a coven, there must be at least nine others in Gloucester. Men and women of no principles committed to the Evil One. The Ratoliers have survived death through some stratagem of darkness and now they are bent on evil. They want vengeance!'

'Why?' Simon interrupted. 'Why don't they stay quiet, secretive, hidden in the shadows?'

'I don't know,' Flyhead replied. 'But they have a vengeance against us hangmen. Even righteous men still accept an eye for an eye, tooth for a tooth, life for life. Why should the Ratoliers be different? They were humiliated, scorned, punished. We should have burned their corpses and that was my mistake. Fire, both in this world and the next, cleanses and purifies.' Flyhead wiped away the spittle from the corner of his mouth. 'We are all for the dark, Simon. But at least I can save you. Now listen. No, no.' He waved a hand. 'I am deep in this sorry state but, at least, I'll show you a way out. Go to the Abbey of St Peter. In the cemetery stands an anchor house. The hermit there was once a member of the same Order as myself, a frail, venerable but very holy man. His name is Edward Grace. Once he was an exorcist in the diocese of Gloucester, now he has given his life over to prayer and sacrifice. There's not much about human evil he doesn't know.'

'How can he help us?'

'Let him hear your confession. Tell him everything you know and act upon his advice.'

'And what will that be?' Simon asked.

'I don't know but he will impose some sort of penance and demand that you do justice though, in your case, there's little guilt.' Flyhead cradled his tankard, rocking gently backwards and forwards on the stool. He glanced sideways at the window. 'God knows what wickedness will happen tonight but you should protect yourself. So listen now.' He unclasped the purse from his belt and shook the contents out on the table.

Simon smiled wryly. There were coins, dice, a few pieces of bone. Flyhead sifted these through his fingers.

'When I am short of a penny or two,' he said wryly, 'I sell them as relics. But this.'

He picked up a small golden locket with a sparkling sapphire in the centre and a gold chain which ran through the loop on the top. Flyhead handed this to Simon.

'Put it round your neck.' he ordered. 'No, go on! Do so!'

'What is it?' Simon asked.

'It's a relic of great value. No, it's none of my trickery: it's a relic of St Dunstan. A great monk, a very holy man who lived one hundred years before the Conqueror came to England. A scourge of demons and those who served them. Wear it constantly, Simon, never take it off. Keep yourself in God's grace and act on the advice of the hermit.' Flyhead's fingers went to his lips. 'And when this is all over,' he added, 'and one day it will be,' he raised tear-filled eyes, 'pray for me, Simon. Pray that, in my journey, in my long pilgrimage after death, I reach a place of light and peace.'

Simon stared in astonishment. Flyhead had changed, no longer the whining hangman.

'I know what you're thinking,' his companion said quietly. 'I'm two people, Simon. I looked at Deershound's corpse and all the evil I've ever done slipped like a heavy bundle from my back.' He tapped the table. 'I watched you in the forest:

you were brave, you're not one of us and I want to do one good deed . . .'

A dog howled in the alleyway beyond.

'The darkness gathers,' Flyhead concluded. 'It's all I can do!'

Chapter 8

John Shipler, furrier, alderman and member of the city council of Gloucester, made his way through the gloomy alleyways. Against the starlit sky he could see the dark mass of St Peter's, its great tower pointing up like a finger. He paused and hitched his costly robe around bony shoulders. Such sights brought back memories of when he was a boy attending the abbey school: his father used to tell him that the tower was actually praying to God. The furrier fought the wave of nostalgia. Those were halycon days when John Shipler was adept at his horn book and applied himself so well, he could translate a Latin verse and fill his father's heart with pride at the way he wrote courtly French.

The years had passed. The furrier, by his sharp mind and keen wits, had become a man to fear and a merchant to be envied. He had drunk well from the pitcher of life, becoming the owner of a great, heavy timbered house, its chambers full of costly hangings and precious cups. A wife, sons and daughters, status in the guild and a seat at the table of power were his. Yet this was not enough. He had other secret pleasures. He sighed and looked down the alleyway. A lantern horn, on a house at the far end, bathed the mouth of the runnel in a pool of light; a cat stepped into it, something dangling from its jaws. It seemed to look directly at the furrier before sliding away. He shivered. An old priest had told him that Death was like a cat, lurking in the shadows from where he could spring. Uncomfortably he recalled that business with the witches, the way they had looked at him in that council chamber.

Shipler leaned against the wall feeling the hilt of his dagger, reassured by the silver and gold hilt. He breathed in and grimaced in distaste at the foul odours from the midden-heaps along the alleyway wall. He shouldn't be here. Then he recalled Lucia's soft, brown neck, the generous swell of her breasts, her waist slim, her skin as soft as shot silk, those black ringlets which came tumbling down to her shoulders. The silver chain around her neck which winked and glittered when she had taken off her gown and stepped into the candlelight of the chamber John Shipler had bought for her off Grays Loan Lane.

The furrier turned, pulled the cowl over his head and walked quickly down the alleyway. A party of watchmen came round the corner so Shipler slipped into the doorway of a tavern. Few people looked up; once Shipler was sure the watch had passed, he returned to the darkness. He wasn't afraid, he just thought it was inappropriate for a man such as himself to be caught slipping through the darkness in the dead of night.

He reached Grays Loan Lane, passed the apothecaries and tapped on the metal-studded door. No sound. He tapped again and pushed it open, cursing quietly.

'I must tell her to be more careful,' he muttered to himself.

He looked down the gloomy passageway, empty, deserted. The mercer who used the lower part of the shop had long gone. Shipler climbed the stairs, a sliver of light from the half-opened door beckoning him on. He went inside. Lucia's quarters really consisted of two chambers, the first a small parlour tastefully decorated, the white plaster walls hung with coloured cloths, good oaken furniture, chests, coffers, tables, chairs and stools. Beyond that lay his place of delight: the bedroom with its turkey cloth hangings, woollen rugs, tables, chairs and, above all, the great four-poster bed with its silk canopy and crisp linen sheets.

'Lucia!' he called.

No answer.

'Lucia!'

Shipler bit his tongue in annoyance. Sometimes the minx liked to play games. He pushed open the bedchamber door. At first he thought it was a shadow dancing in the faint candlelight. The furrier looked again.

'Oh sweet Lord!' he whispered.

He closed the door behind him. Lucia, her body clothed in a linen shift, swung from a rope tied to one of the poles above the bed. Shipler wiped his sweat-soaked palms on his robe.

'What can I do?' he said fearfully.

If he called for the watch how could he, an alderman, a member of the city council, explain what he was doing here? As he tiptoed across, his hands out before him, his fingers brushed the bare leg of the hanged woman, and it was icy cold. Shipler peered into the darkness. He glimpsed the contorted, twisted face of his former paramour. No beauty now, the eyes were staring, the swollen tongue thrust between the teeth. The curtains round the bed had been closed; a stool lay on its side.

Was it suicide, he wondered? Had she taken some rope, lashed it across the pole, stood on the stool and kicked it away? But why? Lucia bubbled with life. Shipler considered her a noddlepate, a butterfly who only thought about today. His hand went out to pull back the bed curtain. He thought again and let his hand drop. He couldn't understand it. The room showed no sign of violence. But why were the curtains closed? He looked at the window on the far wall, which was closed and shuttered, but then he recalled the open door. Shipler looked at the grisly corpse, his mind teeming, wits turning. For Lucia he felt sorry but there were more pressing problems. If he stayed here questions would be asked. Perhaps even the finger of accusation would be pointed at him? And yet, if he fled? Shipler was about to turn away when he saw the bed curtains ripple. Was it a draught? Then he heard it, a low humming sound, like a woman bent over a spinning wheel, chanting softly to herself. He pulled at the latch but the door wouldn't open.

'Why, Master Shipler?'

The furrier's hand came away. He dared not turn round. This was not happening! He was in some terrible dream. He would wake up beside his fat, comely wife and, once again, make resolutions to repent.

'Why, Master Shipler? Are you in such a hurry to leave?'

He turned slowly. The bed curtain was now pulled back and, sitting on the edge of the mattress, was Agnes Ratolier, her face white and liverish, black circles under her eyes, her smile full of malice.

'It can't be!' Shipler exclaimed. 'This cannot be happening!'

He opened his mouth to scream but the sound wouldn't come out. He turned, scrabbled at the latch but it wouldn't move. Now he couldn't care if others heard him. He must get away from this nightmare. So engrossed was he in his own terrors, Shipler began to cry like a baby and hardly noticed the noose being slipped over his head.

The news of the terrible deaths of Shipler and his paramour swept the city, stirring up a delicious sense of horror and scandal. The gossips believed it was suicide, those who knew a little more proclaimed it was murder. Whatever the truth, the two corpses hanging together side by side seemed to represent a judgement of God against a man who had used his power and wealth to offend heaven as well as shock the sensibilities of his fellow citizens. The scandalmongers did a roaring trade, moving from tavern to tavern claiming they had privy knowledge of the truth. They were bought many a free drink and slipped a number of coins to impart what they knew.

Simon heard of it as he broke his fast in the Hangman's Rest. The others were not present. The carpenter had risen early, determined to act on the good brother's advice and visit the anchorite at St Peter's as soon as possible. Mine host told him the news, loudly declaiming against the pleasures of the flesh and how a man should stay with his family and obey God's law. Simon half heard him out, his mind going back to that darkened council chamber, the torches and lights, the dancing shadows, the aldermen and those three malevolent witches.

Simon had risen, determined, eager to see this matter through but he couldn't hide the shiver of fear which turned his skin clammy and his belly against further food. He pushed his trauncher away and fingered the relic Flyhead had given him. Perhaps it was just a coincidence! Perhaps the alderman, fearful of his secret sins being exposed, had killed his paramour before turning his hand against himself? No, Simon was convinced that Shipler's death was somehow connected with the Ratoliers and their malevolent powers.

He drained his tankard and went out into the rain-soaked streets. He pulled his hood up, for the wind was strong and still smelt of rain. Hurrying down the lanes and runnels, he did not wish to meet his companions or anyone else he knew. Were they still in Gloucester? he wondered. Or had they fled? Would they be needed by the Guildhall? Did other prisoners await execution?

Simon crossed Westgate, went up Abbey Lane, through St Mary's and into the grounds of the Abbey, at the far end of which lay the derelict cemetery. The anchor house itself was built of grey ragstone brick, the square window covered by a piece of leather; the metal studded door was off its latch. Somehow Simon had expected something different, more stark and dramatic. He was even more surprised at the small, white-haired, cheery-faced man who answered his impetuous knock.

'I am looking for Edward Grace,' Simon blurted out.

'You've found him.' The sea-grey eyes twinkled in amusement. Grace was old with silver-grey hair and a wrinkled face but his eyes danced with life. A small cat nestled in the crook of his arm.

'This is Satan.'

Simon looked at the kitten, black as night. Grace held him up. The little cat mewed in a display of small, white teeth and pink tongue.

'I found him among the gravestones.' The anchorite put him down on the ground. 'Well, come in, Simon.'

'You know my name?'

'Of course I do. Call me Brother Edward.'

The anchorite gestured at Simon to sit on a small stool on the other side of the fire, a small bed of charcoal in the centre of the room. He put sticks on top of this and peered up at the hole in the thatched roof above him.

'Now, according to what I have been told, the smoke should always go through that, but sometimes it doesn't and I have to open the door again. Well, what can I do for you?'

Simon took in his surroundings. The cell was no more than a stone box containing a bed, a table, a rickety chair near the window, a shelf with some pots and pans, a large crucifix and some chests, battered and broken, probably given to the anchorite by the Abbey.

'It's not much.' The anchorite smiled as he sat opposite, stretching out a hand to the fire. 'But it's been my home for a good two dozen years. It's comfortable enough, however, Simon.'

'You know my name?'

'That's the second time you've said that.' Again the anchorite smiled. 'Flyhead sent me a message. I have been expecting you.'

'Do you know what it's about?' Simon asked.

'Flyhead and I,' the anchorite watched the flames curl round the twigs, making them crackle, 'well, once upon a time we were brothers in the same order. True rapscallions! We took our vows lightly as we did the service of the poor and the worship of God.'

'And what happened?' Simon asked.

'One night I had a vision. I dreamed I was in a room,

something like this. It was bare and cold, no food, no comforts, not even a chair to sit on or a bed to lie on.' The anchorite closed his eyes. '"What place is this?" I asked. "Ah," a voice replied. "Your house for eternity." I can remember that dream is if it occurred last night.' He opened his eyes. 'Brother Simon, I can't describe the dread I felt. I've always thought of hell as a place of roaring flames, demons with grotesque heads and deformed bodies, but the cell I was shown was much more frightening: grey, cold, no doors or windows, nothing at all.'

'Just a nightmare?' Simon offered.

The anchorite shook his head. 'That's what I thought when I woke up. I'd been out drinking in the city and quietly cursed my toping habits – perhaps a piece of badly cooked veal or ale which had turned sour.' He picked up some more twigs and threw them on the fire. 'The following night I had the same dream and the night after. I was a little frightened. However, my fear turned to real terror one evening, just after dark, when I was slipping back, as usual, to my monastery. Brother Luke, or Flyhead as you know him, should have been with me but he was busy elsewhere. I was going down an alleyway. In front of me a dwarf was pushing a barrow piled high with grey rocks. I stopped him, being full of ale, I was a merry soul.' The anchorite paused. '"Why sir?" I asked. "Where are you taking those rocks?" You are not going to believe this.' The anchorite held Simon's gaze. 'But that dwarf had the most foulsome face, twisted and leering. "Why Brother Edward," he replied. "I've been watching you. The rocks in this barrow represent the sins you commit: your drunkenness, your lechery. I am taking them to hell to fortify that room of yours!"' The anchorite put his face in his hands.

Simon hid his despair and glanced at the doorway. Was this Flyhead's help? A lonely, crazed hermit? The anchorite's head came up quickly, his eyes no longer humorous but small, dark pools, his lips a thin, bloodless line.

'I know what you are thinking, Master Cotterill! He's an old fool who has visions and has lost the wit to distinguish between day-dreaming and what is real.' He pulled a face. 'And you have the truth of it. I'll tell you worse. If you go and speak to the good brothers of St Peter's they'll tell you I have the falling sickness. So, if you want, you can quietly tell yourself you are wasting your time and leave.'

Simon sat stock-still.

'Good,' the anchorite murmured. 'So, I'll tell you what happened next. I prayed and fasted for a week for a sign that these were not phantasms of a sickly mind. In my dream I saw a figure, like a pillar of burning fire hidden behind a mist. "Look at your wrists," a voice said, "when you wake, look at your wrists!"'

Simon noticed how the anchorite's sleeves came down almost covering his hands. He now pulled these back, revealing wrists covered in dirty bandages which he slowly unrolled, first the right and then the left. He stretched out his wrists. Simon gasped. Identical, on each, was a wound: shiny-red, open to the air, as if the blood were about to bubble forth.

'I changed my life,' the anchorite continued. 'I renewed my vows. I came and built a house here in the most forsaken part of St Peter's cemetery. Every day I celebrate Mass in a chantry chapel. I fast, I pray, while the good brothers allow me to study their library. In my youth I was a good scholar. I knew Latin and even Norman French.' He sighed and looked towards the door. 'And then the visitors began to arrive, men and women in the dead of night. They bore dark secrets of how they'd dabbled in magic, conjuring, the craft of the black arts. I began to study the books and manuscripts in the library, the works of the Fathers, especially those saints who, in their lives, had to confront the powers of hell.' He smiled. 'And by the way, I apologise, I have no wine to offer you but some will come soon.'

Simon just shook his head, fascinated by what the anchorite was telling him.

'I suppose I've helped many over the years. Above all, I've tried to help my friend Flyhead but he wouldn't listen, at least not till now. He believes it's too late but it's never too late for the compassion of God. However, he has asked me to assist you and I will do so. He has told me something about what has happened. However, before you begin, Simon, let me tell you the power of evil is based on trickery and deception, so that things are never what they appear to be. Sin is an illusion: the pursuit of fame, of fair flesh, food and drink. We know, in our heart of hearts, it will turn to ashes in our mouths. So, Simon, begin.'

'What do we face?'

The anchorite looked up. 'Why, Simon. The powers of darkness.'

'But the Ratoliers, are they dead or alive?'

'Oh, they are alive all right.'

Simon's jaw dropped in surprise. 'But I saw them hang! I was there!'

'You saw them hang,' the anchorite insisted. 'But did you see them die?'

'Is that possible?' Simon asked.

'The witches and warlocks practise great deception. You've heard the stories of how they can fly at night? Or transform themselves into toads or bats, creatures of the night?'

'Children's stories!'

'No, they are not. They are the product, Simon, of certain herbs, particularly the mushroom, the mandrake and other potions. I could brew you a concoction and make you drink it. You would later swear that you flew through the air high above the Abbey of St Peter's or that you'd travelled through the darkness of the night to mysterious places.' He shook his head. 'Nothing but dreams and illusions.'

'But the Ratoliers were hanged! I saw them dangle for hours.'

'And I can tell you stories, Simon, of crusaders, friars who have seen the mysteries of the East. Or men who can walk on fire, lie on sharpened daggers, be buried alive and still survive.'

Simon looked puzzled.

'I suspect,' the anchorite continued, 'that the Ratoliers took some secret potion just before they were hanged, which suspended their minds, their souls. What happened to their bodies was only an illusion. Whereas ordinary men and women would have their breaths cut off, the Ratoliers were in some form of dream, a demonic trance.'

'So, they have no powers?'

'Oh, I didn't say that. I merely work from a logical hypothesis. Flyhead said you saw prints in the ground, rocks and stones being thrown; the death of Deershound the verderer. I heard the brothers whispering in the Abbey this morning about the cruel death of Alderman Shipler. Once you are dead, Simon, you are dead. Yes, there are ghosts but the Ratoliers are different. They are flesh and blood. They can move, walk, run and kill. If they were ghosts I doubt they would have been frightened by Friar Martin's prayers. They are as alive as you are. No Teeth is proof of that.' The anchorite smiled. 'You met him in a tavern, didn't you?'

Simon closed his eyes. Images teemed; of the former hangman eating and drinking.

'Ghosts don't need bread and ale,' the anchorite teased. 'In fact, No Teeth is the key to the mystery. Flyhead told me about him. I suspect your former colleague was a member of the Ratolier coven. Perhaps he was frightened that he might not survive his execution so he took the same potion.' He shrugged. 'I suspect the grave at the Austin Friars was shallow. No more difficult than a boy clambering out of his hiding-place. You know I speak the truth, don't you?'

Simon recalled his meeting with No Teeth, how the man's jerkin came up close under his chin to hide his throat and the marks of a noose. He also remembered the ghastly faces of the Ratoliers and he described these to the anchorite. Brother Edward just chuckled and stirred the fire with a stick.

'Of course they are going to look ghastly. They have hung by their necks. God knows what potions have disturbed the

114

humours of their bodies? But,' he wagged a warning finger, 'they do have powers of the body and mind. They are cunning, they are sly and they can exercise that power over other people's souls. They can also call on the demons.'

Simon's hand went to his mouth. He didn't know whether to believe this man or not. He recalled the terrors of that old hunting lodge but then remembered how the witches had stayed well out of bow-shot.

'Simon! Simon!' The anchorite leaned across and patted him on the shoulder. 'Let me tell you what I think happened.' He held his hands out.

'The Ratoliers are members of a coven. They strive for special powers and made horrid sacrifice to their demon lords in the darkness of the Forest of Dean. If they were so powerful they would never have been caught but they were, by human ingenuity. Like all felons they wanted to escape. From their comrade No Teeth they knew about the secret practices of you hangmen so they bargained for their lives. Friar Martin and, of course, you, rightly refused and in that you were good, such women deserve death. They are nothing but a stench in the nostrils of the Almighty. When you refused I suspect the Ratoliers gambled on their own powers and potions. Oh, there's a lot missing there.' He gestured with his hand. 'But I'll come to that in a moment. They were taken out to the scene of their crimes. Before they were hanged they took a potion. Only the lords of hell know how that would work but, I suspect, their minds and bodies would have gone numb. They danced and they jerked but their souls did not leave the flesh which houses them.' The anchorite jabbed a finger. 'If you had taken their corpses down and burned them, you would have heard them scream as they truly endured death.'

'But they were saved by the storm?'

'Ah!' The anchorite smiled. 'And that was your undoing. I did say they had powers.'

'That rain storm was the work of hell?'

The anchorite nodded. 'I also suspect that, in the trees

beyond that clearing, other members of their coven waited. If the storm hadn't come, perhaps they would have tried some other means: the bodies couldn't be allowed to hang too long.' The anchorite lifted his head and stared up at the hole in the ceiling. 'But everything they had prayed and sacrificed for, happened. You were driven away, the bodies were cut down, the process of revival carried out and the rest you know.'

'How many members of the coven are there?' Simon asked. 'Thirteen?'

The anchorite laughed. 'That is a children's story. I doubt if thirteen people could keep their mouths shut for long. No, no, master carpenter, covens are no more than the square you've drawn many a time.'

'Four?' Simon queried.

'I am sorry.' The anchorite spread his hands. 'I was thinking more of a chamber. Four walls, a ceiling and the floor which supports them all. Six is their number.'

Simon clicked his tongue and listened for the faint bells of the Abbey pealing out for mid-morning prayer.

'We know of four of them,' he said. 'The three Ratoliers and No Teeth.'

'In fact you know five.'

'Ah yes.' Simon smiled. 'The tavern master at the Silver Tabard. So, who is the sixth?'

The anchorite paused at a knock on the door. He gestured at Simon to stay still and went to answer it. A lay brother stood there carrying a tray, a jug, two earthenware goblets and a trauncher covered by a piece of linen. The anchorite thanked him and brought the tray into the room. Placing it on the floor, he filled a goblet with watered wine and offered him the trauncher which bore bread, cheese and some diced, dried meat. They shared this out. The anchorite only ate a small portion, chewing the food carefully, sipping at his goblet.

'I suspect the sixth member is the dominus, their leader,' he declared.

'If they have escaped,' Simon cleared his mouth, 'why

116

don't they just leave us alone? Why kill poor Deershound and Alderman Shipler?'

The anchorite pursed his lips. Pulling back the sleeve of his gown, he rubbed the wound on his wrist.

'Revenge,' he replied slowly. 'Yes, the Ratoliers would like to punish you but, I suspect, it's more than that, much more pragmatic. Deershound needn't have died. I wager the night you left the clearing the verderer came back. He may have felt guilty at deserting you. He wanted to see that all was well. He saw your cart had gone, the corpses had disappeared and that dire warning left upon the stone slab. He would have fled, frightened, as the rest of you, so he had to be silenced.'

'And that's what the Ratoliers intended doing?'

'Yes. And they have the measure of you. You were supposed to stay there, guard the corpses and destroy them. Instead you left. Now the Ratoliers know that you won't come back to Gloucester and confess all but, at the same time, they want to silence your mouths once and for all. You know too much about No Teeth, about themselves.'

'But we could flee. We are little people. Shadbolt and the rest would dearly love to cross the seas, bury themselves at the other ends of the earth.'

'Oh, of course they would but the Ratoliers have to make sure. They must kill you, that is their plan.'

'And, if we flee, they might leave us alone?'

'They might do but I suspect the silence of the grave is better. For any of you who can flee it might be your salvation. But, there again, Flyhead has also touched upon the nub of the problem: confession comes easily to a troubled soul. One of you might present yourselves at the justices and confess what you witnessed. Can you imagine what will happen then? The Ratoliers would be hunted down as would all other members of their coven.' He chuckled wryly. 'I wager a penny to a penny that if you visit the Silver Tabard, no one will know or have ever heard of the Ratoliers.'

'And Alderman Shipler?' Simon asked.

'Now.' The anchorite joined his hands as if in prayer and pressed them against his lips. 'Now, master carpenter, that is a mystery. It would be tempting to say Alderman Shipler was one of their coven and they silenced him once and for all. Or, it might just be revenge on one of their judges but I feel something is missing from the puzzle. It's like a mathematical problem where you are given the answer, but you are not too sure how it was reached.'

'So, what do you propose I should do?'

'Let me warn you about this coven. Perhaps you feel comforted that they are not ghouls from beyond the grave but they are just as dangerous. They do have powers and they can use them. Above all, Simon, they have the power of fear over you. You are like a child in a shadowy room. Because you are ignorant, you don't know what terrors the darkness conceals, and they will play on that. You fight against more than flesh and blood. These beings have the power of darkness behind them. You must have yourself shriven. You must go to Mass and take the sacrament, wear the relic Flyhead has given you. You must clean all disorder from your life. You must become like a castle fortifying its defences against those who lay siege.'

'And what else?' Simon asked. 'Shall I flee?'

'It's tempting. If you hurried, you could be on the London road by nightfall. Yet, this evil has to be combatted. I would urge you to stay and fight. Indeed.' He smiled thinly. 'That is your penance.'

Words Between the Pilgrims

The carpenter paused in his tale. The rest of the company sat in silence.

'What's the matter?' the pardoner asked, playing with his flaxen hair.

'I thought I heard something outside,' the carpenter answered.

Dame Eglantine gave a little scream. Sir Godfrey rose, drawing his sword from the war belt looped over the back of his chair.

'What is it, my lady?'

'A face at the window. I am sure!'

Sir Godfrey nodded at the squire and, together with the yeoman, they hurried out of the hall into the garden, formed like a small cloister garth. The raised flower beds around the turfed seats were bathed in the light of a full moon. Against the four walls the brothers had planted rose bushes and other sweet-smelling plants. The squire, sword drawn, returned and took a cresset torch from its holder. He went out and searched but he could see nothing. So, followed by the yeoman, he strode back into the refectory.

'No one's there, Father. Perhaps it was one of the good brothers looking in?'

'I am sorry,' Dame Eglantine apologised. 'But your tale, master carpenter, fair frightened me. As lady prioress I have the power of axe, tumbril and scaffold.' She waved her hands prettily. 'But someone else always does it for me. Isn't that right, my sweet?' She pushed a piece of marzipan into her little lapdog's mouth.

The miller burped loudly, drawing furious glances from Dame Eglantine.

'I was a hangman once,' he announced.

'Aye, a fellow very worthy of the scaffold,' the summoner said in a loud mock-whisper.

'Shut your fat mouth!' the miller bawled. 'Or I'll knock those pimples off your face!'

'Hush now!' mine host intervened. 'Master carpenter, this is a fearsome tale. Is it true?'

'I've heard of such stories,' the miller continued as if unaware of any interruptions. 'There's many a hangman accustomed to reaching a private accord with their customers.'

'It's a common enough practice,' Sir Godfrey agreed. 'City authorities are always ready to turn a blind eye.'

'But these Ratoliers?' the wife of Bath spoke up. She had lost some of her jollity. She tapped the side of her head. 'They bring back memories.'

'Aye,' the friar agreed. 'And I'm sure I've heard of Friar Martin but I can't remember exactly how.'

'And Sir Humphrey Baddleton?' the man of law asked. 'Didn't he . . . ?'

Sir Godfrey tapped the table with his hands. 'Now, now, sirs. Good ladies all. You know the custom. No real questions till the tale is finished. And, whether it's true or not. Well?' He gestured with his hand. 'That really is not our business.'

'But witches?' the summoner scoffed. 'Human sacrifices!'

'Oh, it goes on,' Sir Godfrey intervened. He glanced quickly at the monk. 'I tell you, sir, your flesh would creep at what goes on under the cloak of darkness.'

'I've been to the Forest of Dean.' the yeoman spoke up. 'Do you remember, Sir Godfrey, you sent me there with letters for my lord Mortimer?' He shook his head fearfully. 'A dark, gloomy place. Do you know, the forest is so deep and dense it stretches for miles. Whole companies of people have been lost there. Gloucester is a pretty enough place but, once you leave its walls, travel west into that green fastness, it is like entering a strange country. I can well believe creatures of the night dwell there.'

The carpenter was playing with a gold chain round his neck. The wife of Bath who, as his story had progressed, had changed seats to study him more closely, noticed the

120

beads of perspiration on his brow. There were strands in his tale which awoke memories in her own soul: whispers of dark secrets, of stories, vague rumours which others had dismissed as tales to terrify the young. If the carpenter's story was true, did it explain why hanging had special terrors for him? Is that why he had fainted? And what was wrong with him now? The wife of Bath felt uncomfortable. She had travelled to Cologne and Compostella. She was frightened of nothing. Yet, she was sitting with her back to the window and she, too, had heard a sound. Dame Eglantine, although pampered and proud, was not given to the vapours or strange illusions. The lady prioress seemed more interested in her pampered little dog or receiving the murmured compliments of that handsome priest of hers, not to mention the hot glances of the dark-faced, enigmatic lawyer. The wife of Bath turned and glanced through the mullioned glass. And why should one of the brothers be peeping in at them when they were welcome to come in here and join their company? She turned back and leaned across the table.

'You did hear someone, didn't you, Simon?'

'Yes,' the carpenter replied. He smiled; only he had heard the wife of Bath use his first name.

'I knew Alderman Draycott,' she whispered.

The carpenter wiped his brow on the back of his hand.

'Come sir!' mine host shouted. 'We'll fill our tankards once more! And then, master carpenter, take us back into this dark and tangled tale of yours!'

Chapter 9

Merry Face sat in the alehouse on a trackway leading down to the London road. For the first time since he had left Gloucester he relaxed, allowing the sweat to cool, sitting back against the plaster wall. He stared up at the hams and onions pegged from the rafters to be cured in the smoke which curled from the log fire in the hearth.

Merry Face felt weary but happy. In the stable yard an ostler, for a penny, stood guard over his sumpter pony and horse. Merry Face supped from his blackjack of ale, allowing the liquid to soothe his sore gums. A tavern wench came across with a trencher of roast duck diced and covered in a mint sauce, an earthenware dish of vegetables and some freshly baked bread. Merry Face smiled but the woman, frightened, backed away.

He sighed. It was the same wherever he went. At least in Gloucester he had been someone, a hangman with the power of life and death. He fingered the money belt beneath his jerkin. He had collected every penny he had earned and, when he reached London or some other city, he'd find a trade.

Merry Face ordered a fresh tankard and ate his meal. He congratulated himself on leaving Gloucester. He would never forget that midnight glade or the awesome occurrences in the derelict hunting lodge. Three witches, undoubtedly hanged, had now returned from the pit of hell to plague their lives. He'd wondered what to do but the news of Alderman Shipler's death had finally unnerved him. Merry Face had collected every penny he owned, sold the meagre sticks he called furniture, bought a money belt, a sumpter pony and a harnessed horse. He would never go back to Gloucester!

The former hangman ate hungrily, pushing the bread and the tasty flesh into his mouth, chewing slowly because of the tightness in his cheek and jaw. He drained the tankard and, against his better judgement, ordered two more pots of ale. After he had eaten, Merry Face dozed and woke with a start. He looked across at the hour candle on its iron spigot near the scullery door and swore under his breath. He must have been asleep for an hour. He pushed away the table, collected his cloak and war belt and strode back into the yard. The horse boy was there sunning himself. Merry Face paid him a penny, collected his mounts and walked down the track towards the main highway.

The rutted path twisted and snaked among the trees. The sun was fairly strong but, every time he glanced to his right and left, memories flooded back of that midnight glade and those three gruesome corpses hanging by their necks. What happened if his companions were right? That the Ratoliers now had power to go wherever they wished?

The forest was silent. Now and again there would be the occasional caw of a rook or a flurry in the bracken. Merry Face stopped and looked back along the trackway. Perhaps he should have waited for someone else to leave; there again, if he moved quickly enough, he would soon be on the main highway enjoying the jostling throng. He would be safe there. He could hide among the pedlars, chapmen, itinerant quacks, wandering scholars, merchants and pilgrims. Then he turned a corner and his heart leapt into his mouth. Two figures blocked his way, hoods over their heads, vizards across their faces. Merry Face's hand went to his dagger but he hastily withdrew it as a crossbow bolt smacked into the earth before him.

'I am armed!' he called out. 'And there are others coming behind me!'

'You always were a liar, Merry Face!'

The smaller of the two figures stepped forward, pushing back his hood, pulling down the vizard.

'No Teeth!' Merry Face exclaimed. 'What is it you want?'

'Where are you going?'

'To London.'

'Are you now? And the others, are they going with you?'

'I don't care what they do,' Merry Face replied.

'And how many people have you told?' No Teeth asked. He winked and smiled slyly.

Merry Face swallowed hard and glanced at the other hooded, cowled assailant. The man just stood there. Merry Face repressed a shiver. A crackle in the bracken made him wonder if the Ratoliers, too, were near. He stared at his former companion. No Teeth didn't look like a ghost. In fact he looked as alive and as ugly as he ever did.

'How many people know what happened?' No Teeth's companion demanded. 'Just answer the question – that's all we want to know.'

'We haven't discussed it with anyone.' Merry Face dropped the reins and held his hands up. 'I swear on my life!'

'That's good enough for me,' the sombre figure replied. 'Your oath's accepted.'

He released the catch and the crossbow quarrel found its mark deep in Merry Face's heart.

Simon had left the anchorite and returned to his lodgings. He felt relieved at the advice the anchorite had given him. At Brother Edward's insistence, he had gone to the Abbey church where he had been shriven and taken the sacrament. He had then broken his fast in one of the hostelries which served the pilgrims who visited Edward II's tomb in the Abbey and made his decision. He would leave Gloucester, at least for a while. It might be a coward's way but, he reasoned, he had done no wrong and what could he do against the evil which confronted him?

He went out and bought saddlebags, panniers and some

new clothes, and drew the silver and gold he had banked with a goldsmith in Iron Leg Lane, supped at a tavern then retired early to bed. He had no thoughts about Alice or anything which had brought him to Gloucester. He just wanted to be away. The city gates would be opened at first light and Simon had decided to travel south. Perhaps even take ship abroad. Yes, he could do that. From Calais he could wander the roads, as he had sufficient monies and could always work to earn his keep.

Simon slept fitfully. He'd wake up, his hand going beneath the bolster to the dagger he had concealed there. Or he checked the candles under their metallic caps which he had lit and placed around the chamber. Simon was afraid of the darkness. When the shadows closed in, he recalled Agnes Ratolier's face.

He woke just before dawn to the sound of horses and the clink of armour from the street below. The candles had guttered out, the chamber was cold. Simon got up and tiptoed to the small casement window. The alley below was thronged with men-at-arms, archers, city bailiffs and the mayor's sergeant-at-arms. Simon turned away. What on earth would they want with him? Or was it something else? As if in answer there was a crash of footsteps on the stairs outside and a hammering on the door. Simon hastily pulled on a shirt and removed the dagger from beneath his bolster.

'Open up!' a voice roared. 'Open up in the name of the King!'

Simon raced back towards the window. Men-at-arms still thronged there. Now some were looking up. He glanced fearfully at the door. He had bolted and latched it the night before.

'Why?' he called out.

'Open up or we'll break the door down!'

Simon glanced quickly around. There was no other way out. Something hard crashed against the door, it buckled on its hinges and lock. He could hear the landlord's vain imprecations and pleas to be more careful. Simon pulled back the bolts and turned the key. The door was flung open, men-at-arms poured in. He was knocked back against the wall. A leather gauntlet smashed into his face, cutting his lip and jarring his head.

'Put the bastard in chains!' a voice roared.

Simon had his arms roughly seized. Iron clasps were placed on his wrists and ankles. He tried to protest but someone seized him by the hair, dragged him to the bed and threw him down. Armed men milled about the room.

'In God's name!' Simon cried. 'What have I done? Where is your warrant?'

Again his hair was seized. He was made to sit up and found himself staring full into the face of Sir Humphrey Baddleton, who tapped Simon on the cheek with a small scroll of parchment.

'You are Simon Cotterill, carpenter, former hangman of this city?'

'You know I am!' Simon snarled. 'You employed me!'

'Not for murder.'

Simon's jaw sagged. 'I've done no wrong!'

The mayor's watery blue eyes remained hard.

'Merry Face is dead,' he accused. 'Taken by a crossbow bolt near the London road.'

'I've been in Gloucester,' Simon stuttered. 'I've never left the city!'

'That's not what we hear. We can produce witnesses that you were at the house Merry Face visited.'

Simon gazed round at the men-at-arms overturning boxes and coffers, shaking out the saddlebags he had so carefully packed.

'And then, of course, there's Alderman Shipler.'

'I didn't even know him!' Simon cried.

'Sir!' The sergeant-at-arms came forward. In his hands he carried a heavy brocaded belt made out of high-quality Spanish leather with a beautifully ornamented brass buckle. The mayor grabbed it and thrust it under Simon's nose.

'Is this yours?'

'I've never seen it before in my life!'

The sergeant-at-arms squatted down next to the mayor. He took off his helmet and rubbed stubby fingers through his close-cropped hair. A soldier's face, thin and harsh, with a scar over his right eye. The stubble on his cheeks and chin made him look all the more sinister. He poked Simon viciously in the chest.

'Is it yours?' he repeated.

'I've never seen it.'

The sergeant-at-arms drew his hand back and smacked Simon across the face.

'You are a liar, a thief and a murderer!'

He snatched the gold chain from Simon's neck, and joined his companions in their search. Simon watched as they began to pocket valuables. He made to rise but the mayor pushed him back. He held the belt up, tapping the leather tongue against Simon's cheek.

'Alderman Shipler was found hanging in his paramour's bed chamber! His belt and the money pouch he carried were missing.'

Simon felt his heart sink. A clammy sweat broke out on his body.

'What trickery is this?' he gasped. 'I did not know Alderman Shipler. I am innocent of any crime.'

The mayor got to his feet.

'You can tell that to the justices.'

Simon swung to his feet in a clatter of chains.

'I know what this is about.' He pushed by the mayor and lunged at the sergeant-at-arms. 'It's the Ratoliers, isn't it? It's your way to silence us!'

The sergeant-at-arms brought his fist back. Simon tried to move sideways but the blow caught him full in the side of the head, knocking him unconscious to the floor.

It was dark when he awoke. The pains in his head were intense and he realised his right eye was half-closed. He lifted his hand and tenderly touched the swelling bruise. He could move but the chains were still on his ankles and wrists. He was on a bed with wet sacking; a pitch torch was stuck high in the wall. Simon glanced around and sniffed. The stench was offensive. A grille high in the wall afforded some light. Sounds from the dungeons, the murmur of voices from the passageway outside, filtered in. He closed his eyes and groaned. He must be in the cells beneath the Guildhall: dark, fetid holes. He struggled to his feet. A dish stood on the rickety table but a rat was already gnawing at the slops it contained. Simon knocked it away.

'I am innocent!' he screamed. 'This is not right!'

The rat scampered away, squeaking in protest. Simon lunged at it but he missed, tripped and crashed to the floor. When he scrambled to his knees he felt pain and sore from head to toe. His tongue was swollen and he had a raging thirst.

'I'm innocent!' he screamed again and beat his fists against the mildewed walls.

'Aren't we all?' a voice shouted back.

A bearded face appeared at the grille.

'Shut up, lad!' the turnkey warned.

'I'm thirsty!'

The key turned in the lock; the gaoler came in. He held a pitcher of water to Simon's mouth. It tasted brackish but he drank greedily.

'Thank you.'

Simon recognised the turnkey, a burly oaf whom Shadbolt had nicknamed the bullock.

'Sad times, eh, Master Cotterill? They say you killed old Merry Face, not to mention Alderman Shipler. You are to stand trial before the justices tomorrow. If you are found guilty . . .' The bullock's ugly face creased into what he thought must be a smile of sympathy. 'They have two new hangmen.'

'Where's Shadbolt? Flyhead?'

'Can't say.' The turnkey got to his feet. 'Disappeared like puffs of smoke they have. Ignored the mayor's summons.' He walked to the door. 'Do you have any money?'

Simon shook his head.

'Ah well.' The turnkey jangled his keys. 'For old times' sake I'll bring you some food. I'll also ask the hangman to make sure you drop quickly.'

The door slammed shut.

'I haven't been tried yet!' Simon bawled.

'Makes no difference, lad,' the reply came. 'From what I gather, hanged they want you, so hanged you will be!'

The bullock strode away. Simon dozed. The gaoler came back with a mess of meat and bread and a battered cup of wine which must have contained some potion; Simon immediately fell asleep and had to be roughly aroused the next morning.

He thought he was dreaming, that this was all part of a nightmare. He was hustled up into the Guildhall court, dragged and chained to the bar before the justices' table. The mayor was one of his judges, the sergeant-at-arms the other while the third was some doddery, local dignitary who seemed half-asleep. The witnesses, whom Simon had never seen before, came forward to say he had been at a tavern where Merry Face had visited just before his death. Merry Face's horse had also been found in a stable frequented by Simon. The ostler claimed the carpenter had brought it there and tried to sell it to him. Next Alderman Shipler's belt was produced. Simon tried to protest but he was told to shut up. He felt dazed, tired and weak, the courtroom was hot and packed with spectators. He was sure he glimpsed Alice Draycott's face.

'This is nonsense!' he cried after the sergeant-at-arms had summarised the evidence against him. 'I am innocent of any crime!'

A soldier smacked him in the mouth. Simon stood horrified as sentence of death was passed. 'For the foulsome murder of three people, theft and a long list of heinous crimes.' The mayor, his eyes steely and hard, glared down at Simon.

'You have no hope of pardon,' he rasped. 'Sentence will be carried out immediately, before dusk this evening.'

Simon was pushed from the court, through the hallway, down the steps and thrown back into his fetid cell. A priest came to visit him. Simon didn't know who he was. He tried to mumble his confession but remembered he had no sins to confess for hadn't he been shriven the previous day in St Peter's?

Late in the afternoon the new hangman visited him, a tall, thickset man who declared he'd filled the same post at Colchester in Essex. He crouched down and tapped Simon's battered face.

'You know what will happen, lad, so no nonsense please.' He scrutinised Simon from head to toe. 'Go up the ladder high.' he urged. 'I'll push you off. It will be quicker that way.'

Some food and wine were brought and, as soon as he had eaten, Simon regretted it. He felt drowsy, his eyes kept closing while his stomach pitched and heaved. He was aware of the rats scrambling over his legs. Vainly, he lashed out against them. Why was the wine drugged? He stared up at the fading light seeping through the grille. Of course, the mayor and his cronies didn't want any chatter. They wanted him to die quickly, no speeches, no declamations.

A short while later Simon heard footsteps in the passageway outside. The door was unlocked and thrown open. The hangman and his assistant, garbed in black, red masks over their faces, bustled in. Simon, just about conscious, was hustled to his feet. He glimpsed men-at-arms milling about. He was dragged out, up the steps, chains still clanking round his wrists and ankles, and thrown into a cart. Guards climbed in after him. He heard voices, the crack of the whip and the gates to the Guildhall creak open.

The grisly cavalcade was soon making its way along the cobbled streets to the hanging ground near High Cross. A small crowd had gathered. Some dirt and refuse was thrown. Simon glanced up; the sky was grey and lonely. Memories jumbled in his fevered brain. He was a boy playing beside the stream or going up to Berkeley Castle. Vague memories of his parents, of the cottage they had lived in; his coming to Gloucester; Draycott's rejection of him and the hurly-burly world of the executioners. Now he was going to hang. Simon felt a spurt of rage. He had hardly lived. He had done no wrong. He had been trapped between the evil Ratoliers and the cunning politics of the mayor. Why were they so insistent on finding him guilty? Or hanging him for crimes they knew he was innocent of?

They entered the area round High Cross. Simon saw the great scaffold soaring above him, the high narrow ladder. He barely had time to reflect before he was dragged off the cart. The crowd was thin, a few curiosity-seekers; the rest had decided to stay away from the threatening rain. Simon was aware of faces and the murmur of voices, the steep houses rising up above him, black-timbered and white-plastered. Some of the mullion-glassed windows were shut, others open. A woman was leaning out of one of them, resting her cheek on her hand.

She's bored, Simon thought. I am going to die and she's watching it as if I am a fly to be hit and forgotten. It was like some mummer's play where the actors mime their parts. The sergeant-at-arms was speaking, reading from a parchment. The assistant was talking to the hangman who was already climbing the ladder: a sea of mumbled words.

Simon walked forward but his legs felt weak. He glanced towards the High Cross and narrowed his eyes. Was that No Teeth sitting on a step, chin propped in his hands? Simon tried to shout but the words wouldn't come. The sergeant-at-arms had stopped reading and he smacked the scroll on Simon's shoulder, the official sign for sentence to be carried out. He was climbing the ladder. It seemed to go on for ever as if he were climbing up into the grey clouds. The assistant was following him, his chains were loosened, his arms pinioned behind his back.

'Where is everyone?' Simon asked. 'Where's Shadbolt, Flyhead, Friar Martin?'

'God knows!' the executioner replied, his voice muffled behind the mask. 'But it's your time now, lad.'

A mask was put over his face. Simon panicked. He felt

something tight around his throat. The hangman was talking to him quietly. He tried to grip the ladder but his arms, pinioned behind his back, wouldn't move. Then he was falling, like he did when he was asleep, lost in some dream. The pain shot through him as he hit the bottom, terrible pains in his back and neck. He scrambled, kicked his legs up, a roaring in his ears. 'Oh, make it quick!' he gasped.

Someone was pulling on his legs. The darkness opened and he fell fast and deep.

Shadbolt, the former chief hangman of Gloucester, hurried along Castle Lane. He stared up at the crenellated wall and glimpsed the sentries standing there. Shadbolt was terrified out of his wits. He'd tried to hide it but the news came in like a shower of arrows. Merry Face had fled, his corpse found on a forest trackway; Alderman Shipler had been discovered hanging by his neck in his paramour's bedchamber! Now poor Cotterill had been taken. Shadbolt felt a pang of guilt. He'd kept to himself; cowled and hooded he had gone round the taverns and heard the news.

Since his return from the Forest of Dean he had lived in a constant state of terror by day and night. He had visited the Hangman's Rest and, when he had lurched out, his belly full of beer and his heart full of false courage, he'd seen those two hags waiting on the corner. He was sure they were the Ratoliers. Shadbolt's nerve had broken. If he could find No Teeth he'd kill the bastard! He'd take his head and stick it on a pole!

Shadbolt hurried on, past the shabby houses, tenements and warehouses and along to the rain-soaked quayside. The river looked swollen, dark and menacing. He slipped into an alehouse where he sat down, pulling his hood over him, his bulging leather saddlebags beside him. Quickly he downed two tankards and shouted for a third.

Flyhead had said he would meet him here, but as yet there was no sign of him. Then a dark shape loomed in the doorway.

Shadbolt gulped and spluttered over his tankard. He put it down and groped under his cloak for his knife but relaxed as Flyhead pulled back his cowl and came and sat opposite him.

'Where are your saddlebags?' Shadbolt asked crossly.

'I'm not going,' Flyhead replied.

'What?' The chief hangman gripped him by the arm. 'What do you mean, you are not going?'

'I don't think it's safe.'

'We face the powers of hell,' Shadbolt hissed. He leaned over the table. 'You were in the forest. You saw those three hanged and then full of life the following morning. And you've heard the news? Merry Face lies in a pauper's grave, gutted like the rabbit he was. And now young Cotterill's been taken.'

'I know,' Flyhead snapped. 'I've just seen his corpse dangling on the scaffold. I'm not going!' he repeated defiantly, his lean, pinched face set and resolute. 'I don't think you should either.'

'It's safer,' Shadbolt insisted. 'We are dealing with demons, Flyhead. I have asked a wise woman.'

'Old Meg!' Flyhead scoffed. 'The one who lives in Mavedeans Lane? What does she know?'

'She says demons and witches can't cross water.'

'I'll believe that when I see it. You take your boat. Travel as far as you can.'

Flyhead ordered a blackjack for himself. Once the slattern had served it, Flyhead leaned his arms on the table and sipped from it, his close-set eyes studying Shadbolt. The former chief hangman felt a pang of envy. Flyhead was no coward. He often boasted he feared neither God nor man. For the first time ever Shadbolt believed him.

'I was a priest, you know,' Flyhead said. 'And do you know why I gave up?'

'What's this got to do with it?' Shadbolt retorted. 'Let's drink up and be gone.'

'You drink too fast and you drink too much,' Flyhead taunted. 'You can hide away but . . .'

'Why aren't you coming with me?'

'I told you, I was a priest once,' Flyhead continued coolly. 'I don't believe there's a God. I don't believe there's a devil, heaven or hell. When you are dead, you are dead. A colourless nothing.'

Shadbolt repressed a shiver of fear and urged his companion to keep his voice down.

'Oh, I suspect everyone believes the same,' Flyhead scoffed. 'Otherwise men wouldn't steal, lust, lie, betray, murder and oppress. To put it bluntly, Shadbolt, if there's nothing after death, the Ratoliers can't be ghosts or demons.'

'But we hanged them. You saw that.'

Flyhead leaned back, laughing. 'Tell me now, Master Shadbolt. How many people have been hanged in Gloucester and lived to tell the tale?'

'That's different.'

'Is it now? All we saw were three women hanged and then we fled that glade. I wished I'd stayed.' Flyhead beat the table with his fists. 'I wished I'd taken a bucket of tar and reduced their corpses to charred cinders. I don't believe in demons.' He drained his tankard and got to his feet. 'Somehow or other those three bitches survived. Now you can run, frightened as a rabbit, that's what they want. But I tell you this, Shadbolt, I've got a feeling none of us are going to be allowed to leave Gloucester.' He stretched out his hand, his face softening. 'But you were a good companion. We drank many a quart and heard the chimes at midnight.'

Shadbolt grasped his hand.

'I don't think we'll ever see each other again,' Flyhead said softly.

'What will you do?'

'I'm not going to stay, but disappear. Why not join me?'

Shadbolt shook his head. Flyhead pulled a face, turned and slipped through the doorway. Shadbolt half rose, meaning to call after him, then sat down.

'What can I do?' he asked himself.

He picked up the saddlebags and walked out of the alehouse, down the lane on to the quayside. A light rain was beginning to fall. It was growing dark but he searched out the trader from whom he'd bought the bum-boat.

'Why not leave it until the morning?' the fellow asked. 'The river's swollen.'

'I'll go up-river, keep to the bank,' Shadbolt offered.

The man shrugged, took the final payment and led the former chief hangman down the quayside steps. The bum-boat was really a wherry, a sturdy craft, fairly new; its woodwork still glistened, the copper ring on the high prow had not yet rusted. The oars looked strong and unsplintered. Shadbolt clambered in and sat on the middle plank. The boatman pointed to a small chest built into the stern.

'As agreed I've put in a wineskin, some dried food and meat. Where are you going?'

Shadbolt just seized the oars.

'Push me away!' he said.

The boatman did so. Shadbolt felt the boat lurch but he was used to such craft. Anyone who had worked as a wherryman on the Thames would have no difficulty.

Shadbolt was glad to be on the river. The Ratoliers and their coven would surely be watching the road and, if they were demons, well, the waters of the Severn would keep him safe. He stretched his feet, kicked the saddlebags a little bit further under the other seat and strained at the oars. The quayside faded. Now and again, when Shadbolt raised his head, he glimpsed pinpricks of light from the city. Once he was away, he'd turn the craft back into shore.

A short while later, he steered the boat towards a clump of willow trees, whose overhanging branches concealed the bank. Shadbolt smiled to himself; he'd rest here the night and, in the morning, continue his journey.

He was free of Gloucester. By this time tomorrow evening he would be well out of the reach of the terrors which hunted him. So engrossed was Shadbolt, so intent on reaching the willow-concealed river bank, he failed to see the pursuing barge slip through the evening mist towards him.

Chapter 10

'Well, well, lad, how does it feel to come back from the dead?'

Simon painfully pushed himself up on the truckle bed and stared round the lime-washed chamber. The sergeant-at-arms slouched on a chest at the foot of the bed. The mayor sat on a stool opposite Simon, so close he could smell the wine fumes on his breath. The mayor had dropped his great cloak on the floor and was turning the beaver hat in his hands round and round. Sir Humphrey smoothed down his silvery hair, his blue, watery eyes intently studying Simon. He leaned over and touched the young carpenter's neck.

'You'll enjoy a purple weal for a week then it'll start fading.'

Simon grimaced at the shooting pains in his shoulders and neck. His head felt heavy, his legs weak.

'Well?' the sergeant-at-arms barked. 'My lord mayor asked you a question!'

'My lord mayor had me hanged!' Simon replied.

'Only pretence,' the mayor scoffed. 'You've been here days.'

Simon stared at the metal-studded door. He'd regained consciousness two days ago. The grey-garbed servants had refused to answer his questions. So had the physician, a whey-faced individual with bloodless lips and red-flecked eyes. He merely poked Simon, scrutinised his neck and asked if he could pass water and food. Simon had lost his temper and had told him to sniff the jakes pot beneath the bed. The physician had expressed himself satisfied and left. Simon had been able to get out of the bed. The door was locked, the windows firmly shuttered though he could hear the sound of carts, horses, people moving about.

'Where am I?' he asked.

The mayor turned to the table and poured two cups of wine and gave one to Simon.

'You are in a house which belongs to the Guildhall. It's sometimes used by the council to house visitors to our noble city. Now it's empty, the physician, the servants and the hangmen are all in our pay.'

'I'm not!' Simon retorted.

'I am sorry. But it was the only way. We made it as quick as possible and, as you surmised, your food and wine were drugged.'

'The pain?' Simon asked, beating his fists against the woollen cover. 'Swinging in the air!'

'It was necessary,' the sergeant-at-arms barked. 'And you made it necessary. Now, tell us everything you know about the Ratoliers.'

Simon sipped from the wine.

'Everything,' the mayor insisted. 'We've learned a little but our chicken at the Silver Tabard has already flown.' He pulled the stool closer. 'We live in troubled times, Master Cotterill; the King's a boy, the French are at sea, peasants grumble and the tax-collectors move like ants, eating up everything they can take. Now, I don't really care if people go off into the Forest of Dean and dance naked around fires. And, to be perfectly truthful, I have very little sympathy with wenches who walk lonely country lanes and take help from strangers.'

'It's Shipler, isn't it? It's because an alderman has been hanged!'

'You should have spiked those bodies!' the sergeant-at-arms broke in. 'You should have stayed and guarded them, then cut them down and spiked their hearts as you were ordered.'

'And so I would have saved Alderman Shipler?'

'Oh, there's more than that.' The mayor put his goblet down. 'Do you remember Shadbolt? His corpse, water-sodden, gnawed by the fish, has been pulled from the Severn. Someone strangled him with a piece of rope.'

Simon sat up, his hands shaking. Poor Shadbolt, despite all his swagger, he must have lost his nerve.

'Tell us everything you know,' the mayor said. 'And when we have finished we'll tell you why we saved you.'

Simon began to talk. He told them about his early life, his joining the hangmen, the secret bargains they made with certain condemned felons. At this the mayor laughed sharply, shaking his head.

'I have heard of such compacts,' he said. 'Master Shadbolt and his crew won't be the first hangmen, and certainly won't be the last, to decide who dies and who doesn't. Indeed, there's a recent royal proclamation, ordering all bodies to be left on the public gibbets for at least a day and a night before they are tarred and gibbeted.'

'So, you knew already?' Simon asked.

'We began to suspect,' the sergeant-at-arms broke in. 'But continue.'

Simon described the hideous journey into the Forest of Dean, the sudden storm, their flight to the hunting lodge and Deershound's death. He also described the advice given to him by Flyhead and his visit to the anchorite in the Abbey of St Peter.

'Why don't you ask Flyhead?' he concluded. 'Or Friar Martin?'

'Ah, that's the problem,' the mayor replied. 'You see, everyone's gone to ground. Shadbolt and Merry Face are dead. We have found neither hide nor hair of Flyhead or Friar Martin.'

'Tell me,' Simon asked, 'whose idea was it to take the Ratoliers out and hang them in the Forest of Dean?'

'You were at the trial. Alderman Shipler . . .'

'And Alderman Draycott,' Simon finished.

'Both are dead.'

Simon's jaw fell. 'I don't understand . . .'

'Alderman Draycott and his only daughter Alice were found dead in their stable.'

Simon felt as if he was going to faint. He dropped the cup, the wine spilling over the coverlet. For some strange reason his legs began to twitch and jerk. His throat was dry. The mayor did not move but the sergeant-at-arms got up. He took a cloth from the lavarium and wiped the wine, picked up the cup and put it on the table. He gripped Simon's hand and squeezed it.

'So, it's true,' he said. 'You were sweet on the girl?'

'That's why I came to Gloucester. The real reason,' Simon stammered. 'But when I got here, Alderman Draycott drove me from his house and Alice would have nothing to do with me!' He gulped for air. 'How did they die?'

'As you know, Draycott was a bit of a miser. Once the day's work was finished the servants and apprentices were put out to fend for themselves. Two retainers remained: an old man and woman who cooked and served at his table. Last night Alderman Draycott and Alice, as usual, supped late. The two old retainers left.

'This morning Draycott's chief apprentice knocked on the front door. He was surprised to see no light as the alderman always had an eye to profit and was up before dawn. There was no answer so the apprentice went down the alleyway which ran alongside the house: the postern door at the back was also locked and bolted. It seemed deserted, then he heard the horses whinnying in the stables.'

Simon nodded. Draycott had a chestnut mare, Alice a small grey palfrey.

'He went inside, where the light was poor. The stable contained two boxes for the horses and, at the far end, some hay and fodder. Alice and her father were found hanging there. No other signs of violence. It was very strange . . .'

142

'I inspected the bodies myself,' the sergeant-at-arms interrupted. 'Their arms and legs weren't tied. There was no sign
of a struggle, just those two corpses, swaying slightly on the
end of a rope.'

Simon put his face in his hands.

'I almost got the impression that they'd committed suicide;
that they both walked through that stable, fastened the nooses
to a beam, climbed the bales, put the nooses round their necks
and stepped off.'

'And the house?'

'The postern door at the back was locked, as I say. I
couldn't find the key so I can't say whether it was from
the inside or outside. Some of my lads broke it down. Inside
everything was clean and tidy with not a pot or cup out of
place, everything washed and cleaned. I interrogated the old
servants. They said they had served a meal and that Alderman
Draycott always left the table for them to clear the following
morning. Only this time he and Alice appeared to have cleared
the table, washed the pots and plates, tidied the kitchen and
scullery and put everything in place. They then left the house,
locking the door behind them, and went into the stable to hang
themselves.'

'But you don't believe that?' Simon asked.

'No, we don't,' the mayor agreed. 'I don't believe in ghosts,
Master Cotterill, but I do believe in demons. You are being
honest with us so I'll be honest with you. For some months
I've had a suspicion of a satanic coven working in and around
Gloucester. Most practitioners of the black arts are slightly
crazed old ladies who believe they have powers. Really, all
they have are their dreams. The Ratoliers are different: they
are demons incarnate. We trapped them once, now we have
to seize them again.' He sighed. 'We wondered if something
might go wrong.'

'I sent scurriers into the Forest of Dean.' The sergeant-at-
arms took up the story. 'We learned about Deershound's death.
We visited the glade. We could see no sign of the corpses being

destroyed while, of course, the inscription on their altar was left for all to see.'

'When the scurriers returned we made careful investigation of our hangmen: Shadbolt, Merry Face and Flyhead. They should have been arrested but they'd disappeared off the face of the earth. Friar Martin is a priest and is probably hiding in his friary, so that left you, Master Cotterill.'

'Why all this mummery?'

'Ah!' the mayor replied. 'Everyone who attended the trial of the Ratoliers and was involved in their supposed death, appears to be marked down for destruction.'

A wild thought seized Simon. He'd been part of trickery to allow people who were hanged to walk away and now it seemed as if the game had turned nasty.

'How do we know Shipler and Draycott really died?' he asked. 'The anchorite told me how it's possible for these practitioners, either through potions or the power they have assumed, to appear as if their souls have left their bodies.'

The mayor laughed drily. 'And the same thought has occurred to me, Master Cotterill. However, Shipler's corpse was kept four days above ground before burial, and the same is true of the Draycotts.'

'I would like to pay my respects to them.'

'You'll do nothing of the sort! Master Cotterill, you are supposed to be dead yourself. You asked the reason for all this trickery, so I'll be blunt. We are going to change your name and your appearance. Your hair will be cropped and dyed black. You'll be armed, provisioned and supplied with monies.'

'For what?' Simon asked in alarm.

'Fifty pounds sterling,' the mayor replied. 'If you help the city council destroy this coven once and for all!'

'How can I do that?' Simon spluttered.

'You have no choice.' The sergeant-at-arms smiled but his eyes were glass-hard. 'You either leave here, Master Cotterill, our living servant or as a corpse.' He emphasised the points on his fingers. 'Firstly, you know about the Ratoliers. Secondly, you know Flyhead and Friar Martin. Thirdly, despite all your bumbling, you, of all of them, seem to have acted with wit and some wisdom. You visited the anchorite. You learned some of the truth. You had yourself shriven and took the sacrament. Fourthly,' his eyes softened, 'we think you are honest. Do this for us and we promise, you'll be allowed to leave Gloucester with honour, well stocked with monies to begin a life elsewhere, take a new name, a new post. Just do what we ask!'

'Silver,' the mayor insisted. 'New clothing, arms and a free passage from the city. Until then you'll live here.'

'Where would I begin?' Simon asked.

'You found No Teeth once. Surely you can find him again?'

Simon contemplated the crucifix on the wall. He still felt weak, sore and shaken and now deeply sad at Alice's death. He had tried to flee but failed. If he tried again he would probably be pursued, not only by the Ratoliers but by all the powers this redoubtable mayor and sergeant-at-arms could muster.

'I agree.' The words were out before he could stop them.

The mayor stretched out and clasped his hand.

'I'm glad,' he said quickly. 'I'm sorry for the pain you had to endure but there was no other way. You had to die, to work in secret.' He let go of Simon's hand. 'I love this city. But evil's swilling down its streets like some rotten rain, all the filthy muck spat up by hell. Now you'll be on your own, though my sergeant-at-arms here will be in the background. If you are caught or discovered, you will have to flee and we'll do what we can. One thing I want to impress upon you.' The mayor's eyes gleamed. 'Forget the Ratoliers.'

'What?' Simon exclaimed. 'Surely they are the leaders.'

'I don't think so. The Ratoliers are merely chaff in the wind. The same is true of the tavern keeper of the Silver Tabard and No Teeth. I want their leader.'

'But the Ratoliers?' Simon protested.

145

'Forget them! They can't change their appearance. They are not really of this city. Don't worry about them. I'll organise a sheriff posse and they can scour the Forest of Dean. The bitches will probably hide there in their filthy darkness and never come out. Unless we know exactly where they're hiding, we'll have to leave them.' He shook his head. 'No, Simon, what you must do, and God knows how you'll do it, is trap their leader.' He smiled. 'And, if you can capture No Teeth and mine host at the Silver Tabard, then all to the good!'

Four days later Simon Cotterill was ready. Before he left the lonely house in a quiet street leading off the Guildhall, he studied his reflection in a piece of shining metal. He was surprised at the change in his appearance. His light-brown hair was now dyed black with pigments the sergeant-at-arms had bought from an apothecary. Yet it was the change to his face which shocked him the most. Whether because of his work as a hangman, the horrors he had witnessed in the Forest of Dean or the hideous agony he had suffered on the scaffold, his face was thinner, more drawn. Furrows had appeared around his mouth. His eyes were deep-set, his nose seemed sharper. Simon ruefully realised his youth was over. He was, in many ways, a forgotten man who really didn't exist. No more worries about carpentry, about joists, joints and carvings or about money or prospects. He was truly alone.

He fingered the relic of St Dunstan the mayor had returned to him. He felt sorry for the Draycotts and he fully understood the mayor's anger. The leader of the coven was probably cloaked in respectability; yet he pulled the strings and made others dance, dealing out death to those marked down for destruction.

Simon, before he left the room, placed his hand over the crucifix on the wall.

'I swear by all the souls!' he muttered. 'And as far as my powers will allow, that justice will be done! For me, for Alice and for all those who have died!'

*　　*　　*

The former hangman, known as Flyhead, lifted the wicker basket of bones and left the reeking slaughter shed in the fleshers' yard of the Shambles near Oxblood Lane. No one would have recognised him. He was no longer dressed in his quilted black leather jacket and his balding pate, so telling in his appearance, was now covered by the makeshift wig he had bought from a whore on the other side of Gloucester.

Flyhead stumbled across the blood-spattered cobbles and deposited the basket of bones along with the rest waiting to be collected by the grinders. He wiped the sweat from the back of his arm and scrutinised the darkening yard. Here, he felt safe.

He had not tried to flee and had kept well away from his usual haunts. He'd secured this job simply because he had been available. No one knew anything about his true name, his past or what he was hiding from. He glanced up at the sky. Soon winter would make itself truly felt. The bedraggled trees which stood round the slaughter yard had already been stripped of their leaves which, thick on the ground, gave the yard a bloody, matted look. A grisly place, the fleshers' yard, with its stench, the gutted carcases of animals, yet a good place to hide. Flyhead would stay here until well after Yuletide and, when spring came, he'd dig up his money from where he had hidden it and flee like a deer.

At the other end of the fleshing shed a bell tolled, the sign that the day's work was finished. Flyhead sighed. He'd collect his pennies, go to the alehouse with the rest and, while they chattered and traded in good-natured obscenities, he would search for eyes watching him.

So far, nothing had happened. He'd heard about Shadbolt's death just after poor Cotterill was hanged on the very scaffold where he had worked. Flyhead breathed in. He felt truly sorry for Cotterill. He would have liked to go out to see the anchorite but that door was closed. He could not bear the reproachful gaze of Brother Edward, to listen to his

147

advice about the Ratoliers being simply evil women who had cheated death.

Flyhead walked back into the empty fleshing shed and tossed the basket down with the rest. Indeed, if he was honest, that had been his saving. The others thought they were being confronted by ghouls and ghosts. They had panicked and fled and it was easy to kill a lonely man on some deserted trackway or a swollen, mist-shrouded river.

Flyhead took his cloak down from a peg and shuffled towards the overseer.

'A good day's work,' the fellow remarked. He thrust two pennies into Flyhead's outstretched hand. 'And there's another one.'

Flyhead didn't even bother to look up but mumbled his thanks, put his cloak about him and left. He did the same every day, trying to avoid the gaze of others or being drawn into conversation. Outside he put the pennies into his purse and allowed himself a smile. He'd be all right. This would join the rest of his treasures, hidden under those ruins on the edge of Gloucester. A lonely, haunted place with crumbling walls. Some said it had been a royal palace. Others, more knowledgeable, said it had been built by the Romans.

Flyhead stepped into the lane. Come spring, he'd be across into Wales then take a boat to Ireland. He walked down the lonely, gloomy runnel. At the corner he abruptly stopped and looked back to ensure no one was following him.

'I don't believe in ghosts,' he muttered. Nevertheless, something dreadful had happened out in the Forest of Dean. Undoubtedly, the Ratoliers had been saved and now they, and other members of their coven, were wreaking vengeance.

Flyhead found the alehouse where the other slaughterers, butchers and fleshers gathered. A dingy, narrow place which stank of blood and guts, but it was safe. The light was poor and Flyhead, to keep his companions happy, would always share a jug of ale, mumble a reply to some question then sit and allow the ale to wash the dirt and grime from his mouth. He did the same as every other evening, hiding in a corner, pretending to listen to his loud-mouthed companions. Now and again he would glance quickly around or watch the door. As usual he drank two quarts and ate a beef stew pie. The food served here was always good, the meat tender and fresh. After all, hadn't it been recently filched from the fleshing shops? The best meat in Gloucester, the ale-master taunted, and he didn't have to pay a penny for it!

Flyhead made his excuses and left. He wandered along the runnels, thin as needles, and eventually arrived back at the dilapidated four-storied house on the corner of Cat's Eye Lane. The door was open. Flyhead climbed the stairs. At last he reached the top and, crouching down in the poor light, checked the pieces of cloth and scraps of parchment he had placed just under the door when he had left that morning. Nothing was disturbed. He took the key out of his pouch and slipped it into the lock. The avaricious landlord had been most surprised when Flyhead had insisted on buying a new lock. He turned the key and walked into the darkness. As he lit a candle he knew he had made a mistake: he should have shut the door. At the sound of a click he turned slowly round. He could make out the outline of a figure standing in the doorway and, in the pool of light from the candle, caught the glint from the barb on the crossbow bolt.

'How did you know?' he gasped.

'You told me yourself, Flyhead. Oh, by the way, that wig does nothing for your appearance.'

Flyhead felt his legs tremble.

'It can't be!' he gasped. 'Is that you, Simon? But you are dead, for the love of God! They hanged you!'

The man who walked into the room and held the crossbow sounded like Cotterill but Flyhead, narrowing his eyes, wondered if he was losing his wits. The face was familiar but it had lost its boyish, innocent look; now narrow and lean, the hair much darker, the eyes not so bright.

'I didn't hang, Flyhead.' Simon kicked the door shut. He

149

put the crossbow down and brought out a small wineskin from beneath his cloak. 'Come on, man. You've got more than one candle. Don't worry.' Simon brought his hand down on the man's shoulder. 'I am as frightened as you, Flyhead. Now, if you light the other candles and bring me a couple of cups, I'll explain what's happened.'

Flyhead hastened to obey and they sat talking in that tawdry narrow chamber. The bells of the Abbey of St Peter were booming out for Compline by the time Simon had finished. Flyhead whistled under his breath.

'And how did you know how to find me?'

'You told me, one night when we were all deep in our cups, how as a lad you worked as a butcher's apprentice.'

'Ah, so I did.'

'And perhaps you told No Teeth the same?'

Flyhead felt a shiver up his spine as if the window had been opened and a blast of icy air swept the room.

'What do you mean?' he demanded quickly.

'I knew you hadn't fled Gloucester. There are six fleshing yards, and I found you in the fourth. I kept well away. One night I stood outside the alehouse and last night I followed you here. Tonight I was waiting for you.'

'You've changed, Simon. A few weeks ago you would have blundered in.'

'I've had to change! What started out as merry japery, a subtle way to make ourselves rich, has turned like a dagger in our hands. You are a former priest, Flyhead, you know how these covens work.'

Simon refilled his cup.

'All those who were involved in the trial of the Ratoliers must die! You, me, the mayor and the sergeant-at-arms, we are all marked down for destruction.'

Flyhead picked up a damp rag and wiped his face.

'You are more cunning than the rest,' Simon continued. 'You think you can hide in Gloucester. For how long, Flyhead? A month, two months? If I can find you, so can they.'

'What about Friar Martin?'

'I haven't visited him yet. He hides behind the skirts of Holy Mother Church. However, I talked to the doorkeeper at the Austin Friars. Friar Martin has turned over a new leaf. He is now custodian of the shrine of St Radegund in the friary church. He sits and listens to the confessions of the pilgrims. Who knows, perhaps he will be safe on consecrated ground? Anyway, he wasn't really one of us. He didn't actually participate in the hanging of the three witches.' Simon chewed the corner of his lip. 'I'll visit him soon.' He half smiled. 'I'll pretend to be a pilgrim.'

'What do you propose?' Flyhead asked. He slurped the cup of wine and cursed his own arrogance. He was surprised both at the change in Cotterill and that he himself had been discovered so easily.

'I want the hunted to become the hunter,' Simon replied. 'But to do that I need your help.'

'Never!' Flyhead vowed.

Simon got to his feet. 'I need you, Flyhead, to lure the bait. I am a dead man and, if you don't help, you truly will be. They'll find you, they'll hunt you down, be it the feast of All Saints or Yuletide. One of these feasts will come and you'll be gone. Yet, if we strike hard, there'll be nothing to fear any more.' He paused. 'In the Hangman's Rest,' he continued, 'you tried to save me: you gave me the relic, you sent me to the anchorite. You judged yourself as dead, and you know in your heart of hearts that hiding is no protection.'

Flyhead stared at his hands. He could still make out the marks from the fleshers' yard. Once his hands were light and soft; they'd held the host and chalice and consecrated the body and blood of Christ. He felt a deep sadness for all he had lost. He glanced up.

'You are right, Simon. Ever since I left my priesthood I have been hiding. So, what do you propose?'

151

Chapter 11

Flyhead lay on his bed and stared up into the darkness. A good ten days had passed since Simon's visit, when Flyhead had agreed to join him. He had given up his job in the fleshers' yard, burned the wig and, once again, been seen in the taverns around High Cross. At first he had been terrified, frightened that the Ratoliers might abruptly strike. Simon, now truly a man of the shadows, had reassured him.

'Never be anywhere by yourself! Avoid the lonely trackway or the deserted alley. They'll watch for that and choose their moment.'

Flyhead's confidence had grown. The coven might be watching him but he was aware of Simon. Flyhead smiled. The young carpenter had surprised him, stronger, more resolute than he had thought. Flyhead never cared for anyone. Well, except for No Teeth's saucy little wench. Flyhead felt his mouth water. She had been so sweet, so kind. He fingered the dagger which lay next to his leg. When the time came he'd also remember her!

The sounds of the night caught his attention: a cat screeching in the alleyway, a bird against the shuttered window. Flyhead recognised all the noises but then he heard it, a slight creak on the stairs outside. He would have liked to seek reassurance, take the tinder and light the candle but he rolled over, his back towards the door, his hand clutching the dagger. He wasn't sure if he heard the door open with just a quick movement. His head was pulled up, the noose was round his neck before he could cry out. The knot tightened behind his ear. He struck out with the dagger at the figure behind him. A scream, foul breath in his face. The room was then bathed in light as Simon, who had remained concealed, as he had every night since they had met, pulled the coverlet away from the lantern he'd primed. Flyhead's two assailants turned in surprise. They both wore vizards but he recognised the back of No Teeth's head. The other attacker was moving, dagger out, towards Simon but a crossbow bolt, thick and squat, smacked full in his face, smashing bone and flesh. The man fell, kicking and screaming, clutching his face. Flyhead needed no encouragement. He knocked No Teeth aside, clambered across the floor and yanked the man's head back.

'Be at peace!' Flyhead whispered and sliced his throat in one quick cut.

No Teeth took off his vizard. He stood trembling, his ugly face white and beseeching, hands extended. Flyhead pulled the noose from around his neck, threw it at him and lunged with his dagger. Despite No Teeth's wailing, he would have struck immediately.

'No!' Simon shouted. 'Flyhead, no! We need him alive!'

Flyhead stopped, dagger extended.

'Go on!' he hissed, glaring at No Teeth's wizened face. 'Be stupid enough, you bloody bastard! You whoreson murderer! Go on, draw your dagger!'

No Teeth fell to his knees, no longer the warlock or the secret assassin. He looked what he was, a pathetic, ageing man terrified out of his wits. Simon slipped another bolt into the arbalest. He moved cautiously, squatting down by the dead assailant, whose blood was now seeping out in great red pools from the wound in his neck. He tore the vizard away. The face beneath was unrecognisable, the crossbow quarrel loosed at such close range had pulped his face as it would a rotten apple. He searched the man's corpse; the jerkin, leggings and shirt were of good quality but the purse was empty except for a few coins. Simon put these on the table.

'That's for the damage caused. Well, well, well!' Simon struggled to control his breathing. 'We meet again, Master No Teeth. You are a most fortunate man.'

The former executioner sat down on the bed. Simon noticed he was so frightened he had wet himself.

'I didn't want to come.' No Teeth's tongue kept flicking in and out. He forced a grin, baring red, chapped gums.

'You're a liar, No Teeth,' Simon replied. 'You are a liar, you are a warlock, you're an assassin and you are a coward. Who's your companion? Mine host from the Silver Tabard?'

'Yes, yes,' No Teeth gabbled. 'It was his idea!'

Simon released the catch and the bolt sped, smashing into the plaster beside No Teeth. He became agitated and, grabbing a blanket, seized it, wringing it between his hands. If it hadn't been for Flyhead he would have fallen to his knees, hands joined.

'Let's begin again,' Simon said. 'This time, the truth. You are a member of a coven?'

No Teeth nodded vigorously.

'For how many years?'

'Three.'

'Why you?' Flyhead asked. 'Why would they choose a worthless knave, a caitiff who's frightened of his own smell?'

'Be . . . because I am a hangman,' No Teeth stammered. 'I was a hangman in Gloucester long before Shadbolt and the rest of you.'

'Ah, of course you were,' Flyhead interrupted. 'But you always resented us, didn't you?'

'I should have been made chief hangman,' No Teeth retorted petulantly. 'I was Gloucester-born.'

'Shut up!' Simon slipped another bolt into the groove of the crossbow. 'The Ratoliers didn't choose you for your good looks, so why?'

'I told you, I was a hangman.'

'Of course!' Flyhead exclaimed. He sat on the edge of the bed playing with the dagger in his hands. 'Simon, witches

and warlocks need the cadavers of hanged men.' He jabbed
No Teeth viciously with his elbow. 'What is it, the hand
of glory?'

'What's that?' Simon asked.

'They use it in their rites,' Flyhead explained. 'Take the
hand of a hanged man; sever it at the wrist, make a candle
fashioned out of the cadaver's fat, light it, place it in the hand
and, with the right imprecations, the demons come, or so they
believe.'

'And you did that?' Simon asked.

No Teeth nodded.

'Who asked you to?'

No Teeth looked at the corpse on the floor.

'Oh, don't bother about him.' Simon smiled. 'He's dead as
nails, no potions, no philtres will save him.'

'He made the invitation,' No Teeth explained. 'He offered
me gold and silver. I met him at the dead of night out in the
Forest of Dean.'

'The coven, how many are there?' Simon asked. He winched
back the cord of the arbalest. No Teeth began to shiver. 'Oh,
don't worry,' Simon reassured him. 'My finger will only slip
if you tell us a lie. How many were there?'

'Six.'

'The Ratoliers. You, your late good friend here and who
was the sixth?'

'I don't know. Honestly!' No Teeth held up his hands. 'Let
me explain. We would always meet in that glade, use the stone
as an altar. We came as we were.' His eyes fell away. 'The
sacrifice was always made; sometimes it was an animal. At
other times beggars, chapmen, tinkers ambushed on the forest
roads. Then, as time passed, further demands were made.'

'You mean the young woman?'

No Teeth nodded.

'And what powers?' Flyhead asked curiously. 'What did
you get in return, apart from the joy of seeing someone die
and revelling in your dark rites at the dead of night?'

'I . . . I can't say!'

Simon moved the arbalest.

'You must understand,' No Teeth gabbled on. 'The coven is like a church, there's a hierarchy.'

'What powers?' Simon insisted.

Flyhead brought up his dagger and pricked No Teeth under his fleshy chin. He muttered something.

'What was that?' Flyhead asked sharply.

'Your heart's desire. Whatever you wanted. Potions, philtres, gold and silver. And for me,' he tried to grin, 'the wench I desired.'

'Do you truly believe that?' Flyhead asked.

'But it came true.' No Teeth shook his head. 'I had more silver and gold than I had ever dreamed of; the choice of the sweetest whores.'

'And the Ratoliers?' Simon asked.

'Oh, they had strange powers. They claimed they could commune with the dark lords. They, too, enjoyed the good things of life.'

'What do you mean?'

'They never came into Gloucester. And in the Forest of Dean they were dismissed as hags, mad women. But, oh, Master Cotterill, you should have seen them when they went to Bristol! They had gold and silver. They changed their raiment. They went as grand ladies.'

'Where do they live?' Flyhead asked.

'Deep in the Forest of Dean at Savernake rocks, where there's a network of caves.' He held his hand up as Simon looked threateningly at him. 'You should go there, Master Cotterill. They are more comfortable there than in any manor house or mansion in Gloucester. They have soft hangings on the walls; goblets of silver and gold; featherdown beds and bolsters; coffers, chests and caskets full of precious cloths and jewellery. Send a courier to Bristol to the White Hart tavern. They will tell you about the three women, under different names, who every so often would sweep in like the greatest in the land and enjoy the sweetest things. Young men paid them court . . .' His voice trailed off.

Simon stared in astonishment and lowered the crossbow. He found it hard to believe that the Ratoliers were no more than cruel outlaws who used their powers to satisfy the gods of their lusts.

'But I hanged you.' Flyhead nicked No Teeth's thigh with his dagger. 'I put the noose round your neck then I buried you. How did you escape that?'

'The Ratoliers always said,' No Teeth explained, 'that because we worshipped the hanged ones, the old gods of the forest, we could always cheat death by hanging. Indeed, I've seen it done. During the rites, one of the Ratoliers would have a garrotte string pulled tight, during which she would offer a prayer to the dark lord and claim to see visions. When the string was released, she fell into a swoon as if dead.'

No Teeth crossed his arms, rubbing his shoulders as if frightened. He kept looking towards the door and window.

'Are you worried?' Flyhead taunted.

'Yes, I am!' No Teeth snapped. 'Ratolier said the birds of the night could tell her what was happening.'

'Fiddlesticks! We were talking about their rites?'

'I asked them once how it was done. Sometimes the woman who had the rope round her neck lay in a swoon for a day as if she were dead. They told me that, before the cord was put round her neck, she took a potion, a mixture of herbs blessed and consecrated during their rites. It put her in a trance as if the soul had fled the body.'

'And you believed them?'

'Why shouldn't I? The Ratolier woman, whoever it was, always revived. They said they were under the protection of the hanged ones and their leader, whom they called "the beloved", "their father", "their dominus".'

'Their leader?' Simon asked.

'Yes. And, Master Cotterill, I assure you, I don't know who he is. Indeed, it could be man or woman. He always came to the glade by himself. Dressed in black from head to toe; a mask shaped in the form of an animal's head covered his face. He spoke very little, just in a whisper. He would sit enthroned before their altar. The Ratoliers and I used to worship him before the rite was carried out then he'd go, as he arrived, like a wisp of mist.'

'And you don't know who it is?'

No Teeth shook his head. Simon caught Flyhead's glance and nodded. The man yanked back No Teeth's head and dug the dagger deep into the flesh under the chin. No Teeth screamed. Flyhead kept pressing until the blood began to drip. No Teeth stamped his feet, waving his hands, terrified that if he moved, if he tried to escape, Flyhead would drive the dagger in.

'I tell the truth, Master Cotterill!' he stammered. 'I tell the truth! I tell the truth!'

'And is that how you escaped?' Flyhead asked, relaxing his grip.

No Teeth nodded.

'The night I killed that man in the tavern,' he said. 'You know the rest. I was taken before the justices and condemned. I was put in the death cart. As I left the gaol, someone came forward with a goblet of wine. Despite her hood and cowl I could see it was Mother Ratolier.'

'I remember that,' Flyhead declared. 'And I let you drink it. You said it would be the last you would ever taste.'

'You were supposed to let me escape,' No Teeth accused. 'But when you put the noose around my neck, I realised there was no leather collar.'

'And then what happened?' Simon asked.

'I remember this,' Flyhead interrupted. 'By the time you reached the foot of the ladder, you could hardly stand. Some of the bailiffs had to drag you up. You were almost in a swoon, it was that wine, it contained a potion, didn't it?'

'What happened?' Simon insisted.

'I remember nothing,' No Teeth replied. 'All I know is that

when I regained consciousness, I had soil on my face and hands. I felt sick and weak. I was in an outhouse behind the Silver Tabard, Mother Ratolier was pouring something between my lips.'

'Why did the Ratoliers save you?' Simon asked. 'How did they know Flyhead would truly hang you?'

'It's part of their rite. They were sworn to save me.' He blinked. 'I asked about Flyhead, old Ratolier just chuckled: "We all know about Flyhead!"'

'And then?'

'As you know, I lived with the Ratoliers out in the Forest of Dean. I thought that was the end of my time in Gloucester. Then one night the Ratoliers were taken.'

'But not the leader or you?' Simon asked.

'I was going to join them. It was the dead of night but, as I approached the glade from a different direction, after I had been out to one of the alehouses, I saw the glow of torches in the trees. I suspected what was happening so I fled.'

'How did the coven meet?' Simon asked.

'Look at those coins,' No Teeth replied. 'The ones you took from my companion's purse. There's a silver piece, different from the rest.'

Simon sifted among the coins. He picked up a small silver disc which he handed to Flyhead. He pulled across a candle and stared at the writing round the rim.

'It's Roman. It's an imperial coin. It bears the head of Constantine.'

'We each received one of those when the coven was to assemble. We usually met once a month: the same time, the same place. The night the Ratoliers were taken we should all have gathered there. We always gave the dominus the coin back.'

'Who delivered them?' Simon asked.

'When I was a hangman in Gloucester I would just find it upon my table; the same for the landlord at the Silver Tabard. God knows who brought them.'

'But that night the Ratoliers were taken?' Simon insisted.

'I don't know, the dominus was not able to warn either myself or the Ratoliers. He later told us that he didn't have the time.'

Simon looked at the floor. If that was the case, he thought, this dominus, this master of the coven, must live in Gloucester and be more than aware of what the forces of law and order were planning.

'And when the Ratoliers were hanged?' Flyhead asked.

'We,' No Teeth pointed at the dead man, 'followed you into the forest. It was easy enough after you called at the Silver Tabard. We watched you in the clearing: we made those noises but the tavern master told me to wait till the storm came.'

'Was that the work of demons?'

'I don't know, I was just told to wait.'

'And the powders and potions,' Simon asked. 'Who gave them to the Ratoliers?'

'They always carried them in small pouches, sewn in their dresses.'

Simon recalled the thick, dirty, dusty gowns of the witches; even if they were searched, such powders would have escaped detection.

'Continue,' he ordered.

'When you left the clearing, I saw where you went. By the time I'd returned, the Ratoliers were already cut down. The nooses taken from their necks. Mine host was pouring liquid into their mouths. I couldn't believe it. I thought all three must be dead, their faces were ghastly. They stirred and coughed, each of them retching, then the colour came back into their faces. Even before I left the clearing to hasten back to the hunting lodge, they were already well revived, full of curses and anger against you all.'

'Who killed Deershound?' Flyhead asked.

No Teeth pointed at the dead man. 'The verderer came back into the clearing. They couldn't take any risk that he might have seen something.'

'But it's more than that!' Simon insisted. 'Every one involved in their deaths must die?'

No Teeth blinked but nodded perceptibly.

'What will happen to me?' he wailed. 'I'm telling you the truth. Surely I can be given another chance? Even a pardon! I'll lead you to the Ratoliers' caves.'

'In heavens' name, No Teeth, you're an arrant coward.' Flyhead punched him on the shoulder. 'You'd sell your mother for a bowl of broth.'

'Keep telling the truth,' Simon advised him. 'And, No Teeth, you might be given another chance at life.'

'The coven met again,' the rogue went on. 'The dominus issued an order: we were to slay all those involved in the hanging of the Ratoliers.'

'Why?' Simon asked.

'Revenge, punishment, to keep your mouth closed and because of the rite. The dominus said it had to be done. Deershound had already gone. We killed Merry Face out on the forest path. Shadbolt in his barge on the river; the poor bastard thought he could flee. We caught him napping on a bank under a willow tree. The Ratoliers also killed Shipler.'

'And the Draycotts?'

No Teeth lifted his hands. 'Master Simon, I know nothing of that.'

'Who killed them?' Simon persisted.

If Flyhead hadn't stopped him, No Teeth would have slipped to his knees.

'I swear, Master Simon, by all that's holy . . . !'

'Don't blaspheme,' Flyhead interrupted. 'Just tell Master Cotterill the truth.'

'I don't know,' No Teeth sobbed. 'Believe me, I don't know. I suspect the dominus did.' He wrung his hands.

Simon watched those cunning, weak eyes. A dangerous man, he thought, who could wheedle, importune, beg and plea but, if he had the upper hand, he'd have as much compassion as a weasel closing in for the kill.

'How many more people must die?'

No Teeth put his face in his hands and began to cry even more loudly.

'Answer the question!' Flyhead insisted.

No Teeth took his hands away. 'All of you,' he muttered. 'The mayor, his sergeant-at-arms. Everyone who was in that chamber that night. Even the Dominicans, in time, will feel the wrath of our master.'

'Aren't you frightened, No Teeth? I mean, you are confessing all?'

'Anything's better than another hanging.'

'So keep confessing,' Flyhead taunted.

'You were all marked down for death,' No Teeth continued. 'Each one of you. But the mayor and sergeant-at-arms are well protected. The dominus said they would have to wait.' He pointed at Simon. 'I saw you hanged.'

'Do you know, No Teeth, there'll be a joke soon, that the best place to be hanged is Gloucester. You always get a second chance!'

'You were looking for me, weren't you?' Flyhead jibed.

No Teeth shrugged and licked his lips.

'Can I have some wine?'

While Simon held the crossbow, Flyhead splashed some wine into a cup and brought it over. No Teeth drank greedily.

'The Ratoliers wanted to kill you,' he went on. 'But the dominus was insistent. They were not to go into Gloucester. They caught Shadbolt on the river. The tavern master knew how Shadbolt was going to leave.'

'How's that?' Flyhead asked.

'The poor bastard made no pretence, wandering around like a dog that's lost its tail.'

'But I was harder.'

Flyhead banged the knife on No Teeth's bony knee.

'We thought you'd disappeared,' No Teeth winced. 'But the dominus has the gates watched. I don't know how.'

'Are there other members of the coven?' Simon asked.

No Teeth shook his head. 'The Ratoliers know gipsies, the moon people, tinkers and chapmen who collect a lot of the news.'

'Of course!' Simon said. 'No one was supposed to know that the Ratoliers had been condemned, let alone hanged.'

'And Friar Martin?' Flyhead asked.

'Oh, the dominus is insistent that he dies. Twice he's tried to break into the Austin Friars but cannot. Our fat brother is never alone. When he sits near the shrine of St Radegund, there are enough people milling about. The dominus has sworn a terrible oath that Friar Martin is to be left to him and him alone. He has a special hatred for the man.'

Simon studied No Teeth. On the one had he accepted that their prisoner was telling the truth but, on the other, there was a shift to his eyes, too swift a patter to his talk. He was apparently terrified but had he told them the full truth?

'Is there anything else, No Teeth?'

The prisoner shook his head.

'Are you sure?' Flyhead insisted. He jabbed the point of his knife into No Teeth's fleshy neck.

'Nothing at all.'

'Aren't you forgetting something?' Flyhead asked.

No Teeth blinked quickly, mouth opening and shutting.

'There's one person you've forgotten,' Flyhead whispered. 'Little Lucia with her ripe, full breasts, firm buttocks and a waist you could span with one hand. Delightful in bed.'

No Teeth swallowed hard.

'Are you sure there is nothing to tell us?' Flyhead again asked.

'You shouldn't have taken her!' No Teeth accused. 'She was my wench. She swore oaths to me.'

'Lucia would swear anything as long as the coins kept falling into her hands. Well, Master Cotterill, what shall we do with him?'

Simon ran a finger round his neck. 'The rest have to be warned,' he said. 'Friar Martin in particular. Letters should

164

be despatched to those Dominicans in London and the mayor should hear what No Teeth has told us.'

'Oh Lord, no!'

Simon pointed to some rope lying on top of a coffer.

'Bind his hands, Flyhead. It's late but, perhaps, we may find someone at the Guildhall.'

Flyhead went to a coffer and brought out a white hanging mask. He dangled this before No Teeth's face.

'We don't want anyone to see your pretty visage. Hooded and bound, that's the way we'll take you. Turn round!'

No Teeth obeyed. As Simon rose and crossed to open the door, he heard a moan followed by a rasping gurgle. No Teeth was sitting on the edge of the bed staring in disbelief at the blood pouring from the terrible wound in his throat. His eyes rolled up and Flyhead pushed him, sending him sprawling on to the floor beside his companion.

'For the love of God!' Simon strode back.

Flyhead stretched his dagger out. 'That's as far as you go, Simon.'

He leaned down and rolled No Teeth's corpse over. The blood was now saturating the shabby jerkin and shirt. He glanced up.

'It's the only way, Simon. No more powders or potions, no spells or tricks. There's not a power on earth that can heal a slit throat.'

'He might have told us more.'

'I doubt it. I am not too sure whether he has told us the full truth. No Teeth wouldn't know what a lie was even if it jumped up and bit him on the nose.' Flyhead got to his feet and re-sheathed his dagger. 'He came here to kill me, Simon. More importantly, he killed Lucia. I had a fondness for the girl.'

He crouched down between the corpses and began to remove their boots and belts.

'I'll tell you what we'll do, Simon. I'm going to strip these of every valuable then leave you on guard. I'm off to the fleshers' yard. I know where I can get a small handcart and a barrel of oil and, before daybreak, we'll burn these corpses like the offal they are! When we catch them, the Ratoliers will die the same way.' He paused. 'Go down and ensure the street's safe.'

Flyhead was already stripping the corpses, looking for anything valuable such as rings, or hidden money pouches. Simon went down the stairs then suddenly stopped. One thing was certain: No Teeth did not know the true identity of the dominus, the master of the coven. It was obvious that such a person lived in Gloucester but, for all he knew, it might be the mayor, or his sergeant-at-arms. He looked back up the stairs. Or even Flyhead himself?

Chapter 12

On the morning after No Teeth's death, Simon and Flyhead slipped secretly into the Guildhall for a meeting with the mayor and sergeant-at-arms. The two officials listened carefully to all they said.

'It saves us the trouble of hanging them,' the sergeant-at-arms commented. 'And the two corpses?'

'Like their souls, black ash!'

Four days later the mayor held secret meetings with the chief verderer and foresters about launching an attack on the caves at Savernake. No soldiers were to be used, only royal huntsmen who knew the paths, lanes and byways of the forests. They all agreed that the caves were almost inaccessible.

'Very few go there,' the chief verderer commented, his seamed, sunburned face looking even darker, more menacing in the dancing torchlight of the council chamber. He and his companions had come into Gloucester, being lodged at the corporation's expense.

'Why is that?' Simon asked.

The verderer shrugged. 'There are many parts of this kingdom, young man, where very few people go. The area around these caves is one of them. The forest there is very ancient, the trees group together like a wall. It's very difficult to hunt in and it has a bad reputation.'

'So, how will you attack?' the mayor demanded.

'Couldn't we wait for these three beauties to go on one of their trips to Bristol?' Flyhead asked.

'We might wait years,' the mayor replied. 'No, if it's to be done, it's to be done before winter really sets in. Let's hope and pray the Ratoliers have not moved on.'

Three days later Simon and Flyhead accompanied the verderers into the Forest of Dean. At different points and locations they collected more of the forest people, all those who lived and worked in that great, far-flung community: verderers, foresters, even men who toiled in the royal mines deep in the forests. They were promised a good bounty and a tenth of whatever they found. About the Ratoliers, however, the mayor had been most explicit.

'No prisoners,' he specified. 'I don't care how they die but the Ratoliers must be killed and their bodies burned immediately!'

The verderers had no qualms about this. Flyhead later whispered that this was the way the foresters worked.

'Outlaws are killed on sight. In the forest, Simon, no mercy is asked and none is given, as you will find out.'

As when he had travelled to the Ratoliers' hanging, Simon was struck by the vastness of the Forest of Dean, as if he had entered another country. Even he, who had been born in the Vale of Berkeley, had not realised how deep and dark this ancient place was. By the time they had mustered all their men, the chief verderer must have had about sixty to seventy under his command, a wild-looking gang. Some were dressed in brown leather but most of them in stained lincoln green, well armed with sword, mace, axe and club. Above all, they carried long bows and deerskin-covered quivers crammed with feathered shafts.

They moved in single file, threading their way through the trees like ghosts. Occasionally they would find a clearing to pitch camp. No fires were lit. Simon and Flyhead were ordered to keep to the back, protected by two foresters, who made sure they didn't get lost.

'Wander away,' the chief verderer warned them, 'and God knows what will happen! People have entered here and never come out alive!'

Only faint rays of weak sunlight pierced the green canopy. Simon felt as if he were in some cathedral which stretched on and on with only faint glimmers of light to show him the way. There were streams difficult to cross and, more dangerous, quagmires, marshes and slime-covered morasses ready to trap the unwary. Wild animals blundered across their path. The chief verderer explained how the boar still lived here as well as varieties of deer not seen elsewhere in the kingdom.

Their scouts were two old men, grizzled and sunburned. Five days after they had left the main mustering point, these came back whispering their news: the caves of Savernake were ahead and they glimpsed wisps of smoke. Later that day they camped in a small glade.

'How do the Ratoliers know of this place? How can they find their way out?' Simon asked.

The chief verderer pointed a thumb at one of the scouts.

'Oh, there are easier paths but they are secret. If we had followed them, the Ratoliers would have known we were coming. It's a bit like London,' he continued. 'I was there just before the old king died. I wondered how any man could find his way through that warren of alleyways yet I met those who could do so, blindfolded. The forest is no different.' He laughed softly. 'Or no less dangerous. You'd best sleep.'

They shared out some of the dried meat and stale loaves of bread; a wineskin was passed round.

'Eat, drink and sleep,' the chief verderer whispered. 'Tomorrow we climb.'

Simon and Flyhead whispered about what might happen.

'Are you glad you are here?' Simon asked.

'To be sure.' Flyhead smiled back through the darknesss. 'Master Cotterill, I have few things left in life and I would give everything I own to see the Ratoliers burn.'

Simon was aroused when it was still dark, a cold, cloying mist creeping through the trees. Weapons were prepared, bows strung. Anything they didn't need was left under a rear guard. They left the glade and abruptly the ground began to climb.

Sometimes the tree line would break, so that for the first time for days, Simon glimpsed the sky and the rocky crags at the summit.

The sun began to rise, weak and faint, but Simon was soon coated in sweat. He found it difficult to control his breathing. Now and again a man cursed as he missed his footing or slipped. Closer and closer they drew to the top. At one point the chief verderer, imitating the call of a bird, ordered them to pause and rest. They did so for a short while and then continued to climb. Simon felt as if he were dreaming. Would anyone in Berkeley ever believe what had happened to him since he'd left the village? A pauper, a hangman, a condemned felon and now, at the beginning of this mist-cloaked day, a man intent on killing three evil warlocks?

The climb became easier. Simon glimpsed the mouths of caves. He felt elated. Ratolier would be taken by surprise. Then came the chief verderer's bird call, loud and clear. Simon froze and glanced up. He was sure others could hear the pounding of his heart. On the rock above them, gazing out over the forest as if she could sense the approaching danger, was Mother Ratolier, her grey hair streaming in the wind, her black dress flapping. She reminded Simon of some evil raven perched on a wall.

'She knows!' Flyhead whispered behind Simon. 'The old bitch suspects they are in danger.'

Mother Ratolier now had her hand cupping her eyes. She turned and said something. Her two daughters joined her at the mouth of the cave. All three clustered together. Simon felt his fingers ache as he hung on grimly to a piece of rock. He dared not let go. He was frightened that if he slipped, he would raise the alarm. He glanced quickly to his right and left. Others were the same, crouched flat against the rock face. There was little they could do. They must go on and reach level ground before they could draw weapons or the archers could bring their bows to good effect. Simon sniffed and caught cooking smells and something else, a fragrant perfume. He peered up.

The Ratoliers were now standing in line, hands joined, all three staring down the rock face. Somewhere behind Simon, a verderer missed his footing or couldn't keep still any longer. There was a slither of gravel, a crashing in the undergrowth.

'They are coming!' Mother Ratolier's voice rang through the air.

All three disappeared into the caves.

'Now!' the chief verderer screamed. 'Before they can bring weapons to bear!'

Simon gazed in horror up at the cave mouth. No soldier he, yet he was quick enough to realise the chief verderer's warning. Spread out on the rocky escarpment, hidden by a few trees and bushes, they were all exposed and vulnerable. A few defenders, armed with bows and rocks, could hold the heights and wreak terrible damage.

The whole party surged forward, slithering and cursing. Now and again someone missed their footing. There were shouts and cries. Everyone was eager to reach the level ground beneath the cave mouth where they could use their own weapons.

Simon moved forward as quickly as he could. His knees and hands were cut and bleeding, his face scarred by the bushes and vegetation. His body was sweat-soaked, his weapons seemed to hang like weights around his waist. He then heard a whir followed by a scream. He glanced up. The Ratoliers had reappeared. All three carried crossbows, loosing their deadly quarrels. If Simon and his party stayed still they were targets. If they moved, they had to break cover. The Ratoliers commanded the approaches using their arbalests to good effect. Simon stared in horror as the verderer in front of him came slithering down, screaming and writhing at the crossbow bolt which had taken him in the neck. Simon tried to help but the man slithered by him, fighting against his pain, not caring what happened.

'Climb on!' the shout came. 'Forget the wounded!'

At last a bowman reached the rocky ground beneath the caves. Simon came up behind him. The bowman moved fast.

They had appeared on the left flank of the Ratoliers and, before the witches knew what was happening, the man had loosed a shaft, sending it deep into the chest of one of the witches. The other two fled. The rest of the verderers now surged forward, swords drawn. They reached the level outcrop and fanned out towards the cave mouth. Simon was one of the first to step into the large, cavernous entrance. Pitch torches spluttered on the walls. He gazed in astonishment. It was like entering the solar or hallway of some wealthy merchant's house. Hangings and tapestries on the walls; costly items of furniture, small coffers, chairs and benches. The hunting party, already sensing easy plunder, began to loot and pillage until the chief verderer imposed order with the flat of his sword.

Flyhead and Simon, however, ran deeper into the cave where further signs of the Ratoliers' ostentatious wealth were apparent. Off the main tunnel stood small chambers, all tastefully furnished. Simon realised how difficult their hunt would be along this honeycomb of passages and tunnels. Eventually he stopped, sitting down on a ledge, fighting to regain his breath. He loosened his jerkin, trying to seek some respite from the exhaustion and fear which had drained his strength in that terrifying climb. Flyhead was eager to go on.

'Don't be stupid!' Simon snarled. 'They could be in any of these passageways or tunnels! The first we'd know about it is a crossbow bolt or a dagger!'

He glimpsed a jewelled goblet lying on the floor and stretched out to pick it up. That movement saved his life. A crossbow bolt smacked into the rock wall behind him. Simon, crouched on all fours, peered down the passageway. In the dim light of a smoking torch he saw a figure move. He edged his way along, Flyhead behind him. When the air grew cooler, Simon realised this must lead to another entrance. The wall, as it curved, afforded some protection against the crossbow bolts the shadowy figures loosed. Behind him he heard the chief verderer and his party, so he shouted a warning. Soon the entire hunting party crowded at the mouth of the tunnel.

Simon narrowed his eyes. The figure kept moving out from behind a buttress of rock. He glimpsed the arbalest and drew back just before the bolt slapped into the rocky wall.

'One of them is going to get away,' Flyhead whispered.

Simon peered out, ascertaining that it was the old Ratolier who was holding them back. She had proved to be a cunning adversary. None of the huntsmen dared move. One did and yelped in pain as a crossbow bolt took him in the fleshy part of his shoulder. His groans were greeted by a raucous scream of triumph. The verderer whispered to some of his bowmen to creep forward and they loosed arrows in reply. Eventually one of them caught the old Ratolier deep in the throat. She staggered towards them. Simon leapt to his feet and ran down the tunnel, ignoring the shouted warnings of the verderer. By the time he reached the old woman she had collapsed to the ground coughing and jerking, choking on her own blood, but her eyes gleamed defiance. She opened her mouth to speak, feebly beckoning Simon to draw closer. He did so. She moved but he caught her other hand and the sharp pointed stiletto it carried. He forced the hand round and, holding her malevolent gaze, drove it deep down into her chest. He gripped the handle as her body jerked beneath him. Only when she lay still did Simon let go, crouching back on his heels. He stared at that ghastly, evil face which had brought him so much terror, so much pain.

Flyhead came up, kicking at the corpse, screaming curses. The chief verderer ordered more of his men down the tunnel to find the hidden entrance. Simon heard them go. He sat fascinated, staring at the corpse as if he couldn't believe she was gone.

'She's dead.' The verderer patted him on the shoulder.

Two of the huntsmen came and lifted the corpse and carried it out to the mouth of the cave to lie by the other. The bodies were searched but nothing was found. Simon insisted that he examine them once again. Mother Ratolier looked more powerful, stronger than he thought; her daughter was attractive.

Indeed, their shabby dress and dishevelled hair made a perfect disguise. It wouldn't take much to transform either of these into comely women. All around him the huntsmen were helping themselves, plundering the caves, exclaiming in surprise at the treasures they found. Simon, however, waited for the others to return. Eventually they did, shaking their heads.

'There's another entrance,' one of them said. 'At the far end of the caves. It leads down to the forest.' He shrugged. 'We could search for a year and a day and never find them.'

'She might not survive long,' the chief verderer declared. 'She'll know not to come back here. We'll be visiting this spot quite frequently. She dare not go to Gloucester and, if I know my lord mayor, he'll have writs issued to Bristol and Bath and the other towns.'

'They've got to be burned,' Simon said firmly, getting to his feet.

The chief verderer agreed. A funeral pyre was hastily built, the corpses thrown on top, then covered in dry kindling. A pitch torch was brought from the cave and, within the hour, the flames were blazing up to the clear blue sky.

'Burn now! Burn in hell!' Simon whispered.

Once he was certain the bodies had been consumed and he could no longer stand the foul smell, he joined the chief verderer in the cave. Two of the hunting party had been killed, three wounded. The corpses were taken down, the wounded tended to but, really, the huntsmen now saw themselves as victors after a battle and were intent on plunder. Simon was surprised by the amount of treasure that the Ratoliers had accumulated over the years as well as the number of potions and philtres, powders and dried herbs all neatly stacked on shelves in one of the small caverns. He had these broken and smashed; his real search was for any documents. Parchment coffers were found, leather bags, especially made to contain manuscripts, but these were empty. Any books, letters, household accounts, every scrap of document, seemed to have been removed.

'I suppose this was done,' Simon mused, 'when the Ratoliers were first arrested. Someone came here and removed anything incriminating. I wonder who?'

They did find items of black magic: figures of clay, inverted crosses, amulets and charms. One small cavern at the end had definitely been used as a chapel in which they venerated their demons. It was a dark, sombre place with a rocky ledge stained with blood, but everything else had been removed.

'I think we arrived just in time.' Flyhead grinned. 'I think the Ratoliers were preparing to move.' He patted his wallet full of coins he had seized. Other items were pushed down his jerkin and the leather bag he carried clinked and clattered as he walked. He held this up. 'Reparation and compensation. The Ratoliers owe me something. It's a pity we didn't slay the other bitch!'

'I doubt if she'll survive,' Simon declared. 'The coven is nearly destroyed and she had little time to take any wealth with her.'

He returned to the mouth of the cave and looked down at the funeral pyre. The flames were now dying, the foresters becoming more and more drunk by the hour as they feasted and revelled in their victory. Simon wished to be away. Flyhead, too, now convinced he was safe, wanted to return to Gloucester.

'I'm going to collect everything I have,' he said. 'And move to the far corners of the earth. You'll never catch me again in the Forest of Dean.'

The chief verderer was only too willing to help. Now the Ratoliers had been caught and killed, Simon could see they wished to keep most of the plunder for themselves. Three guides were provided with instructions to bring carts from Gloucester.

'We'll camp here for the night,' the chief verderer said. 'The cart should be with us by tomorrow afternoon. Tell my lord mayor we will not enter Gloucester.' He tapped the side of his nose. 'Discretion is still important. We'll journey down to the village of Stroud. There's a tavern there, the Flambard. If he wishes his share of the booty, he can come and collect it!'

An hour later, Simon, Flyhead and three of the verderers left Savernake. The journey back was swift and uneventful. This time the verderers took them by forest paths and trackways and, early the following morning, they reached the outskirts of Gloucester. As they were about to enter Northgate, Flyhead plucked Simon by the arm and stretched his hand out.

'I'll be leaving you now, Simon.'

'Are you sure?'

'I'll stay one more day in Gloucester but this time tomorrow I hope to be out of this city. I'll shake its dust from my feet.'

'And where will you go?'

Flyhead pulled a face. 'Probably north. There's a lot of business on the Scottish march for a former priest, soldier and hangman.'

'You should take care,' Simon warned. 'We still have to hunt down the dominus, not to mention the last Ratolier woman.'

'They are finished,' Flyhead scoffed.

Simon clasped his hand and sadly watched as this final companion slipped down an alleyway.

Simon found it strange to be back in Gloucester, with its close-backed houses and narrow lanes. The merchants were putting out their stalls, their apprentices piling them high with goods. At High Cross the market beadles were assembled, horns in their hands, watching the light-blue sky. The bells of the Abbey of St Peter began to toll. On the final chime, the market beadles blew their horns declaring the market open.

For a while Simon just wandered about. He had remained hidden before he left Gloucester; his long journey through the forest and the attack on the Ratoliers' stronghold had made him feel unreal, as if cut off from life. Now he found it soothing to watch children play with a hoop; two women studying a roll of linen and haggling volubly over the price; a water tippler claiming his water was the purest from the Severn. A pie man, hustled through the crowd by bailiffs, was forced to stand in the stocks. The putrid pastry he'd sold the day before was tied beneath his nose and the bailiffs shouted an invitation for all to come and witness. A hunting party rode through the crowd causing consternation as their lurchers and limners barked and yelped. A wedding group appeared, the groom slightly the worse for wear for drink; they wound their way, garlanded with flowers and accompanied by relatives, up to the main door of St Wilfred's church.

Simon went into a tavern, the Griffin of Wales. He ordered a tankard of ale and slices of venison covered in a red sauce with freshly baked loaves and a pot of butter and honey. He ate and drank slowly, taking in the other custom of the tavern. A tinker was busy selling a whippet. The prospective buyer claimed that the dog was blind in one eye and tried to lower the price. Two relic-sellers had, by chance, met and caused deep merriment when the taverner pointed out that both claimed to have among their goods the right hand of St Sebastian. Other customers joined the ribaldry, loudly demanding how any man, even a saint, could have two right hands?

Simon finished his food and went out. He felt tired and rather sad. His return to Gloucester had awoken memories of when he had first arrived here, his heart burning with love, his hopes full of winning the hand of Alice Draycott. He walked and found himself outside the dead merchant's spacious, half-timbered house. The doors, guarded by bailiffs, had been sealed by the city corporation. He went down an alleyway and into the stable yard. A bailiff, sleeping in a corner by the water butts, got up and waddled across. Simon took out the mayor's commission and showed it to the fellow, who held it upside down, gazed blearily but recognised the seal.

'I am on secret business from his worship,' Simon lied. 'I have his permission to search both the stable and the house.'

The fellow agreed. Simon broke the seal on the stable door and went in. The place was warm, musty and reeking of horse dung. Simon walked down and looked up at the beam. Two strands of rope still clung there. He went out across the yard,

where at his insistence the bailiff opened the postern door.
Simon entered the deserted scullery. The kitchen beyond was
large and spacious, the flagstone floor neatly scrubbed, as was
the oaken, polished table, where the merchant and his daughter
must have taken their last meal. Simon sat down on the chair at
the top and blinked away the tears. His love for Alice seemed
a lifetime away. A dream he had enjoyed and lost. He looked
up at the window. The thick and mullioned glass broke the
sunlight which streamed through. He watched the dust motes
dance in the empty kitchen. Was Alice here, he wondered?
Did her shade, her ghost still linger in this place?

He joined his hands, closed his eyes and prayed. Could she
help him now? Could she intervene? Simon sighed and opened
his eyes. The power of the Ratoliers was now destroyed. No
Teeth and his companions had been killed. But who had come
into this house that night? Surely someone Alice and her father
trusted? And why had they so obediently gone to their deaths?
Surely they would have struggled, resisted? Simon heard a
cough from outside. He half rose then remembered the bailiff.
He walked deeper into the house, into the spacious, ornately
furnished parlour. The window looked out on to the street so
he kept well away, fearful that the other bailiffs might see him
and object. He went upstairs but, although the chambers were
tidy, he noticed that all papers and other documents had been
removed from the counting-house, the little chancery office
Alderman Draycott must have used. Simon sat at the top of the
stairs. Who would come here? Someone the alderman trusted.
The mayor? The sergeant-at-arms? Or even Flyhead?

Simon rubbed his hands together. He recalled the attack in
the caves in the forest. If No Teeth had been a member of the
coven then why not another? And the Ratoliers? They seemed
to be anxious, fearful that an attack might be launched. Had
someone warned them? Simon put his face in his hands. What
if Flyhead had got a message to them? They had slept in the
forest, near the caves, before the attack was launched. Had
Flyhead stolen away, used some secret path? But, if that was

the case, why hadn't the Ratoliers fled? Simon beat his fist against his thighs. Yet there was that attack in Flyhead's chamber. Was that all a pretence? Had Flyhead known those two assailants would appear? Was that why he had cut his former companion's throat, to silence him, fearful lest he make other revelations?

Simon went downstairs, thanked the bailiff and made his way back. He recalled Friar Martin. He must tell the good friar what had happened, even if it meant revealing himself. If Flyhead was the killer, then perhaps he had unfinished business? And what about himself? Simon touched the hilt of his dagger. Perhaps Flyhead would wait a while? Simon made his way across the bustling city to the Austin Friars. The main gate was open, pilgrims thronging up the causeway into the church to pray at the shrine of St Radegund. Simon joined them. Soon he was inside the cavernous church, humming with the murmur of pilgrims.

Inside the porchway a lay brother sold ale and refreshments. A little further up a stall displayed badges and other keepsakes to entice the pilgrims. Simon avoided these. At last he reached the shrine of St Radegund to the right of the high altar. It was a large, spacious chancery chapel. The saint's tomb stood in the centre surrounded with a praying ledge, covered in red leather. Pilgrims were kneeling on this, pressing their faces into the small enclaves around the tomb. At the far end of the chapel stood a statue of the saint with dozens of red candles blazing before it. Simon glanced across. Behind the shrine, in a corner, was the shriving pew. The penitent would kneel on a small prie-dieu sheltered from the priest by a small buttress jutting out; on the other side sat Friar Martin. Simon went over, crossed himself and knelt.

'Bless me, Friar Martin.'

The friar peered round the pillars, his eyes rounded in amazement.

'It can't be! My good friend, Simon! Your hair, your face!'

Simon smiled back.

'I thought you were dead,' the friar stammered.

Simon studied him closely. Friar Martin had changed. His face was paler, his beard and moustache neatly cropped, his eyes weary.

'I heard you were hanged,' he whispered behind a cupped hand.

Simon shook his head. 'I've been through the valley of death, Father, and, if God is good, he'll bring me out. The rest are dead. Shadbolt, Merry Face, as well as the good Alderman Shipler, Draycott and Alice!'

'Oh no!' the friar groaned.

Simon nodded. 'Both hanged.'

'And Flyhead?'

'He still lives. He has fled the city, says he'll travel north. No Teeth and the taverner from the Silver Tabard are also dead.' Simon beamed. 'As is Mother Ratolier and one of her daughters. The other bitch escaped.'

Friar Martin began to tremble, his face in his hands. For a few minutes he just sat there, shoulders shaking. Simon glanced over his shoulder, to where other pilgrims were becoming curious. The friar took his hands away. Simon was shocked at the change in him.

'So many deaths,' he said quietly. 'Simon, so many, many deaths!'

'But you are safe, Brother. I had to come and see you. I owed you a debt.'

'I'll never be safe. And neither will you, my son.'

'You are safe here,' Simon insisted.

Friar Martin sighed and got to his feet.

'You'd best come with me!'

180

Chapter 13

They left the church, going through a sacristy smelling of beeswax and incense, along a tiled corridor and into a small parlour. Friar Martin immediately fastened the shutters on the window and locked the door. He lit a lantern horn and slung it on a chain which hung down from a beam. He then sat down behind a table. Simon could see that the friar was in a parlous state. His eyes were bright as if suffering from fever, his face had turned a mottled hue and he found it hard to stop trembling. He pointed to a flagon and a tray of cups on a table and asked Simon to fill two. No sooner had Simon done this than there was a knock on the door. He unlocked and opened it. A tall, severe-looking friar stood there, hands beneath the mantle of his robe.

'I heard Friar Martin had left the church.' He peered down at Simon. 'And that he came here with a stranger. Who are you, sir?'

'Don't worry, Father Prior!' Friar Martin called out. 'This man is a friend.'

Simon stepped back as the prior came into the room.

'You are well, Friar Martin?' he asked anxiously.

'Yes, Reverend Father.'

The prior, uninvited, sat down on a bench just inside the door. He gestured at Simon to sit on a box chair near the table.

'Are you sure, Brother?' he repeated. He turned an eagle eye on Simon and studied him from head to toe.

'This is Simon Cotterill,' Friar Martin said. 'He is my friend. Reverend Father, he brings me news.'

'We live in very troubled times,' the prior declared.

'Friar Martin who, perhaps, was not as strict in his vows as he should have been, has now decided to stay here. Have you told him what has happened?'

Simon looked swiftly at Friar Martin who swallowed hard and shook his head.

'Friar Martin is welcome to come and go as he wishes,' the prior continued. 'But he has chosen to stay here. His life is under threat. On two occasions wine has been left here as gifts for my brother. He forced a smile. 'On both occasions the wine was poisoned.'

Simon gazed in astonishment at Friar Martin.

'The Ratoliers?' he asked.

'It must be,' the friar replied. 'And there's worse, isn't there, Reverend Father?'

'Oh yes, other gifts have been sent: sweetmeats, pastries, left at the friary gates, all heavily tainted. Even in the chapel of St Radegund . . .'

'You didn't see them?' Friar Martin broke in. 'But there's a small choir loft as you come in the door. It's so our order can guard St Radegund's shrine. Two lay brothers watch from there, just in case the coven send someone in to wreak revenge.'

'Friar Martin has told us of how he tried to help destroy this coven.' The prior got to his feet. 'And for that he has our thanks. So, you can see, Simon, why I came along.' He sketched a blessing in the air. 'Though I can tell from your eyes that you are a goodly man. Friar Martin, Master Cotterill, I bid you adieu.' The prior left.

Simon sat and listened to his footsteps fade along the passageway. Friar Martin was still agitated, lost in a reverie, hands clasped together. He was staring at a point beyond Simon's head, his lips moving wordlessly. Simon wondered if this jovial friar was losing his wits. At last he seemed to remember where he was. He blinked, rubbed his face and, lifting the cup, toasted Simon.

'And where to now, master carpenter? Is it back to Berkeley?'

'Like Flyhead, I would love to flee this city,' Simon replied. 'But there is unfinished business: the dominus!'

'The dominus?'

'The dominus,' Simon confirmed. 'The master of the coven.'

'How do we know it's a he?' The friar tugged at his fleshy jowls.

'It must be.'

'I always thought it might be old Mother Ratolier,' Friar Martin said. 'But come, Simon, tell me everything you know.'

Simon did so, aware of the time passing, broken only now and again by the slap of sandals outside and the clanging of the friary bell. Friar Martin sat, arms folded on the table, head down, listening intently. Occasionally he interrupted Simon with a question. Simon paused when a lay brother brought in a tray of food from the kitchens. Simon found he was ravenous but he noticed Friar Martin only picked at his food. At last he finished and sat, face in hands.

'Who do you think the dominus is?' he asked, tapping his nails on the table. 'I do wonder about our lord mayor.'

'But why should he become involved in such trickery?' Simon scoffed. 'A man of such status and power? No, no. Sometimes I suspect Flyhead.'

'Why?' Friar Martin asked curiously. 'He was in hiding.'

'Who was he hiding from?' Simon asked. 'The coven or the power of the law? There are many questions to be asked.'

'Such as?'

'The Ratoliers. A mother and two daughters. I wonder who the father was?'

'What makes you ask that? She could just be an old widow who turned to evil and took her daughters with her.'

'I wish I could go back,' Simon replied. 'I wish I could go

back in time to that glade. I feel like a carpenter again, Brother, working with wood, but there're vital pieces missing.'

He got to his feet. Friar Martin did likewise. He came round and, grasping Simon, held him close.

'You'll come back, won't you Simon? You'll come back and see me again and tell me what happens?'

Simon agreed and stepped back.

'You'd best go to the mayor,' the friar said. 'But, Simon, be very, very careful!'

Simon left the friary a short while later and went straight to the Guildhall. He found that he no longer slipped along the alleyways, keeping to the walls, but walked boldly. The master of the coven, he reasoned, might not be discovered but the power of the Ratoliers was broken once and for all.

He had to wait for a while in an antechamber until Sir Humphrey agreed to see him. They met in his small chancery office. The mayor closed the door and, leaning across the table, listened carefully to Simon's report; what had happened in the forest and the attack on the coven at Savernake. Simon also described his visit to Friar Martin and his suspicions about Flyhead. The mayor sat back, flicking his thumb against his teeth. Simon surveyed the wainscoted chamber, a dark, close place, the table before him littered with manuscripts. The mayor's face was hidden in shadows sent dancing by the cresset torches and the candlelight. A wild thought occurred to Simon. Was he alone with the dominus? Was the mayor the master of the coven? Sir Humphrey looked at him, narrow-eyed.

'What do you find so interesting, Simon?'

'I wonder if we think the same thoughts, my lord mayor?'

'Which are?'

'Are you the dominus or am I?'

The mayor threw his head back and laughed. He clapped his hands.

'You should have been a clerk, Simon.' He wagged a finger playfully. 'If you had learned your horn book, you'd have been a good clerk. Sharp-witted, quick thinking. And haven't you changed? No longer the bumbling young carpenter. But, I suppose, life is like a piece of your wood, isn't it? You are carved out, chipped and clipped, fashioned into something else.' He spread his hands. 'I admit the thought had occurred to me and, I suppose, for the same reason. Someone who knew the Draycotts entered their house. Someone they trusted.' He breathed out noisily. 'They were drugged first, weren't they?'

Simon nodded. 'They must have been, sir. A potion added to their evening wine. The house was deserted, and they were then dragged out to the stables and hanged.'

'And this business of the Ratoliers?' the mayor asked. 'You say there was great wealth in the caves? I wonder how they accumulated that?'

'By their powers,' Simon replied.

'I wonder?' The mayor was lost in a reverie. 'You can read, Simon?'

'Despite what you say, my lord mayor, I was good at my horn book. A carpenter has to read drawings, study measurements, list figures and costs.'

'Then come with me.'

The mayor took him out across the council chamber, down a passageway and into the muniment room. Two scriveners sat there, busy filling out a tax roll. The mayor clapped his hands. He introduced Simon and then told them what he wanted.

'I want you to look for the name Ratolier,' he instructed them. 'Anything you can find on them. Anything at all. Master Cotterill here will help you.'

The scriveners looked nonplussed and, when the mayor had left, grumbled under their breath at their new task.

'How far back do we go?' one of them asked.

Simon recalled the eldest daughter, a woman of perhaps twenty or twenty-five years.

'Thirty years,' he said.

The clerks groaned.

'And what are we looking for?'

'As my lord mayor said, the name of Ratolier in any of the tax rolls for the city or environs of Gloucester. I am afraid I can't tell you the reason why.'

The clerks at first proved unwilling workers but their mood soon changed when Simon opened his purse and shook out four pieces of silver on to the desk.

'The labourer is worthy of his hire,' he declared. 'And the sooner we find it, the sooner I'm gone!'

The clerks became busy as bees. Chests and coffers were opened; greasy, yellowing tax rolls were taken out going back to the twenty-second regnal year of King Edward. There wasn't enough room to work in the scriptorium so they used the council chamber, laying the great rolls along the table. Simon found that each roll had an index at the back, a list of names and places which the clerks showed him how to use.

As the day wore on, more candles were lit. Sir Humphrey came back to see how matters were progressing and was kind enough to send in pies and wine from a local tavern. Darkness fell and, although Simon felt exhausted after his journey, the energy and commitment of the two clerks kept him to the task.

'The name Ratolier is not of these parts,' one of the clerks said. 'We've been through a number of rolls, Master Cotterill, and there's no mention of it.'

'Which means?' Simon asked with a heavy heart.

'Whoever they were,' the clerk went on, 'they may have moved into the area from any part of the kingdom.'

They continued with their searches. Simon's eyes grew heavy and he began to doze. He woke with a start when one of the clerks shouted, 'It's here! It's here!' He pushed across a manuscript roll.

Simon studied the entry. It mentioned Agnes Ratolier, 'seamstress', and her half-brother Edward: 'two orphans in the parish of Stroud'.

'Let us see if there are any more.'

The clerks went back to their studies. Simon, restless, paced the floor. He no longer felt sleepy but invigorated by what they had found. An hour passed.

'I am sorry, Master Cotterill.' One of the clerks shook his head mournfully. 'But I think that entry is the only one we have.'

Simon thanked them both.

'We'd best leave things as they are,' the clerk said. 'We can clear our desks in the morning. Master Cotterill, you are welcome to stay.'

'Will his worship the mayor return?' Simon asked.

'Perhaps.'

The clerks began to blow the candles out but they left two capped lights as well as the huge lantern horn they placed near the door. They collected their belongings and cloaks, shook Simon's hand and wished him good night.

Simon sat for a while going back to what had happened since this business had begun. He dozed for a short time and was woken by a rat scurrying across his boot, making him jump in alarm. The chamber was empty. The candles had burned low. Simon thought he heard a door opening and closing but, when he went to investigate, it was only some clerk working late and preparing to leave. Simon decided to make himself useful. He picked up the taxation rolls and took them back to the chancery office where the clerks had been writing. He put these away on the shelves. He promised himself that, if the mayor did not arrive by the time the candles had gutted, he would leave.

He stowed the manuscripts away and sat at the clerks' desk, looking at the different parchments strewn there. He picked up one of the papers; the handwriting was cramped. He recognised the name Adam Draycott and guiltily realised he was reading the alderman's will, waiting to be approved by the city corporation. He went through the different clauses. Alice was to be her father's principal heir and, if she died before him without issue, his wealth and goods would go to certain kinsfolk, a niece in the city of Bath and others. Different items caught his eye, then Simon's blood ran cold. He pulled a candle closer and studied the entry carefully.

'Heavens above!' he whispered.

Simon feverishly searched among the manuscripts but could find no trace of Alderman Shipler's will except a reference to where it was lodged. When he heard voices speaking in the gallery he put the will down, blew out the candles and left. The mayor was standing talking to the sergeant-at-arms. They fell silent as Simon came across to join them.

'Master Cotterill, you are working late.'

'The clerks found one entry,' Simon replied evasively. 'But nothing of real import.'

'We've been busy on your behalf,' the sergeant-at-arms remarked. 'I think it's best if Master Flyhead didn't leave Gloucester for a while. We've searchers out, scouring the city for him.'

'Hasn't he returned to his old haunts?' Simon asked, trying to hide his nervousness and surprise.

'No.' The sergeant-at-arms clapped Simon on the shoulder. 'But don't worry, we'll find him. Rest assured of that.'

Simon made his farewells and clattered down the stairs, glad to be away. Outside a light drizzle was falling. He wondered where Flyhead would hide. But what could he do? He had to make other searches for himself.

The streets were still fairly busy as traders made their way home and shopkeepers put up their boards for the night. Doors were flung open, lights from candles and lantern horns streaming through. Apprentices chattered as they sat on the cobbles outside the shops, ignoring the light rain, grateful for a rest after a day's labour. Simon made his way across the city and into the sweet-smelling taproom of the Silver Tabard. The mayor had told him that the lease had been abruptly sold; a new taverner and his family had moved into the deserted chambers above the taproom.

Simon introduced himself and gazed around. It looked

ordinary enough, tables and stools, hams and onions hanging from the rafters. Its new owner had given it a touch of paint. Little children staggered about the entrance to the scullery and kitchens. A fire burned in the hearth. It was hard to realise that this homely place once housed a member of the Ratolier coven. Simon ordered a bowl of jugged hare and a tankard of ale. The taverner himself served him.

'Are your slatterns and pot boys also newly hired?' Simon asked.

'Most of them are.' The taverner wiped the sweat away from his red, chapped cheeks. 'The previous owner was a solitary man. He hired slatterns, anyone who wished for the job, but no one slept here except him. Now Isolda, over there, she worked for him for a while.'

'May I have a word with her?' Simon asked.

The taverner shrugged. The slattern came over. She had mousey-coloured hair which framed a thin, peaked face; her nose was slightly crooked and she had a cast in one eye. She was surly tempered but changed her mood when Simon put a silver coin down on the table.

'You served here before, with the previous owner?'

'Yes, master.'

Her chapped fingers went to take the silver piece but Simon put his hand over it.

'What was his name?'

'Joscelyn. Joscelyn Blackwell.'

'And what do you know of him?'

'The mayor's men have asked me the same question. I am a seamstress during the day. I have a chamber further down the alleyway. I came here at his request. He paid well and some of the customers were generous.'

'But the man himself?'

'He was secretive. He kept nothing here. At night the tavern was always closed when the curfew sounded. He wouldn't let anyone stay. Nor would he allow us upstairs.'

'Did he talk to the customers?'

189

'Hardly ever, his mind seemed elsewhere.'

'And he had no family or friends?'

'None that I ever knew.'

'Did you notice anything untoward?'

'I wondered why he hired me and paid me so well. But he seemed very interested that I could read and write. On some evenings he would leave early and return, just before the curfew sounded. Other evenings the tavern would be closed, the doors bolted, the windows shuttered.'

'Why?' Simon asked.

'I don't know. I think he went away.'

Simon took his hand away from the silver piece.

'But you are a sharp-eyed girl,' he coaxed. 'You must have noticed something?'

'He was solitary.' The slattern watched the coin and licked her lips. 'Sometimes, when the tavern was closed, well, I used to walk down here. You could tell when it was deserted and Master Joscelyn was away. At other times I'd glimpse a light. I had a feeling people were here. But I could never really tell. As I said, the doors were barred and bolted. It was none of my business so I never asked.'

'Do you have a writing tray?' Simon asked. He placed another coin on the table.

'Certainly.'

The slattern came back with a battered, wooden tray, a scrap of parchment, an ink horn and a quill. Simon carefully wrote out the list of names.

'You can read?'

The slattern nodded.

'Look at these. Do any prick your memory?'

The girl took the scrap of parchment over to where a lantern horn hung from a pillar. She peered at it, her lips moving wordlessly. She came back and put the list on the table.

'I recognise none of them.'

Simon's heart sank.

'None whatsoever, but one thing . . .' She narrowed her eyes.

Simon put down another coin.

'One night when Blackwell locked up, I was preparing to go. There was a knock on the door. I went to answer it but he insisted on going.'

'What happened?' Simon asked.

'Blackwell said . . .' she closed her eyes. 'Yes, that's it. "Go away, there's none of your sort here!" The other person replied, "I bear a message from the dom . . ."'

'Dominus?' Simon asked.

'Yes, that's it. Dominus, the word was clear. Blackwell came back in. I could see he was distracted. He had a small roll of parchment in his hand. He snapped at me to go, I did. That was the end of the matter.'

Simon handed the coins across, re-tightened his sword belt, picked up his cloak and left. He was halfway down the alleyway when he heard the sound. There was a trickle of cold between his shoulders, he whirled round. The figure came at a run from the shadows. He saw the blade held high and glimpsed a young woman's face, the surviving Ratolier. Simon backed away, desperately trying to draw his own dagger. He tripped and fell. Rolling over in the mud he lashed out with his hands, fearful of the killing blow. When he looked up the figure was gone.

Simon picked himself up. So soon? He remembered the fight in the caves. He had been one of the first up that rocky escarpment and the Ratolier must have recognised him. If he had arrived back in Gloucester early that morning it wouldn't have taken much longer for the Ratolier, who knew the paths as well, to slip back into the city. He walked backwards, dagger drawn, looking over his shoulder.

'Master Cotterill!' The woman's voice sounded eerily on the night air. 'Master Cotterill, don't worry. We shall, undoubtedly, meet again!'

Simon sheathed his dagger and ran, quietly cursing his own

stupidity. He thought the Ratolier coven had been wiped out but, of course, the dominus was still alive and the Ratolier woman must have come into Gloucester to seek him out and tell her master what had happened. Nevertheless, he drew comfort from what he had seen in that will. He paused at the mouth of the alleyway before walking out into the thoroughfare, close to where a group of beadles sat near the stocks. He stood there, calming his mind, grateful to be close to anyone. He would never make that mistake again. Where on earth could Flyhead be? By now the beadles were becoming curious. Simon walked on. He had to make sure, clear all doubts from his mind.

When he arrived at the great square before the Abbey of St Peter he went across to the monastery gate and, using the mayor's commission, demanded to see Father Abbot. The lay brother shook his head.

'He's away,' he said. 'But one of the sub-priors may be able to help?'

Simon was taken across the cloisters to well-furnished chambers. The sub-prior was helpful. He listened to Simon and his questions about the will of Alderman Shipler. A copy was brought. Simon studied it closely, trying to control the tremors in his body.

'It's too late for Flyhead!' he exclaimed. 'I can do no more!'

'What do you mean, my son?' The sub-prior rose, anxious about this strange young man bearing the mayor's commission.

'Nothing, Father.' Simon got to his feet. 'I thank you and bid you good night.'

Chapter 14

Simon was awoken early in the Guildhall house by a rapping and kicking on the door. He shouted at the person to wait, dressed hurriedly and fastened on his sword belt. A tipstaff was standing on the stairwell, his face sweaty under dishevelled hair.

'You must come, sir!' he rasped. He showed Simon the mayor's seal. 'Sir Humphrey himself wishes to see you in the Guildhall chamber.'

The fellow would say no more. Simon hurriedly put his boots on and followed him through the mist-filled streets to the Guildhall. Very few people were about, the silence only broken by the occasional creak and rattle of a cart along the cobbles and the peals of the bells of churches clanging to the cloud-covered heavens for the first Mass of the day.

Sir Humphrey was waiting in the main porchway, walking up and down. On a stone seat the sergeant-at-arms lounged: both men looked as if they hadn't slept. The mayor dismissed the tipstaff and gestured at Simon to follow him. They went across the great courtyard through a roofed archway and into an outhouse.

Simon's heart sank at the body sprawled out on the handcart, the head lolling over the edge displaying the slashed throat.

'Flyhead! Oh Lord, have mercy!'

Simon knelt down, sitting back on his heels, the hard ground grazing his knees.

'Christ have mercy on him!' he prayed. 'In many ways you were a good man, loyal and brave.'

'His body was brought in this morning. He was found outside Eastgate. From what I can gather,' the sergeant-at-arms continued, 'he left just before the curfew sounded. He didn't travel far before they attacked.'

'They?' Simon asked.

'It must have taken more than one to kill poor Flyhead.'

'I don't know.'

Simon told them about the attack on him the previous evening. He went through the dead man's pockets. As he did so he noticed red candle grease marked Flyhead's tarry jacket.

'What is that?' the sergeant-at-arms asked.

'Candle grease.' Simon got to his feet. 'Sir Humphrey, how soon could you arrange a posse of archers and men-at-arms?'

'Give me an hour,' the sergeant-at-arms barked, 'and I'll have a good dozen of my lads ready.'

'Why?' the mayor asked.

Simon plucked him by the sleeve and, taking both men out to the cobbled yard, told them the conclusion he had reached and the reasons for it.

Two hours later, just as the city of Gloucester stirred, the mayor of Gloucester, his sergeant-at-arms, Master Simon Cotterill and a large comitatus of armed men, both mounted and on foot, surrounded the house of the Austin Friars. Sir Humphrey, jangling the large bell before the main gate, demanded an immediate meeting with Father Prior. The sleepy-eyed lay brother objected.

'The brothers are all in church,' he whined. 'It is the hour of Matins.'

'If he doesn't come out now!' Sir Humphrey barked, 'I'll have him arrested and take the consequences!'

The lay brother hurried away. A short while later Sir Humphrey, the sergeant-at-arms and Simon were ushered into the prior's parlour. Soon a pale-faced Friar Martin joined them. The prior, all a-fluster, protested at such high-handed treatment, but the mayor cut him short.

'I'll write to the bishop's palace,' he said. 'Ride to Westminster and come back with all the warrants I need!'

'What is the matter?' the prior asked, sitting down on his throne-like chair, hands gripping the arm-rests.

He gestured at Friar Martin, pointing to a chair at the side of the desk then nodded brusquely at the mayor and his companions to sit. Simon did so but the sergeant-of-arms went over and leaned against the door.

'I am here on the King's business,' the mayor began. He pointed at Friar Martin. 'I accuse that man, that so-called friar, that Judas priest, of being a cunning, deceitful murderer. Of being a member, nay, indeed the leader, of the devilish coven he so hypocritically declares he is hiding from.'

The prior stared back, speechless, his face pale, his mouth sagging. Friar Martin, however, half rose in the chair, his face in a snarl.

'Have you lost your wits, sir?' he sneered. 'Simon, for the love of God!'

'Sit down, Friar Martin!' Simon told him. 'Or shall I call you by your real name? Edward Ratolier. Once an orphan in the parish of Stroud, half-brother to Agnes, a well-known witch and warlock recently killed in her lair at Savernake.'

'This is ridiculous!' Friar Martin hid the lower part of his face behind his hands. 'Simon, have you lost your wits?'

'Which house were you professed at?' Simon began. 'Come on, Friar Martin, tell me which house? We'll go back through the records. It may take weeks, it may take months, but, by that time, your sole surviving daughter will be hanged. My lord mayor's men have her in the Guildhall dungeons. She has been put on trial and has confessed. She'll hang before noon.'

'Eleanor?' Friar Martin's hand went to his mouth.

'How do you know which one?' the mayor intervened. 'The only thing that will save your daughter,' the mayor continued Simon's bluff, 'is if you confess, full and true.'

'Wait! Wait!' the prior intervened. 'Friar Martin is a cleric, he's under the protection of Holy Mother Church!'

'Friar Martin is a heretic and a killer!' the sergeant-at-arms retorted. 'If you wish, Father Prior, my men can take him by force. All of Gloucester will know what has happened here.'

Friar Martin now sat, his hands on his lap, staring down at the floor.

'This is truly ridiculous!' the prior continued. 'Friar Martin has, true, wandered from the path of righteousness, not been as faithful in his vows as, perhaps, he could. However, over the last few weeks, he has reformed. He has made himself a virtual prisoner in this house.'

'True, true,' Simon agreed. 'And a man who pretends to be frightened, who expresses a wish to hide away, is scarcely watched. Tell me, Father Prior, where is Friar Martin's cell?'

'Behind the shrine of St Radegund. You know that!'

'And if he wished to leave at night? Let us say, for the sake of argument,' Simon insisted, 'that Friar Martin wished to sneak out of his cell?'

The prior blinked, his lips moved wordlessly. Simon caught a look of uncertainty in his eyes.

'I speak the truth, don't I, Father Prior? If Friar Martin wished to leave, to steal away in the darkness, he could do so. Please! Answer me, yes or no?'

The Prior nodded. 'It's possible,' he conceded.

'Flyhead's dead,' Simon said. 'He came to see you yesterday, didn't he, before he left? He wished to say farewell to his comrade-in-arms. Poor Flyhead! Once a priest, always a priest, I suppose. Before he left he must have lit some of those red wax candles at the shrine of St Radegund. When they brought his corpse in I found wax on his jerkin, and only churches have red candles. Flyhead would never enter a church unless he had to. The only hallowed place he would visit would be St Radegund's shrine to bid his former friend farewell.'

Friar Martin kept his head bowed.

'Did you hear his confession? Or pretend to?' Simon asked. 'Did you give him good comfort? Did you tell him that you might even join him? That he should leave by Eastgate?'

'What is this?' the prior asked.

'Flyhead was a former hangman,' Simon explained. 'A comrade of mine and of Father Martin's. I am sure, Father Prior, that, if you asked among those lay brothers who watch the shrine, they may have noticed this pilgrim. He'd have pulled back his cowl when he entered the church, and his bald pate was covered in black spots.' Simon paused. He couldn't tell whether Friar Martin was even listening. 'And I wager, too, my lord prior, that if you ask those same lay brothers, they will tell you how a young woman also came into the shrine and asked our good Friar Martin to hear her confession. She'd have sat in the pew and told her father.' He paused at the shock in the prior's face. 'Oh yes, I suspect Eleanor Ratolier is Friar Martin's daughter. When I last visited this friary, he was deeply shocked by my news of the Ratoliers' deaths. I thought the cause was fear. I now know it was grief. Anyway, Eleanor escaped from Savernake. She would immediately seek the protection of her father and her dominus, the friar we know as Brother Martin. He would tell her about Flyhead's visit. How she could wreak vengeance for the destruction of the coven and the deaths of her mother and elder sister. Flyhead was always partial to a pretty face. He paid for his mistakes with his life. But she'll hang! Not secretly. She'll jerk and she'll dance. It may take a good hour for her to die.'

'How do you know all this?' Friar Martin lifted his head. His face was smoother, younger-looking, as if the mask had slipped; his eyes were watchful, calculating and full of mockery.

'How you must have laughed,' Simon jibed. 'How you must have laughed and sneered at everyone. Nevertheless, my first question: where were you professed?'

'In our house in London.'

'And where to then?'

'To Royston in Hertfordshire.'

'And then?'

'To St Asphs in Wales before coming here.'

'And your name, your true name?'

'Will she hang?' Friar Martin spread his hands. 'Give me your oath, Simon, and yours, my lord mayor. Will Eleanor Ratolier hang?'

'She'll go free,' the mayor replied. 'She was captured by horsemen fleeing Flyhead's corpse. We'll say a mistake's been made. She'll be taken to the nearest port.' The mayor continued Simon's lie. 'And told to go to foreign parts.'

'I have your oath on that?'

'You have my oath,' Simon replied.

'How did you know it was me?' Friar Martin cocked his head sideways. His eyes were full of curiosity as if he'd posed Simon a riddle and was surprised the carpenter had found the answer.

'From the beginning,' Simon said, 'you knew the Dominicans were visiting Gloucester, that some search was being carried out. However, you were not given enough time to warn the rest of your coven. During the Ratoliers' trial you recommended they be executed in the forest. Aldermen Shipler and Draycott followed your advice. I will come to the reason for that in a short while.' Simon cleared his throat. 'Secondly, after their trial, the Ratoliers wanted to see a priest, but why? They had no intention of being shriven! They hoped against hope that the hangmen might secretly agree to their freedom. Of course that was futile! You probably knew that. Now, when we visited them in their cell, you told them that they were going to be hanged in a forest glade, thus alerting them to the danger ahead. You'd also insisted that I accompany you down to the cell. I was green and fresh, soft-hearted. I agreed to be their messenger to the landlord at the Silver Tabard.'

Friar Martin shook his head knowingly.

'Clever boy!' he murmured.

'If the Ratoliers weren't to be shriven,' Simon continued. 'Why did you come out to the Forest of Dean? I mean, to spend three nights in some lonely, rain-swept glade? You travelled with them in the cart and, unobserved, passed them the potions and philtres they needed to survive the hanging. After their executions, you put the hoods over their faces just in case we noticed anything untoward. You agreed that we should leave the glade. When the Ratoliers attacked us, you told Shadbolt not to waste his arrows. And, of course, how would the Ratoliers know about the sins of their hangmen? You remember, they called them out? You knew all there was to know about our companions. You pretended to be frightened and, in doing so, heightened our own terrors. We were nothing more than a quivering bunch of cowards unable to cope with the phantasms before us while you played the role of the devout priest. Once you returned to Gloucester, you could hide away in the priory. In truth, you were intent on vengeance, slipping out whenever you wished. The hangmen had to die because of what we had seen. The same fate befell poor Deershound but the aldermen were more dangerous, weren't they?' Simon paused, studying the friar. 'They were dangerous, weren't they?'

Friar Martin nodded.

'First, they might remember how you advocated the witches be hanged in the forest. They might reflect on what had really happened. Now I wager that you, Friar Martin, had heard rumours about the mayor's interest in this coven. You said as much to Shadbolt and myself in the Hangman's Rest. Did you approach Aldermen Shipler and Draycott to find out more?'

'Why should I do that?'

'You might be confessor to condemned men and chaplain to the council but you were also confessor to both Draycott and Shipler. You knew all about them. You approached them, making enquiries about rumours of a witches' coven, about the mayor's suspicions! About the arrival of the Dominicans in Gloucester!'

'You made similar enquiries of me!' the prior hissed.

Friar Martin gazed stonily back.

'I saw their wills,' Simon continued. 'Draycott's in the Guildhall, Shipler's in the Abbey of St Peter. Both men had left bequests "to their good friend and confessor Friar Martin". You might be their confessor but, in time, they might have become suspicious. Of course, you also wanted revenge. Being Shipler's confessor, you knew all about his paramour, where she lived and when he visited her. Only on that fateful night the Ratoliers were waiting for him, weren't they?'

'He was a terrible hypocrite,' Friar Martin mocked back.

'And the Draycotts? Good Friar Martin comes to see them, to share a jug of wine. How easy it would have been to slip a potion into their cups and then, in the dead of night, drag their bodies across to the stable to hang them! A busy night's work eh, Friar? Done under the cloak of darkness. You hanged those unfortunates, returned to the house, cleared the table and kitchen and returned to your hell hole.'

'Hell hole?' Friar Martin queried.

'Be it a church or a cave in the forest, anywhere you lurk is on the path to hell!'

'But the poisoned wine!' the prior exclaimed.

'Oh, the work of the coven, done to depict Friar Martin as an angel of light.'

'Go on!' the mayor insisted.

'The rest were easy to kill. Poor old Merry Face on the forest path. Shadbolt trying to escape along the river and, of course, Flyhead. I suppose, in the last resort he was well named: he walked straight into the spider's web.'

The prior now reasserted himself. 'I can scarcely believe my ears. These accusations are horrible, a blasphemy in the eyes of God! What is your real name?' He banged his knuckles on the desk. 'I can, if you wish, send couriers to our house in London.'

'There'll be no need for that,' Friar Martin replied languidly.

Simon studied him intently. The friar was revealing himself as a colder, harder man than before: the bluff bonhomie had disappeared. His eyes were dangerous, cold and implacable. His only reaction to his accusers was the occasional licking of his top lip with the tip of his tongue.

'I have your word,' he grated. He snapped his fingers at the prior. 'And you, Reverend Father, must remember that, whatever you think I am, I am still a cleric under the governance of Holy Mother Church. I cannot be handed over to the secular arm.' He paused and took a deep breath. 'I am Edward Ratolier, a native of Cripplegate in London. My mother was English, her second husband, my father, came from Brittany. Both died in the great pestilence, leaving me and my half-sister Agnes as orphans. Have you ever been a child on your own, Simon? Thank God you never were.' He smiled thinly. 'If there really is a God. Agnes and I knew evil. Men with their lusts and their wants. We wandered the roads and byways of the kingdom. Eventually we arrived in Stroud. A few months later we moved to Norwich where a fat merchant took a fancy to my half-sister Agnes. I was given a good education in Theobald's School. Agnes and I, to escape the attentions of our so-called father, fell under the true care and protection of Mother Cressingham.' He saw the mayor start.

'The same woman who was tried before King's Bench in London?'

'Ah, so you have heard of her?' Friar Martin pulled a face. 'Mother Cressingham was hanged and burned as a witch but she was the only parent we knew. She introduced us into the mysteries . . .'

'Devil worship!' the prior snapped.

'Shut up!' Friar Martin sneered. 'Shut your prattling little mouth!'

'Continue!' the mayor barked.

'Oh, we learned the mysteries. The use of potions and, above all, the secret death.' He put a hand to his throat. 'Do you know, Simon, that before Christianity ever came to these shores, the tribes worshipped those who lived in the trees. Their priests used to take potions and strangle themselves; in their dreams they'd enter the halls of the gods and peer into the visions of the night. By the time we were adults, both Agnes and I were masters of the mysteries. We also became handfast.'

'Married!' the prior exclaimed. 'Half-brother and sister!'

'I know, Reverend Father,' Friar Martin replied sarcastically. 'But let's be honest, I'm not the only priest who's sinned. That old goat of a merchant had one son. Agnes took care of him and became sole heir. She also became pregnant. The old goat thought it was his doing and Agnes did not disabuse him. To allay suspicion I, who loved no other woman, became a friar. The old merchant died and Agnes sold his property.'

'So that's where your wealth came from?' Simon interrupted.

'Oh, we have gold and silver deposited in many a city. Where I went, Agnes always followed. She reared our daughters and became steeped in the mysteries.'

'Of course!' Simon scratched his head. 'You are a friar. Your order is well known for its libraries. You would have access to books and manuscripts denied to others.'

Brother Martin smiled. 'I was right about you, Simon. Sharp and bright as a new pin. I told Agnes that! I had great hopes for you. At last we came to Gloucester,' he continued. 'Now, when Agnes and I had been orphans at Stroud, we made friends with an old forester, a verderer. During the few months we were there, he took us out to show us the old secret byways of the woods and we hadn't forgotten them. It's easy for a friar to leave his house, to slip out of his cell at night and climb the wall.'

'And, being chaplain to the hangmen, confessor to the condemned,' the mayor noted.

'Sir Humphrey, your wits are not as dim as they appear.'

Friar Martin laughed softly to himself. 'Ah well, we set up home in the caves of Savernake. We had another hiding place in the forest but we won't mention that. It would take you years to discover. No, on second thoughts.' He grinned. 'It would take you a thousand lifetimes. Now our appetite for the truth behind the great mysteries grew. We had sacrificed before to the hanged ones. Now Agnes insisted that these sacrifices be constant to please the dark lords.'

'Demons!' the prior murmured. He sat slumped in his chair, wearied and shocked at these revelations.

'We took whores,' Friar Martin continued, dismissing the prior with a look of contempt. 'Whores and slatterns, poor creatures who would never be missed. I would mark them down. Agnes would seize them.'

'And the others?' Simon asked.

'Every coven must have six members, just like our society.' He sniggered. 'Or a priory. I was their Father Abbot. It wasn't long before mine host at the Silver Tabard was recruited and, of course, No Teeth was invaluable.'

'But they were dispensable?' the mayor asked.

'Naturally. When they had served their time and fulfilled their purpose, they would have gone like the others.' Friar Martin flicked his fingers. 'Like that! No Teeth was a problem. He became arrogant, too fond of soft flesh and strong wine. When he killed that man, I said to Agnes, let him hang! But Agnes said, "No. Let us test the true strength of our potions!" Sacrifices were made. No Teeth was spared.' Friar Martin closed his eyes and chuckled to himself. 'Agnes was there when I dug him out of that shallow grave. She took him away. I was very angry that you saw him, Simon.' He wagged a finger. 'Trust me. No Teeth's days were numbered. If he had been more vigilant that night, Agnes and my two daughters would never have been taken. He had a huge debt to pay.' He paused and sighed. 'I did wonder at first if Shadbolt would agree to his usual trickery but then I thought no, the lord mayor himself wants the death of my women.

And so I plotted. I urged the court that they be executed at the place where they had carried out their sacrifices. It wasn't too difficult either, to convince those noddlepates the Dominicans.'

The prior put his face in his hands. 'They came here,' he said. He was almost talking to himself, waving his hands like a bird. 'They came here and told me a dreadful story. How such sacrifices had been carried out in other parts of the kingdom. They mentioned Norwich. Yes, and other places.' He glanced sideways at Friar Martin. 'Everywhere you went, you left blood and chaos behind you.'

Simon, too, felt a chill of apprehension. Were those women the only victims, he wondered?

'Whose idea was it?' he asked. 'To spare the hanged, the felons who should really have died?'

Friar Martin's head went down.

'Answer the question, sir!' The mayor beat the table with his fist.

'There's no need to, is there?' Simon declared in a horrified whisper. 'Those who were spared, whom you revived in the lepers' corner of the graveyard. Many of them were also marked down for sacrifice!'

'What is this?' Father Prior demanded.

'I shall tell you later, Prior,' the mayor interrupted with a sweep of his hand.

'You would tell the lonely ones where to go, wouldn't you?' Simon urged. 'To hide in the Forest of Dean. Many of those poor men and women, who thought they had been spared, were handed over to your wife, put under the slaughterer's knife.'

Friar Martin raised his head.

'A tangled web, eh, Simon? And I will answer neither nay or yea to your question. However, I was there when Shadbolt and Merry Face died. Agnes took care of old Shipler and I visited the Draycotts. He was an old fool but you are right, Simon, Alice was bright of face and keen of wit.' He glanced round. 'In the end they would have had you all, little by little, bit by bit, except No Teeth. He was always trouble. I reserved that pleasure for myself, to wring his neck like a chicken.' Friar Martin's face turned ugly.

Simon stared at this horror in human flesh.

'And me, Brother Martin?'

'Oh, you would have died last, Simon. I would have given you the opportunity to come across, yet things are never what they appear, eh boy? I sensed that from the beginning. You were different from the rest. Most men, Simon, are like animals. They eat, drink, whore and fornicate but you have a spark, hidden by those plough-boy looks.' He gazed fondly at Simon like a father would at a favoured son. 'But it's all come to a pretty pass now, eh?'

The prior stood up and went to kneel on the prie-dieu beneath the crucifix.

'That's right, priest! Prattle on!' Friar Martin glared venomously at his kneeling superior. 'You were a great help, Father Prior,' he jibed. 'You really should keep the Rule more strictly. It is easier to slip in and out of here than it is the door of a tavern. Of course, being custodian of the shrine of St Radegund, that bundle of mouldering bones, I could meet members of my coven when they visited as pilgrims.'

'You are wicked!' Father Prior turned his head slightly sideways. 'You should be taken out, hanged and burned!'

'But you won't allow that, will you?' Friar Martin mocked. 'How the tongues would wag! And what would you say to your superiors? And how can my lord mayor punish a priest? Every cleric in the city would be in uproar. All the shaven pates clapping their hands and clucking their tongues. And you, my lord mayor.' He poked a finger like a vicious child jabbing the air. 'Are you going to put me on trial, eh? Tell the city your mistakes? And what evidence will you produce? Who'll stand at the bar and clack their tongues?'

The prior got to his feet and turned. Simon had never seen

a man look so stricken, torn between anger and fear.

'My lord mayor, I must remind you that Friar Martin is a member of this order and a tonsured cleric. He comes under the authority of Holy Mother Church.' He held a hand up to stifle the mayor's gasps of protest. The prior kept his hand up as if swearing a great oath. 'Friar Martin, you called me Reverend Father, your superior, and so I am. I have the law and the authority to punish you.'

Friar Martin's face lost some of its arrogant malice.

'What will you do?' the sergeant-at-arms asked.

'Beneath this priory is a cell with only a small grille in the roof to allow in some light and air. The floor is of stone, the walls thick, the roof is as hard as rock. I am going to order the sergeant-at-arms to take you there. I am going to allow him to bring his men into this monastery.' He paused. 'By the authority of Holy Mother Church I shall call our lay brothers, men who have been masons. They will remove the door of that chamber and, apart from the small grille, they shall brick you up alive. You will eat and drink what is pushed through. You will relieve yourself in the latrine provided. You will be given a fresh robe of horse-hair every year. You will be served by someone who is mute. You will never be allowed to meet anyone. You will never leave that room alive. I swear this by all that's holy! No matter how long you live, you shall, for the rest of your natural life, be immured in a living hell!'

The sergeant-at-arms came across. He pulled the loop from his belt and expertly tied the prisoner's hands. Friar Martin, white-faced, stared at Simon.

'But Eleanor will not hang? You'll keep your oath?'

Simon rose to his feet and leaned across the desk.

'I told a lie,' he admitted. 'Eleanor is not our prisoner. Yet, if I ever meet her, Friar Martin, she will not draw many breaths!'

Friar Martin would have sprung at him, his face a mask of fury.

'You whoreson bastard!' he grated, struggling in the sergeant-at-arms' grip. 'Remember this, Simon Cotterill, we shall meet again! I tell you, we shall meet again!'

Words Among the Pilgrims

The carpenter finished his story. The pilgrims assembled in the long, candlelit hall stared expectantly at him. Was he Simon Cotterill? This man with his greying hair and kindly face? Could he possibly be the same person who had crossed swords with that evil coven in the Forest of Dean? Mine host leaned forward but Sir Godfrey squeezed him by the wrist.

'Remember,' he cautioned. 'We must not embarrass the man. It may be a fable or it may be the truth.'

'It is the truth, isn't it?' The rubicund-faced friar down the table lifted his goblet, eyes sparkling.

'Why do you say that?' the carpenter asked.

'You have a fear of hanging, we know that.'

'Why, don't you, Brother?' the carpenter retorted, provoking a ripple of laughter.

Sir Godfrey glanced at the monk, who had his cowl pulled over his dome-like head. His eyes glittered, his bright red lips stained with wine were slightly parted. Aye, Sir Godfrey thought, you'd savour a story like that about creatures of the night!

'I have heard something about this.' The man of law ran a finger round the collar of his chemise, fingering the jewelled gold pendant hanging there. 'Sir Humphrey Baddleton, yes, he was mayor until recently. He was killed in an accident, or so they say, along with his sergeant-at-arms. A fire in a tavern where they were staying while travelling to Bristol.'

'How do you know that?' the carpenter asked, but he didn't raise his face.

'Oh, it was suspicious circumstances,' the man of law declared, glancing quickly at Dame Eglantine. 'Yes, yes. Foul play was suspected. Something about the windows and doors being sealed and both men being unable to break free.

The commissioners of assize were despatched to the area, I was one of them.' He nodded proudly. 'But no proof was found. We upheld the coroner's verdict: death by misadventure.'

'So, it is true,' the friar continued. 'Brother Martin's a common name, but I did know of such a fellow in our house at Norwich. I'm sure he was sent to Gloucester.'

The carpenter stole a glance down the table at the Wife of Bath. Usually this red-faced, gap-toothed, middle-aged woman was full of jests and opinions. Now she had fallen silent, staring into her cup, her mind elsewhere.

Sir Godfrey got to his feet. 'I think, good sirs, ladies, this tale is done, is it not, Master Carpenter?'

'It is told as far as it can be,' the fellow replied evasively.

Sir Godfrey nodded imperceptibly. He knew the tale was true. Anyone could tell that from the haunted look on the carpenter's face. Sir Godfrey, who'd worked at the House of Secrets in London, quietly promised that, after he had finished his pilgrimage, he would go there and search among the records. He glanced quickly at the monk. He would also deal with Brother Hubert. Sir Godfrey was intent on hunting down and crushing all such creatures of the night: men and women in league with Satan. But now was not the time; the day had proven a long one. The miller was fast asleep, resting on his bagpipes. The summoner was, once again, trying to get close to the franklin, for the rogue seemed intent on slitting that white silk purse. Sir Godfrey clapped his hands.

'We should go now! Retire to our beds!'

'All those who can afford them!' a voice shouted from down the hall.

Sir Godfrey spread his hands. 'My son and I will sleep here. I suggest we make ourselves comfortable.'

As the pilgrims got to their feet, some glanced through the window and shivered. They recalled the gibbet, those dangling figures and the grim tale told by the carpenter. What monsters moved, they wondered, at night? Did the unhanged follow them here? They busied themselves. They were in good company; tomorrow would be fine and they would continue their journey.

The carpenter waited quietly until he was no longer the object of attention and, getting to his feet, he walked out of the refectory and along the passageway. He opened a door and entered the cool, sweet-smelling priory garden. He sat on a turf seat and looked up at the stars.

A beautiful night, he thought. He wondered if Alice's spirit followed him. He heard footsteps and turned. The wife of Bath stood there, her usual merry face was solemn. She had taken off her broad-brimmed hat which she now held between her hands.

'You are Simon Cotterill, aren't you?' she asked.

The carpenter nodded.

'May I sit with you?'

The carpenter smiled. The wife of Bath was not accustomed to make such pretty pleas. When the spirit took her she could be as coarse and uncouth as the miller.

'Of course, my lady.' He half rose as she took her seat.

'I come from Bath,' she began. 'I trade in cloth. Thanks to my uncle, his legacy has made me a wealthy woman.'

'Alderman Draycott?' Simon asked.

The wife of Bath nodded. 'I am the kinswoman mentioned in the will you saw in the Guildhall at Gloucester. I will not tell you about my life. Suffice to say, I always wondered about Uncle's death.'

Simon turned and studied her. In the moonlight, if he looked hard enough, he detected glimpses of his beloved Alice, a family likeness.

'That's why you were frightened of the hanging, wasn't it?'

Simon nodded.

'But there's more to it, isn't there?'

'Yes.' He sighed. 'There's more. I left Gloucester two weeks later, lavishly rewarded by Sir Humphrey. I travelled to Hereford, Worcester and then I settled in a small village,

Woodford, in Essex on the Epping Road. I have a good trade there. Even the merchants from London hire me. Sir Humphrey sometimes wrote to me. I regarded the Ratolier girl and Friar Martin as ghosts. I consigned them to the realm of the dead.'

'And then?'

'Two years ago Sir Humphrey sent me an urgent letter. By sheer force of will and subtle trickery, Friar Martin had escaped from his cell.'

'Oh, sweet Lord!' The wife of Bath breathed.

'Shortly afterwards news came of Sir Humphrey's death and that of the sergeant-at-arms. I made careful search at Blackfriars, the Dominican house in London. The Dominicans involved in the trial of the Ratoliers had also met curious deaths. One was hit, crushed by falling masonry. The other hired a wherry to go across the Thames to Southwark. The boat, its master and the Dominican never reached the far shore. God knows what happened! Whether it hit another craft or was caught in the sudden swirl around London Bridge?'

'But you know different, don't you?'

'Yes, I know different. I believe Friar Martin and his daughter Eleanor Ratolier are like hunting dogs loosed upon their quarry. They could be anywhere, here in Kent or the wilds of Cornwall. They will not have forgotten me. Every time I see a hanging, the memories flood back.

'I journeyed to Gloucester. Edward Grace, the anchorite, is still alive. I asked him what I should do. He said pray, do God's will and, as an act of penance and as a plea for help, every April I should pray for protection before Becket's shrine in Canterbury.'

The wife of Bath slipped her arm through the carpenter's.

'Come in,' she urged. 'Come back to the warmth. I'll take you to the buttery. I'll pay one of the brothers to pour us two cups of wine.' She grinned impishly. 'Are you married?'

'No.' The carpenter smiled. 'I'm not.'

'Good! Oh Lord save us!' the good dame replied. 'Perhaps I'll pay the good brother for a full jug, not just the goblets!'

They walked back into the priory. Only when they were gone did the figure, one of the hangmen who had executed the felons at the crossroads, come out of the shadows where he had been lurking. He listened to the fading footsteps, the chatter and the laughter of the wife of Bath. He re-sheathed his dagger, climbed the priory wall and raced through the darkness to report back to his dominus what he had seen and heard.

Author's Note

The phrase 'to be hanged by the purse' is a medieval one and, like charity, covers a multitude of sins! There was quite a roaring trade in medieval England, and long after, in condemned men reaching a private compact with the hangman and escaping execution. Even as late as the eighteenth century rumours were rife that Jack Shepherd, the master housebreaker, escaped execution at Tyburn, an event which was attended by thousands of people.

Medieval witches and warlocks used to be dismissed simply as people having rather wild parties in the depths of some forest; their claims to 'fly through the air' or be skilled in other powers were dismissed as fanciful nonsense. It may well be, however, that, although drug companies did not exist in the Middle Ages, many people knew the value and power of hallucinogenic drugs contained in the natural properties of certain plants and herbs and the effect these could have on the human mind.

P.C. Doherty